Praise for **THE**

"*The Night Language* is a rare achievement: lush language and classic storytelling with a contemporary feel that renders its history palpable. It is also a love letter to the artist, the outcast, the othered. Keep it by your bedside, read it in the early hours— it will not fail to inspire you."

—Garrard Conley, author of *Boy Erased*

"Not since Michael Ondaatje's *The English Patient* have I read a novel in which a character—the story and skinsong of Alamayou— has haunted language, history, and heart so intensely. David Rocklin's novel *The Night Language* is a book of longing. Longing for history to unravel and retell itself around those whose buried voices and bodies truly mattered, longing for time to reverse and make decolonization possible, power giving way to intimacy, longing for art to bring a body back home, longing for language to unmoor itself and bring us back to life. If you read one novel this year, let it be *The Night Language*. It is still possible for a reader's heart to be broken back open."

—Lidia Yuknavitch, author of *The Book of Joan*, *The Small Backs of Children*, and *The Chronology of Water*

"Rocklin does a beautiful job capturing the raw emotions that bring Alamayou and the queen closer together, all the while exploring the forbidden intimacy between him and Philip that permeates the novel...a moving and inspiring novel that shows what happens when those in power listen to foreign visitors."

—*Kirkus Reviews*

"This novel of otherness is made all the more compelling by its basis in true events. Giving voice to suppressed stories is worthy work, and Rocklin warns readers of repression's lasting damage."

—*Booklist*

THE NIGHT LANGUAGE

a novel

A GENUINE VIREO BOOK | RARE BIRD BOOKS
LOS ANGELES, CALIF.

THE
NIGHT
LANGUAGE

a novel

DAVID
ROCKLIN

THIS IS A GENUINE VIREO BOOK

A Vireo Book | Rare Bird Books
453 South Spring Street, Suite 302
Los Angeles, CA 90013
rarebirdbooks.com

FIRST TRADE PAPERBACK ORIGINAL EDITION

Set in Janson
Printed in the United States

10 9 8 7 6 5 4 3 2 1

Publisher's Cataloging-in-Publication data
Names: Rocklin, David, 1961–, author.
Title: The Night language : a novel / David Rocklin.
Description: First Trade Paperback Original Edition | A Genuine Vireo Book | New York,
NY; Los Angeles, CA: Rare Bird Books, 2017.
Identifiers: ISBN 9781945572487
Subjects: LCSH Alamayu, Prince of Abyssinia, 1861–1879—Fiction. | Victoria, Queen
of Great Britain, 1819–1901—Fiction. | Great Britain—History—Victoria, 1837–1901—
Fiction. | Ethiopia—History—19th century—Fiction. | Gay men—Fiction. | Historical
Fiction. | Love stories. | BISAC FICTION / Literary | FICTION
Classification: LCC PS3618.O354465 N54 2017 | DDC 813.6—dc23

*To the love of my life
And to yours.*

I turned silences and nights into words.
What was unutterable, I wrote down.
I made the whirling world stand still.

—Arthur Rimbaud

All alone in a strange country, without seeing a
person or relative belonging to him, so young
and so good, but for him one cannot repine.
His was no happy life, full of difficulties of every kind,
and he was so sensitive, thinking that people stared
at him because of his colour, that I fear he
would never have been happy.

—The Journal of Her Majesty Queen Victoria
14 November 1879

Chapter One

17 December 1900

Villefranche

AT LAST, SOME DAYLIGHT.

The sun broke through in the afternoon, following two days of thick black clouds and downpours that had him spending his holiday running from doorway to café canopy. Now, finally, he could paint.

He unpacked his canvas and set up his easel on the path that ran along the blue ribbon of sea between Nice and Monaco. Mixing his oils, he gazed at the vista before him, acquainting himself with the particular shades of sunlight and the way they teased both color and shape from the land. Already he'd painted a good deal of the distant village, and in just two days' time.

A wonderful two days, he thought, in which he got thoroughly lost in his composition while occasionally humming a forgotten adagio. He worked without interruption, oblivious to everything around him. Thinking of nothing, only colors, tones, rims, and borders. Fellow visitors may have passed by him as he worked, or not.

Villefranche clustered under the soft gold dust of the sun's rays breaking through the last cloud cover left by the passing storm. It was built up against a striated wall of rust-colored rock some six hundred feet high. Above the tile roofs of the homes and the cathedral, wispy tendrils lifted from the cooking fires of restaurants and cafés.

Gulls soared down from the ledge in a tight arrow, passing the zigzagging switchback trails carved into the cliff face. In the light they resembled falling bodies clad in white. Their shadows bent across the cliffs as they abruptly pulled out of their dives just before hitting the foaming waves. They flew close, their outstretched wings ruffling the surface of the sea. The wind they rode was cold and strong.

He weighted his easel with smooth stones, then daubed at the cliff paths with a mix of sienna and bay to catch the smoothing effect of the last days' rains. As he worked, enjoying the pleasant briskness of the air and the faint sounds of Villefranche's townspeople emerging from their homes, he took notice of a sleek *canot* drifting in on the tide toward the natural stone jetty that stood as the town's lone port. Such an unremarkable thing, visitors on an outing to the Mediterranean town. The area had gained a reputation for its agreeable weather, its flourishing casinos and fine hotels. The fact that the boat he spied was filled stem to stern with finely dressed ladies in broad seaside hats and immaculate dresses of milk and wheat shouldn't have held his attention for more than a moment. And yet he couldn't reclaim the sense of disappearing into his work that he craved, not while the ornate canot drifted toward land.

Muttering curses at his own inability to concentrate, he watched the ladies gather around a figure on the canot, a woman dressed entirely in black. It seemed that they were trying to shield her. *The chill*, he thought, *or the prying eyes of others*. Perhaps she was someone of note.

He'd come to Villefranche from Paris for the same reason he always did. The city would grow too hot, too cold, or too close, and he'd find that he needed to step away from his days living and working in the Marais to be alone at the water's edge, staring at the low leaden horizon line. There had been far too many tourists on his last few visits, and he'd begun considering other destinations he could escape to before deciding to give this spot one last chance.

In any event, it was best to catch the light before him while it lasted. If he just set to working again, he felt confident that he'd make progress.

The painted cliff paths looked good, so he turned his attention to the cove at the base of the village. An excuse to watch the canot, its oars lifted in surrender to the pull of the tide.

A local piloted it, he could tell. They knew how fruitless it was to row once they got close to the stone jetty.

I'll watch just a bit longer, he decided. *Maybe this is a new painting, presenting itself to me.*

The black-clad figure struggled to her feet. She was immediately surrounded by the finely dressed women.

A rich invalid, no doubt.

He selected a thin horsehair brush and daubed a bit of gray on Villefranche itself, on its narrow sidewalks that a grown man could span wall to wall with outstretched arms, its descending stairways, down to the sea path and the first shades of aqua.

The woman in black got out of the canot, followed closely by the others. Her baggy, overly billowing clothing was in fact a formal dress. It was dark and jeweled with some sort of stone that ignited from the sunlight. The woman herself appeared small, stooped, unsteady, and slow.

A rich, old *invalid*, he thought with a shake of his head. Still, he couldn't stop staring. A sense of unease slowly rose in him.

This is ridiculous, he thought, but the feeling wouldn't go away.

As the rest of the elderly woman's entourage stepped onto the jetty, a second boat floated in. It was as full as hers had been, with similarly dressed women. They got out en masse, dislodging the feral cats sunning themselves atop and between the jetty stones.

So this was some sort of idyllic invasion—the first wave of dowagers on holiday marching their staffs across the path to the small-stakes baccarat tables in Monaco.

He tried to amuse himself, but his hands were trembling. Without being aware, he'd put down his brush. He was stepping away from his canvas, gazing around his position on the path for places to hide. It had been years since he felt so conspicuous and exposed. A voice from long ago filled his head.

We could run.

Calm yourself, he thought. *What will passersby think of me?* A Negro among good white faces, searching for where to go to ground like a criminal. There's no reason for this. There's nothing to be afraid of. Nothing.

He stared at the black-clad figure until she was close enough to make out.

Dear god, it's her. Victoria, queen of England.

The shuffling old woman's companions produced parasols. One held hers high above her head, blocking the sun and extinguishing the flare that burst from the queen's crown.

Move, you idiot, before she sees you.

He ran for cover behind a tall row of wild heather. From there he spied her no more than twenty feet away. Those few villagers out walking were now realizing who moved among them, as if such a thing were normal. They bowed and curtsied and cheered her. *La reine! La reine Victoria!*

God, how old she'd become. How ungraceful. *Time,* he thought, *wins every argument.*

It was her daughter Louise who held the parasol up like a shield against the insistent sun. More than thirty years had passed since he'd last seen either of them at Windsor and suddenly there they were, walking together in another country and not fifty feet from him. Behind them came the usual downstairs help, brought from their normal posts in liveries and dressing rooms out into the light. A lady-in-waiting, a footman, a valet. No one he knew anymore.

The queen walked toward the shoreline, passing his easel while her entourage huddled together against the wind. She lingered a moment at his painting, studying it and smiling wistfully. She looked around for the artist, but he was well hidden.

At the sea, the queen stared at the coming tide. Clouds crept in from the south, covering the sun. The light dwindled. Villefranche by the sea descended into the steely gloom he'd grown used to over the last days.

He remembered that way the queen had of losing herself in her surroundings. Watching her, he wondered if she ever thought of him anymore. Perhaps the passage of all those years had finally swept his name away.

Her time alone lasted fifteen minutes, maybe longer. As the breeze grew bitter, Louise covered her mother's shoulders with an ermine wrap. The queen leaned against her daughter for support.

They returned together to the sea path. There, the queen paused again near the painting. Fleetingly, he thought he saw something alight in her expression. Then it was gone, replaced by a familiar stony resolve.

"Are you well?" he heard the princess ask. "You look pale, Mother. Perhaps we should return home."

"No." The queen's voice was hushed and trembling. "Let us have our holiday. We ought not allow the odd memory to ruin our time."

"Memory? Is something troubling you?"

"No more than any day."

Together they continued toward the path and soon to the crags of the jetty, where their entourage split into two. The larger group clambered onto the waiting boats. The canot pilots poled them away from land, onto the swelling crests of the port current.

The remaining few walked behind the queen and princess. Every so often, the queen paused to rest. Her servant staff waited, heads bowed, for her to move again.

Well, of course, he thought. *She's old. Ill, maybe. Nothing and no one is forever. Feeling a pang for someone I haven't seen in three decades is sentimental and foolish.* Any moment, the queen and princess would be so far away that they'd never see him, and he could emerge from his hiding place and pick up where he'd left off, carrying on as if nothing had happened.

Yet he wanted to cry out to her, to see if she'd turn around. She would come back to him. What would she say? What would he? *Your Majesty, you can't simply appear as if out of a cloud, rain down all that you carry that rightfully belongs to me—the names, the faces, the nights—only to leave while these memories invade me without regard for my life to demand that I find a place for them. You can't.*

When she was merely a speck on the path alongside the light-dappled sea, he emerged from the hedgerow and told himself that it was time to go. There'd be no more painting and it was useless to pretend otherwise. His focus and desire were gone. Tomorrow, he'd get things sorted. Yes, he'd seen her, true enough, and maybe some memories were dusting themselves off and presenting themselves, but that was all. Nothing had changed. It didn't matter. He could simply paint in the early morning, return to Paris on the evening train, arrive near dawn a few hours sleep, then unpack and resume the day's work, and the next. The life he'd made was still there, waiting for him. He was in no danger of being revealed.

He didn't hear the villagers' excited talk of glimpsing the queen, or the sea that had silently brought her here. Only his panicking heart and long-ago words ringing as clear as the bell at Saint-Paul. *What is love, in the end?*

Love is language.

He packed his easel, then turned around on the path that led back to his villa and walked along the sea, trailing the queen until she came to a far dock near one of the fine hotels dotting the coastline. There, she stopped again. In time, she gathered the strength to go inside. By evening, she hadn't come back out.

It was over, this unexpected unearthing of old things from another, far different life. All he had to do was leave.

He took a seat on a rusted seaside bench and watched lights come up in the hotel windows. Over the course of the night those lights extinguished. The storm clouds returned but didn't bring rain, only a covering that smothered the stars and took the light away.

He could scarcely make out the contours of his hand, held up to the sky. It was as if he'd been erased from the world.

Somewhere inside, the queen slept. He wondered if the ghosts of her own past gathered around her as they did around him.

When she departed in the bright morning, he was still there. For the next three days, he followed her throughout France.

§

HE LEARNED THAT THE queen wasn't on a state visit. One of the royal physicians had ordered a holiday out of concern for her ailments. She was suffering from pains, loneliness, and the real and imagined afflictions of the shut-in she was. She chose to spend that prescribed holiday in Cannes, Versailles, and the Exposition Universelle in Paris.

She visited Cimiez for a day, before journeying to Monte Carlo—he snuck onto an adjacent train car to follow. From the window he took in scenes of pastoral beauty. Local shepherds in knee breeches, white stockings and leggings, large black felt hats, tended to flocks as the train swept by like a meteor, making a blurred dream of the passing landscape.

Reginald Manfrey, the shipping magnate, had a villa in Menton. The queen journeyed there and he followed. In the evening she dined at the Royal Opera House in Versailles. The stalls were cleared to make room for more than one hundred guests, with the sovereigns seated on the right of the Royal Box, beneath garlands hung from vaults and chandeliers. From outside its walls, he heard the musicians perfectly execute pieces from Strauss and Dufresne. Their swelling crescendos swept away the cacophony of the street.

She made other stops. The stuff of tourism, like visits to the Louvre and the Palais de Saint-Cloud. Once he spied her through a window, enjoying a private moment with Princess Louise over a drink at the Grand Hotel in Nice. Away from her own country, the simple act of sitting across from her daughter's open and adoring face must have felt like a moment of pure serenity.

He chose to believe that. She didn't deserve to be lonely. No one did.

§

ON THE LAST DAY she toured the Avenue des Nations at the Exposition Universelle in the company of her daughter, their servants, and a dozen gendarmes. They boarded a small locomotive and slowly rolled along a gauge railway, past careful reconstructions of the Bastille and the Galerie des Machines. Occasionally, someone called for the car to halt, and she got out to the astonishment of the other visitors to the grounds.

Police kept the crowds well clear of her, affording him ample cover. Moving with the masses, he watched her stroll through the remnant gardens from the Paris World's Fair, past exhibit buildings constructed from jute, a Parisian invention. She continued by stalls featuring the newly minted discoveries by which the coming century announced itself. Bell's telephone. Arc lighting of the most fascinating sort, installed along the Avenue de l'Opéra and the Place de l'Opéra, powered by Zénobe Gramme dynamos that pulsed like blood flow.

Her expression, as far as he could make out from behind a display of Edison's phonographs and megaphones, suggested fear. It troubled her, the changes to life as she knew it.

They followed the winding garden paths. She didn't stay long at anything she saw until she and her entourage found the Human Zoo.

Signs boasted that the Human Zoo exhibit featured four hundred natives from Africa and the Orient. A man in a heavy woolen coat and top hat bowed deeply to the queen and princess, then raised a walking stick. On his silent signal, a chorus of guttural howls rose up from deep within a display of a mock tribal village. Thirty or more half-naked Negroes rushed out from behind grass huts and shrubs as if on the attack. They gnawed at bones, leveled spears at stuffed prey animals, shimmered before burning tribal fires, dancing and singing gibberish that made him ill.

There's no stronger cage for a Negro, he thought as he watched, *than the white man's imaginings of him.*

The display went on for ten minutes until the show's finale. The natives acted out the sacrifice of one of their own behind a curtain of fanned feathers. A boy, cut down and carried off to pagan gods.

Her Majesty's hand rose to her lips in disgust.

At the foot of a jute statue, the natives lay the boy down and began to club him with the blunt ends of their spears. They made contact with the boy, who was just into his manhood. Sixteen, maybe. The beating was light by the sound of the wood against his back. It was all for show, for her benefit. Every few strikes, the natives paused in their violence and their war cries to glance at the top-hatted barker for direction. Their pale eyes pleaded. *Do we have to keep doing this?* Then they resumed hitting the boy.

"Stop," the queen said softly. "Make it stop."

"Your Majesty?" one of the women accompanying the queen said.

He moved through the crowd, closer to the front and the African village. It smelled like the lie that it was, plaster and woodrot. He feared being seen, but the queen's face beckoned to him. She was in some sort of agony.

"Stop this." Her voice was hoarse and weak. "It's awful, that you should do this in front of us. We cannot see this."

"Mother," Princess Louise said, "are you unwell?"

"I sent him away."

The queen spoke those words to the natives. He saw her do it. He heard her, as clear as anything anyone had ever said.

The natives dropped their spears. They stood uncertainly around the boy, who winced confusedly as he rubbed his neck.

The queen looked at them with such obvious clarity that he no longer cared if he might be seen. Whether she, the princess, or anyone recognized him didn't matter. It didn't matter that there had always been a wall separating him from everyone else.

Look at her, he thought.

Princess Louise took the queen by the arm. "I sent him away and I knew he'd die," the queen blurted as her daughter tried to turn her from the exhibit. "Of course I did. I could have fought on. I could have hidden him or just told him to run. I could have done something. Oh, *God*."

"There were no choices left to us," Princess Louise argued. "You know that, don't you? After all these years, Mother, please don't torture yourself now. Not now, of all times."

"Oh God, I killed Alamayou, I *killed him*."

She crumpled to the cold pavement. "Alamayou!" she cried as the princess cradled her head in her arms. The gendarmes joined her. The natives vaulted their exhibit's fence to aid the queen. They made a tight circle around her, closing in fast.

"Leave her alone!" the princess screamed, and they all backed away. "Can't you see she's dying?"

§

IT WAS A BRILLIANT blue afternoon in the Marais district of Paris. On Rue Malher, in front of Congregation Ha Kehilot, the late daylight made a calliope of pale white buildings.

He let the warm flickers of the synagogue's candles draw him to its windows. Looking in, he was soothed by the sight of its pews and its ark behind doors and musty curtains that no amount of washing or fresh air could fix. Nothing new or unexpected, and that was what he craved. That the places he knew stayed as he knew them. No startling, upheaving changes. Nothing akin to a queen coming out of nowhere, floating on the sea, and crying out as she collapsed.

Everything kept shifting around him as it always did at that strange hour bridging day to night. When he felt so alone that it was impossible to accept that he could belong anywhere, to anyone, it was good to step outside and let a bit of life turn itself toward him. And it did. The sun threw faint shadows, then a lone cloud came from some far place where perhaps it once carried rain, and slowly the shadows and the light were erased.

It was hard to believe that this was his life he peered at. For almost eighteen years he'd lived in the modest *appartement* above Ha Kehilot, working in the synagogue in exchange for rent. The Jews were good to him. They believed his kind shouldn't be vilified for the color of their skin. The Jews concerned themselves with the manner of living here in the world, not in any imagined hereafter. He respected them immensely, even if he didn't always understand them.

He understood one of them, at any rate. The man he knew best, a rabbi named Ariel. Ever since the day they'd met on the streets of the Marais, the rabbi had asked only that he clean and do the occasional repair, and for such paltry work he was able to live well enough and without any unwanted attention. He'd even set up a clinic of sorts, and he used his medical knowledge to care for Jews old and young. Like him, they weren't wanted and had few options when they became ill.

He supposed that made him a doctor of sorts, in a quiet vein, which protected him. Sometimes, those he treated would stare. It didn't take a mesmerist to know their thoughts. *If I weren't desperate, I'd never resort to the likes of you.*

As a result of his work and Rabbi Ariel's kindness, he'd been able to carve out a decent life in Paris, at least in comparison to some. At night he returned to an appartement, built a fire in the hearth, enjoyed suppers of game and glasses of good port, and retired to a book by the firelight.

But things were different now. He knew it in his heart. There was no going back to the man he was before. Seeing Queen Victoria rise out of his past into the pale Villefranche sun was shocking enough, but in a way she'd always been there, silently accompanying him on all his journeys. Now, for the first time in three decades, he was thinking of London. Of his once-life in that unimaginable city. Of war and Windsor.

Dying. Princess Louise said she was dying. And the word on the queen's lips, if she really was at the last turn of the earth, was that name.

Alamayou.

He stood in the street outside Congregation Ha Kehilot like an imbecile, hoping something might magically give him a reason not to do what he increasingly felt he had no choice *but* to do. God, the wind, the dead sunflower clusters in the window of the bakery next door; really, he wasn't picky and any sign would work if it calmed his racing mind.

Inside, the rabbi would be preparing for Shabbat. There was nothing left to do but go in and tell the old man what had happened over the three days that he'd been away, even as the sight of the crumpling queen swam through his head.

He wouldn't tell Rabbi Ariel what it all meant. Never that.

And when he calls you by name, respond, and keep from him what you've always kept.

He found the rabbi in the *oratoire*, dusting the carved doors of the ark. He was an old, stooped man with a thorny white beard. His eyes were a rainstorm gray, abundant with patience and friendship.

"Philip!" the rabbi cried.

He waved to the rabbi as he closed the synagogue door.

"*Boruch aschem!*" Rabbi Ariel walked unsteadily toward him, his arms outstretched. "Where have you been? I've been worried sick. I thought something happened to you."

"You're dusting. I should be doing that, *rebbe.*"

"You'd deprive an old man of the only exercise he gets? Now, let me sit."

He helped the rabbi to a rickety pew and lowered him down.

"Seeing you relieves me," Rabbi Ariel said, breathing hard, "and yet I can feel my heart like a hammer. What happened?"

"Did you know that Her Majesty Queen Victoria is visiting France?" He tried to be light and airy.

"Yes," the rabbi said. "I read it in the papers. Such a fuss over an old woman. I might travel more if everyone parted like the Red Sea for me."

"I saw her. I was out walking and there she was."

"Philip, *meyn zun*, tell me what has happened to you. You look sick."

For a moment he wanted to say everything that he'd been hiding for three decades.

"Help me up, Philip."

Rabbi Ariel rose with some difficulty. It reminded him of the queen, the way the old Jew's body failed him.

The rabbi went to the door of the synagogue and opened the wooden flap above the knob. There was a sign underneath that he revealed to the street, *Closed—illness*, and the address of another Jewish congregation a few streets over.

He'd made the sign for the rabbi a few years earlier, painted it, sanded and polished it, cut it to fit, and built a wooden cover that could be opened and closed over it. *Only when I need it*, the rabbi had said, *only when I'm too ill to help my people. May the day never come.*

There had been more and more of those days.

"But the congregants will be here soon, rebbe, and you're perfectly well to lead *Shabbos* services."

"Don't tell me how I am," the rabbi said.

"Stubborn. I'll tell you that."

"From one who knows stubbornness all too well. Come, have tea with me. We'll talk awhile. If you're not too long-winded, maybe I'll get to evening services after all."

Together they climbed up one flight of chipped wooden steps to the rabbi's appartement. Down a dark hallway from his own, it was larger and full of smells that carried the old country. Schmaltz, potato, sweet wine, onion, the sulphur of tinders struck at evening, the sourness of age wrapped in Paris heat and damp. The rabbi's walls were barnacled with Stars of David and mezuzahs, gilt-edged portraits of long-dead rabbis, and sketches of the Torah scrolls.

Ariel was a widower, and he missed her. He'd heard the old man on some nights reciting the *kaddish* and crying her name, Devorah. There were sons, though he never saw them. The rabbi once said the new world took them away with promises of beautiful *vomen*, music and dancing, a life in normal clothes with no *tefillin* wrapped like chains around their arms. It had been years since the rabbi had heard from them. They'd succeeded in losing themselves among the multitudes.

He often wondered what that would be like, to lose himself out there among the millions like the rebbe's sons. To be so much like others around him that no one even saw him. Just one raindrop in a storm.

Rabbi Ariel brewed a weak tea and brought him a cup. It wasn't the beefy English tea that he still craved each morning, but it warmed him as it seeped into his crevices.

The rabbi's hand trembled badly as he set his own cup down on a modest table. It hurt to see the ravages of age overtake his friend. The old man was ill, their gentle teasing of each other aside. He'd become so frail over the last few months.

Rabbi Ariel was the one he most often saw, a kind and even fatherly man. One day he'd awakened to the realization that he feared the loss of the curmudgeonly old Jew, and he wasn't used to such notions. It had been far too long since he'd let his heart open.

"Tell me what's on your mind, Philip."

The rabbi's was a honeyed and startling voice when heard in private, in a close and cluttered appartement. He never tired of it despite its harsh edges when speaking the Jewish language. It carried a melody of mild complaint that he'd come to learn was natural for a people herded throughout history to deprivation and death.

We never sound like that, he would tease the old man, *and we Negroes have plenty to complain about.*

Then the Negro should learn to speak up a little more, the rabbi would say.

"I think I have to go to London, rebbe."

"Many years since you were there, yes?"

"Yes. Many years."

"But now, a need?"

"I suppose. Yes, one could put it as such."

"This language of yours, my friend. You think you should go. One could. Consider, *kavana*. To live life with intention. Purpose."

"'Kavana.' Yes, it's a good word."

"*Oy*, Philip. You're missing my point as usual. A good word? A good *life*. There in London, a good life waits for you?"

"I didn't say I was going to a new life."

"You didn't need to. Who disappears for days to consider a brief voyage across the Channel? So where will you live?"

"I've made some arrangements for what I'll need. There's a property on Frith, in Little Britain. Not that you'd know. But it ought to be suitable for me, and I've learned it's available. Who can say its condition. It's as good a place to begin as any."

"That's important, to have somewhere to begin, or begin again. Yes?"

"I listen to you, rebbe, and suddenly I don't know if I will come back. I truly don't."

"Then my friend, have you not already departed?" Rabbi Ariel smiled, clearly enjoying being right. "How much will have changed since you were there? Can you even imagine?"

"I can't."

"You've told me where you need to go, Philip, but you've said nothing of why. What's happened to do this to you?"

"Do what?"

"Make you leave your home."

He felt undone by that word. "Home." It carried too much.

"This is hard for me, rebbe."

"I know. Such a quiet man must forget he has a voice. Do you have work tonight?"

"No. Not tonight."

"Good. Nor do I. Let's sit awhile. I'd like to hear."

He took one breath and hoped that it was pure, and told Rabbi Ariel all that he'd seen at Villefranche and the Exposition.

The rabbi listened patiently, until the last word.

"'Alamayou'? I know that name."

"The Abyssinian, rebbe. The orphan taken in by Queen Victoria thirty-odd years ago."

"I vaguely remember the story. He was the son of the emperor of that country, right? He came to England after the war his madman father started."

"Yes."

"I want to say I heard about this Alamayou's story from you, when you came up to me that first day on the street."

"You did hear it from me."

"I'm so sorry, Philip. How horrible to see such a thing as that zoo. Men can be monsters."

The rabbi refilled both of their cups. He looked into the tea and saw his reflection there. Tapping the side of the cup, he was swept away by the tiniest of waves beneath the steam's cloud cover.

"But London?" the rabbi asked. "I don't understand. From such a story, bad as it is, all this? It shouldn't cause so much *tsoris*. A troubled heart. A sudden need to go back where you came from after so much time's passed. I can see the pain it's bringing you. You're a good man, Philip. Take that with you wherever you may go."

"You don't know me, rebbe. I'm no good man." A breath. "I lie."

"Listen to me." The rabbi put a fatherly hand on his leg, patting it. "I've known you these many years and though we don't dine together or take long walks in the moonlight, still I think I know enough. You have a human heart, yes?"

"Of course. Though some believe men like me to be no better than apes."

"So to those people, you lie. You present yourself as a gentleman when you're tied in knots with anger, as I've seen you more than once. You show yourself to be quiet and contrite when you know more than they do. The heart has many rooms, my friend, but only room to hold so much. The rest is a facade, not meant to be inhabited."

"Well said."

"We Jews have the gift of gab, you know."

"Three decades with you. Yes, I think I know." They laughed quietly. "You're a wise and good man yourself, rebbe."

"You see how skilled a liar I am? Stay in Paris with me, and learn from the very best."

He blurted it. "I knew Alamayou. And the queen. I was there at Windsor. I lived there with them for a time. God, such a short time before it all ended."

"Philip, I've seen more of you in a day than in the years I've known you. What you want to say, say. My son, my son."

It was more than he could bear. In three days' time he'd heard too many words cast skyward in surprise and loss. *My son.*
Alamayou.

He quickly left, knowing the rabbi wouldn't follow.

§

QUEEN VICTORIA AND THE princess left France the following day, on a morning of quiet, steady rain. She crossed the Channel in the ivory light of a sky wrapped in silky gray cumulus to the fanfare of a brass band and hundreds of onlookers. The *Journal des débats* reported on her visit and her departure in bold headlines, but it made no mention of her visit to the Exposition Universelle or her breakdown before the dreaded dark race, and said nothing about the name she cried out before falling.

No one in Paris recognized that name. Certainly not in the Marais where he'd found the closest thing to belonging that he'd known after his own Channel crossing so long ago. Shortly after his arrival in Paris, he'd made a test of it, asking several people on too many streets to recall. He said the name out loud, saw their utter confusion or indifference, and never uttered it again.

After so many years of silence, one spoken word could be louder than anything. Louder than rockets, louder than war.

Alamayou.

He packed his trunk as if he wouldn't come back. Atop the bed he placed a note for the rabbi.

Hold my apartment for as long as you think reasonable. Await word from me. Sell what can be sold if I don't return in that time. My gratitude is yours. I wouldn't have taken offense if you'd refused to speak to the likes of me thirty years ago.

To the Channel.

§

HE MADE HIS WAY by train and carriage to a quiet dock at Menton. Soon the boat would emerge from the bank of sea-clinging clouds to carry him away. In all he'd travel some thirty hours.

London waited.

The rain slowed to a fine mist. Paris was transformed, made a dream as he left it. Behind him, the storm lidded the city in woolen light. The rain smudged Paris's steel, making it appear impressionistic and suggested, both beautiful and impossible to see clearly. Soon, though, the city would explode in foliage, blossom, earthen-toned umbrellas and children in boarding school lines, shedding their coats despite the warnings of the *proviseurs*, to play where now he saw only puddled reflections of the battleship clouds passing overhead.

Over the years he'd lived there, he'd witnessed the city evolve in a wondrous geometric progression. Roofs of tar and flinty stone gave way to spires, to gleaming metal, and to artisan glass. The open sky became stitched with wire, along which the voices of the age carried. Dirigibles floated like clouds and, because of them, the world below came to think of its hemispheres as something to be measured and traveled.

It was a time of marvels. So much to consider. Almost too much to take in.

He stood at the boundary Channel and thought of Alamayou as London first saw him. A stranger who emerged from the war that leveled the only world he'd known, who came with nothing but a legacy too large and terrible to put into English words, who grew like London and Paris until there was no more room and the truth of his life burst into the open, at last. An orphan, accused of murder before the queen and Parliament.

There had been a moment back at Ha Kehilot when he was certain he'd say it all, but he'd been too terrified of the destruction doing that would surely cause. How could he even begin to save a human being, a life? The only thing he knew how to do was what he'd always done. Hold that life inside of him. It had been enough until his glimpse of the queen. Now, it felt as if there was nothing left inside but the secret he carried.

The boat came for the Channel crossing. He let the others board first so they wouldn't take offense. Porters carried their possessions, but he carried his own. While they were seated and attended to, he provided papers proving him fit and free to travel.

When it was clear that his presence was an undeniable fact, he dragged his trunk and found a seat well apart from the others.

A few passengers appeared queasy at the insistent turn of the water. He could have suggested Doan's pills or a pressure point to push to lessen the nausea. But he wasn't called upon, and besides it wasn't any of his business.

"I brought you some of my tea, Philip. I knew how much you'd miss it."

Rabbi Ariel took a seat next to him. He held a fat cloth valise packed full for a journey.

"What are you doing, rebbe?"

"All my life spent in one *arrondissement*. What use does anyone have for a man like me, who lives his whole life without seeing the world? Now you, you've seen things. Perhaps you'll tell me about them as we travel. It will help pass the time, or so I'm told."

"It's better that I'm alone. In London I don't even know what will happen to me. If you understood, you'd want no part of this. You'd turn around and go back to the Marais while you still could."

"I've decided I can't live with the not knowing. Like it or not, you matter to me. So if it's complaint about my being here, *sha*. Go back to your silences. But if you'd like to entertain me with some stories of Abyssinians and royalty, you'll find me an amiable listener."

He looked as any good father might look at his child. There was tolerance and concern in his eyes, along with a pervasive weariness.

He pitied the rabbi's ungrateful missing sons, that they somehow decided their father's eyes weren't worth the hard work of remaining.

The ferry got underway. His thoughts came untethered to drift on the winds, across the water to London.

"How did you meet such people?" Rabbi Ariel asked.

"It began in the Abyssinian war."

"Simple as that, eh?"

He sighed. "During the battle at Meqdala, there was a small cottage on a mountain peak. It was on fire. After that we returned to live at Windsor for a year, give or take. That's all there is to it. You can go home now."

"*Sha.*" The rabbi settled back, making it clear he wasn't going anywhere.

"War isn't an easy thing to talk about."

"Nothing's easy for you to talk about," Rabbi Ariel said sourly.

War. No words could hold it. It was vividly death, but also vividly life. He'd seen the faces of the men waiting to be turned loose to charge the battlefield where they knew they'd die. He'd seen the impossibility in their eyes. No one was so alive.

It's a long ferry ride to London, he thought, *and I ought to say something more. I guess the rabbi's right about me, though I won't give him the satisfaction. He knows me better than anyone has for a long time. I've forgotten my voice for some things.*

"You'll tell me it's none of my business," the rabbi said, "but I don't understand the point of this trip."

"My trip."

"Our trip now."

"The queen is ill. Terribly ill. The princess said so."

"A sad thing. Are you her doctor?"

"I need to see her before she's gone and it's too late. That's all."

The rabbi opened a book and began to read, his lips moving with the words.

Reaching into his coat pocket, he withdrew an aged, yellowed letter and unfolded it along its well-worn creases.

9 January 1869

> *Love is language. It comes to us before we can speak it. It demands our fluency. Learning it undoes us, or brings us home.*

Maybe it's finally time, he thought, *for my life to be this. These words. Nothing in my life has ever brought me home. Maybe the only thing that will is the truth.*

He got up and walked to the bow of the ferry, away from the rabbi and the rest of the passengers, as a curious sensation settled over him. A ship, the water, viewed from this spot as it steered away from all he'd known, making its way to a strange place. He'd been in this precise place before. Each time he found himself crossing a boundary body of water, it was because the world was changing right out from under him.

Now look at me, he thought. *Crossing the Channel as if no time has passed since the first crossing, when I was someone else.*

ONE

Chapter Two

22 August 1868

Aboard the Feroze

Royal Victorian Harbor

ALAMAYOU FOUGHT TO STAY on his feet as he followed the curve of a narrow pitching corridor that spanned the entire hull bottom of the *Feroze*. He was in search of the ship's cargo hold, where much of what the English had taken from Abyssinia was kept.

The fever that had gripped him for weeks was finally receding. His chills were subsiding to slight tremors beneath his skin and his vision was clearing of the hot fog that mottled everything from the ship's lamps to the stars.

It was late and most of the *Feroze*'s crew slept in their thatch and metal bunks. Above every returning soldier was another, and one above him. Each cabin lined its war-weary men along the walls as if they were trophies from a hunt.

He'd spent most of the night before up on deck, wrapped in a thin blanket that offered him no warmth. There he'd kept watch from the rail, staring at the coming sea as if it could give back what it had taken from him. Clouds had covered the waves completely, hiding everything. If not for the constant roar of the water as it swept against the ship, he would have sworn the *Feroze* could fly.

Where he was now, below deck, it was almost easy to pretend the night before hadn't happened. He hadn't stood on deck with the salt air lacerating his skin and the starless sky a pitiless canopy over the ship, watching the clouds gather low above the waves like a white dream. He hadn't stood there for hours, thinking of how it would feel to jump.

He descended through holes, down ladders and steps. Night persisted in the lower ship no matter what time of day it was, so he carried a lamp and walked behind the pale yellow space it opened in the dark. The shuddering flame cast a rippling circle against the floor, and as he watched the motion inside the circle of light, he thought, *That's what wind would look like if it could be seen.* As he stumbled along, he ran his hand along the hull's wood. It was always cold and carried the sense of water even though it was dry.

After what seemed like hours spent wandering, he arrived at the cargo hold where his country's treasures were kept. On their first night at sea almost four months before, Philip—the one he'd stayed with over the many months at sea, the one he'd seen for the first time at the fire that killed what remained of his family—had held up a finger outside the same room. Alamayou hadn't understood what that meant at the time, but he understood now. Philip had held up his finger that first night aboard the ship to say, *One thing.* Take one thing from the room that once was part of his life in Abyssinia. As a comfort, Alamayou supposed. He hadn't that day. He wasn't ready.

He pushed the door open and went inside.

Beyond the lamp's weak glow, a cavern full of crates, suspended nets jutting out at odd angles from the mismatched shapes stuffed inside, and rugs piled high with carelessly strewn trinkets stretched almost the length of the ship's bottom. Things he'd used, held, knew every day of his childhood, had been pulled from the wreckage of his father's fortress after it collapsed under the English assault. Now it all lay in pieces alongside each other. The English had put it here in pairings that never happened in life. His father's crosses, Bibles, and muskets lay gouged and bent next to his mother's broken jewelry, her torn clothes, and shattered pottery. None of it looked real anymore.

In the corner of the cargo hold there was a fragment of the shield given to him by his father, or one so much like it that he almost blacked out. He steadied himself against the corner of a crate, waiting for the months at sea, the war, the sight of his mother and father in the fire at Amba Geshen, all to stitch itself back together and make sense. He waited and looked around the hold for anything to keep while the lamp's wick sputtered in its own flame.

He left the remains of his country behind and walked to the other side of the hold, where the English kept the weapons they'd used in the war. Armstrong batteries. Eight-inch mortars. Snider rifles. All the things they used to pour steel into Abyssinian men.

This room held the end of Abyssinia. He already had enough pieces of that inside of him.

There's no use pretending, he thought. The lie didn't keep him warm any more than the rag of a blanket had. He sat on the cold floor, in the orphan space between the English weapons and the wreckage of his father's fortress at Meqdala, and said it out loud.

"Last night at the rail of this ship, I thought about joining you."

He'd been alone on deck the night before, at least for a time. He'd tested the rail's ability to hold his weight. He'd run his fingers along its damp, pitted wood to see how slippery it was. Too slippery and he'd fall before he was ready.

Had he jumped, it all would have been over by now. The fever, the loneliness and fear, the terrible things he'd seen—real, imagined, some awful mix of both—everything would be silence. Whatever fate waited for him in the days and weeks ahead would never find him.

The moment his body would have hit the water, he surely would have filled with horror even as his lungs froze and his heart stopped and dank seawater pushed inside of him. Had he done it, he would have known a moment of flight, then falling, and, longest of all, the hopeless fear of dying alone, cold, and suffocating.

No one would hear him cry that he'd been wrong, that he was afraid to die and wanted to be saved.

In the last moment before it all went away, he wondered if he would have seen them again. *Abat. Anat.*

And then he'd heard a noise, turned away from the sea and the horror his fever had made him believe he saw in the waves, and there was Philip. He couldn't understand why. He'd been quiet when he'd left their cabin and, what was more, they barely knew each other. They didn't speak each other's language and could only communicate with their hands, with gestures and grunts. Their only connection was the war and their skin. They were the only two blacks aboard.

Philip didn't owe him anything, and when he'd awakened and seen Alamayou's bunk empty, he could just as easily have rolled over and gone back to sleep. But there he'd been and at just the right time, staring at him with the same expression he'd worn at the fire on Amba Geshen. Like he needed to say something, but there were no words for it.

It was as if Philip had known that dark thoughts were gathering on the deck, like the clouds gathered above the sea. All he had to do was look at Alamayou and he could see Alamayou conjuring it, to see if throwing himself off the ship's rail was the right and only thing left to do, and now it mattered that Alamayou turn away from the waves and stay on board with the living.

Maybe there's something about me, Alamayou thought. *A mark of some kind. This ruined hand, maybe, or something else, and everyone can tell I'm not meant for living in the world. Maybe Philip has it too, and that makes it easy for him to see it in me.*

We're two black monsters, not fit for anything but fires and oceans.

He left the hold without taking anything.

Finding the steps out of the ship's bottom, he climbed as the sounds of the *Feroze* began to rise with the dawn. Men called to each other and it sounded like a dirge. The clang of metal and the thud of booted footsteps echoed like drums, like the *negrit* at Meqdala.

He didn't want to see the deck again so soon after the long night, but the ship was beginning to slow. Wherever it was that they'd been heading, it felt as if they were close. He needed to at least see the rumor of the land, and see for himself the place where they'd been taking him all this time.

§

THE THUNDERCLAP OF BELLS woke Philip. He bolted upright in the dark of the cabin, the way worried men do at late hours. The bells brought him to the cabin's porthole where he saw little. The lightening sea, the steamers and frigates splitting the water on approach to the *Feroze*.

Home at last, he thought bitterly before turning to rouse his cabinmate.

Alamayou's bunk was empty, its threadbare blanket gone.

Panic burst brightly in his chest. He leapt to his feet and began to dress in the murk, his thoughts bounding wildly from one possibility to the next. The Abyssinian was lost. He was wandering the corridors or, worse, grief stricken at being alone in the world. Back on deck, with that haunted look he'd seen the night before. What in bloody hell had Alamayou been thinking there at the rail?

Philip wished he had words the Abyssinian could understand. *You're sad and scared and sick with fever. You're wondering, where life's left you off? You and me both, mate. Alone in this shitty world, and me longer than you. Just stay above ground. You may starve for just one good thing in your life, but maybe each day you'll see something worth the trouble of the next day. Don't let these bastards see you looking like you did on deck. Worse than afraid.* Beaten. *Don't give them any more ground than what they were born with, and what they've taken from you since the day their mothers spat them out.*

Philip had spent a year at war and at sea, putting his hands into the dead and dying alongside the doctor he'd apprenticed with, Marcus Baker White. White had already gone to his own death thanks to a sick and pathetic love of drink that the war only deepened. Soldiers had wrapped White's body in a sheet before heaving his corpse over the side of the boat. That was only a day into the voyage home from Abyssinia.

Since then, he and Alamayou had spent four months at sea, on a ship of white men returning from a campaign of killing black men—men like him, men exactly like Alamayou. Philip could feel their utter contempt every day. The soldiers of the Second Regiment had no need for two Negroes sharing the *Feroze's* limited rations of food and potable water, its cramped space, and its dwindling stores of medicine.

Seeing the Abyssinian at the fire on Amba Geshen, and last night at the rail, felt the same as the war, though Philip couldn't put his finger on the reason. Alamayou standing at the fire, watching it consume his parents. Alamayou at the ship rail, no doubt mourning his country and his life, maybe looking for the impossible: a way out. Somehow, the sight of the only other man on board who looked like him standing alone at the rail made Philip painfully aware of how tired he was. He was bone-tired of bearing witness to the destruction of black men like him.

Like them.

Christ, you fool, he'd thought the night before as he watched Alamayou. *Don't be another one of their dead men. Come away from there.*

Now the sight of the empty bunk made him sick. He finished dressing and left the cabin, already breathless. If something happened to the Abyssinian prince before they reached London, the soldiers wouldn't need him anymore. He was no doctor and his stupid pride prevented him from being their servant. With no other use, they'd surely kill him. They'd lynch him—like rumor had it was done with the Negroes in the old colonies.

He'd be no better off than a runaway slave. They'd string him up like a chicken, sear him head to foot in tar, and leave him to strangle in the sea sun beneath a coat of pitch blacker than his skin.

He made his way through the dim veins of the *Feroze*. Its bottom hull had been built in tribute to a ship that broke apart in a storm at sea some forty years before. Bearing the name of a dead man, the *John Mackenzie* met a terrible gale that sent veins of wind and light through its hull until it burst. Parts of it washed ashore for a month. Whole pieces of its frame that were still seaworthy made their way into the skeletons of new ships.

He located the deck by following the salt smell and the raucous bellowing of the men putting things in crates and tying it all down while great-necked machines moved through the port water to the *Feroze* to lift it and take it to the decks of other circling ships. There was never silence. The sea never lost its voice. Neither did the soldiers who cursed, laughed, or cried in the corridors outside their cabins at night when they thought no one could hear.

When he found Alamayou at the same rail, wrapped in his bunk blanket, he nearly buckled with relief. He walked over as his anger rose. "Jesus, nothing good comes of you wandering off. What is it with you and this bloody deck?"

He put a hand on Alamayou's forehead. It was cooler to the touch than it had been for weeks. "Fever's breaking. What were you thinking last night? Wandering to the rail as if someone was leading you by the hand. Never seen a man so sick and still standing."

Why bother trying, he thought as he stood with Alamayou at the rail, where the ship shuddered most urgently as waves cut into the sea by the cargo ships swept into its hull. *Him in his shell, me in mine. Most likely we part ways the moment we set foot on dry land again, and then we'll be bound for who knows where. It doesn't matter if he wanders off, or jumps, or stands on his head. Soon I'll be on the street with no prospects. Best to worry about that, not him.*

He opened his mouth to tell Alamayou all that. Words Alamayou wouldn't understand, though the tone of them ought to be clear enough. The deck of a hostile ship at open sea, and exhausted men returning from a war with his father. A man either uses his head or loses it.

There at the rail, the overwhelming spectacle of London came. The murmurings of white men behind them, cold air, and a ceiling of sky stretching far past the landfall where railroad tracks ran the lengths of the quays, below the sooty plumes of the train engines that rose and drifted across the graineries and mills, over the slow-rolling railcars and out again to sea to shroud the forest of swaying ship masts. Farther out, the ghostly shapes of spikes, blocks, domes, and towers huddled in the quilted gray fog.

Jesus Christ, he thought. *Look at what he sees. He's terrified. Who wouldn't be if he never saw a white man's city before.*

London at near dawn, viewed from the sea, was a ceaseless machine with no edges or endings. A man would have better luck searching for the end of the world.

He softened. "London." He pointed, making a wide sweep of the visible city with his arm so Alamayou would understand, London meant everything. "London, Alamayou. And stay off the rails, eh? I've had quite enough of that."

A soldier came to them as the *Feroze* pulled closer to the docks of the Royal Victorian. He wore the uniform of the Second and carried some papers. "Layard, Philip?"

"Yes."

"And you speak for the Abyssinian? The prince, Alamayou?"

"No, I don't. I've had a change in fortune and prospects, is what. I'm here with him now, and no one but me tries to talk to him. That's all it is."

"Be sure that I don't care," the soldier said. "What you take yourself to be, fit company for good men, is wrong. All wrong. You and he are unfit for white men. Soldiers, no less. But Her Majesty called for him to come back because she has a heart. That's why you weren't heaved overboard or sold off."

"England's no slaver," Philip said. "Not in my lifetime."

"A change in your fortune, like you say." He glanced at his documents. "Once ashore, you'll report to a coach bearing the crest of Windsor and the number twenty-two. Do you understand?"

"Yes."

"Tell the bonnie prince. Use your hands or whatever it is you *kaffirs* do."

"What will happen to us then?"

"I don't know what will happen, but I know what should. Tell the Abyssinian, from me. It's a fool who crosses the world thinking there'll be anything of home to be found. A bigger fool walks out of his own war expecting to be welcome. The chances for either of you to be included in the course of your lives, the devil's got better odds of being christened."

The soldier left them on deck to fend for themselves.

Philip studied Alamayou's face, trying to figure out if the Abyssinian understood his circumstances. He didn't envy the task before Alamayou, now that a city so immense as to invite madness in an orphan of a far-off war stood right in front of him, daring him to come set foot onto its hard heart.

"You can't understand me," he told Alamayou, "but maybe if you listen you'll find something you can hold onto. You're alone. You've got no one. Your mother and father are dead and gone and it's best not to think of them too much anymore. Maybe they'll do what they ought with you, the people who'll deal with you from here on, but it's not much against what's been done to you. Then you'll just be you. Not a damned prince but a colored man like me. I'm alone too, hear? You'll get no help from me though my heart's good, or so I choose to believe. It's my pockets that lay bare and that's all that matters, eh? So don't hope, is what I'm telling you. Hate England if you want. I suppose you've a right if anyone has. Just live how you can, and I will, too."

The Victorian docks loomed. He set his hand on the rail, next to Alamayou's. "See that? We're alike as two shadows. So maybe we're not alone, really. You hear that? Not alone."

As he listened to Philip's indecipherable gibberish, Alamayou watched boats full of cheering Londoners row out to greet the soldiers atop the last waves before the jut of shore. He was on the other side of the world from the only one he'd ever known. The whites were everywhere he looked, like a swarm of locusts. Beyond the visible port was some sort of horizon built of fortresses unlike anything his father could have dreamt from his tent on the plains of the Falah Saddle.

He watched it all come, and he thought of how far away the night before seemed.

"We need to get our things," Philip said. "It's time." He held up a finger. "One thing—"

Alamayou clasped Philip's hand. Some of the soldiers whispered and laughed.

"Why?" he asked Alamayou, but didn't pull his hand back. Warmth pulsed from Alamayou's fire-ravaged palm into his own skin.

After a moment, Alamayou walked away, into the teeth of the white soldiers. He held his head high, as a prince, a *lij*, would do. Holding Philip's hand hurt; he felt the fire in his palm even still. But it was all he wanted to take from the *Feroze*. Just an unbroken moment to hold skin like his own. To not be alone.

§

THEY STUMBLED DOWN THE gangplank to the dock of the Royal, where constables by the hundreds cleared a path from the pier to the limits of the city, forcing cheering onlookers to either side.

At the queue for carriages they were presented with letters and ushered into a modest trap bearing the crest of Windsor and the number twenty-two. Soon they were clattering along Cumberland Terrace on the east side of Regent's Park, passing white balconies,

Ionic columns of granite polished to fine neoclassical bone, and endless blocks of sculptural pediments and arches.

Their carriage passed the Royal Zoo and its signs depicting the animals donated by Queen Victoria for the benefit and enjoyment of her subjects. The hippo, the orangutan, the tigress, the 150-year-old tortoise sent in loving gratitude to Her Majesty by a family left standing after the plunder of the Cape of Good Hope. One colorful drawing, a rhinoceros, came beneath the bold claim: *The unicorn of faerie tale come to true life!*

From the carriage window they saw a large cage with a lone elephant inside. The creature picked at the low boughs of a beech tree, releasing a cascade of leaves that whirled to the ground.

Soon the lane ahead lay clear and the larks sang high above. A light wind tossed leaves into the carriage's path. The day warmed and the Thames murmured somewhere to the west. The visible world transformed from open road to Dutchett and its ribbons of color bursting elms, the fetlock of the Horseshoe Cloister, the Norman Gate, and the motte upholding all.

Windsor rose before Alamayou's disbelieving eyes.

He searched Philip's face, hoping for some sleight of hand to make it understandable; the people that destroyed his country could also put immeasurable beauty and immensity into it. But Philip's hands were silent, so he sat back in the carriage, staring at the barrel of the Round Tower.

Where his father's fortress was a crude extension of the mountains it stood against, this was a dream of glass and stone, the work of artists with imaginations beyond anything he'd ever known. The castle pressed up against the continents of cloud gathering up from the east. Its silhouette was an upturned key at the vanishing point of the Long Walk.

Up on the range of rolling grasses, there was a magnificent ball, as big as a ship, tethered with netting to a basket large enough to hold ten grown men.

"A balloon," the coachman explained. "It rises at twilight from Chisholm Hill in the shadow of the tower. From up there ye see London. Some of 'er lights never go out. Like stars below ye. Like ye left the very world."

"He doesn't understand a bloody word," Philip said.

"I wager ye he will when it flies."

The royal grounds already bustled with activity. Huntsmen walked leashed mastiffs past show horses of rare breed cantering gracefully along the paths encircling the lawns, prodded gently by men of the royal livery. Children ran out of the anxious reach of their nannies, trailing kites with ribbons for tails through the warm light.

In the midst of the chaos was an artist sitting alone and peaceful, considering the fog and the castle while mayflies swirled above open jars of turpentine.

Her Majesty's Guard thundered past, startling Alamayou. He shrank against his seat until they were gone. The horses' eyes seemed to linger on him as they went by. They held the madness of the whip that drove them.

Alamayou winced at every whip crack. His head snapped back as if someone had slapped him. The welling red stripes were easy to see despite the dark hides of the horses. They didn't leave his sight even when he closed his eyes. It didn't matter how dark the skin was. When the whip's tail struck, you could see the wound it made. You could see it for days.

For days after he'd left Amba Geshen with his mother to go to his father's fortress at Meqdala, everyone could see the whip marks. All the servants, all the soldiers. They knew who'd done it.

There were so many things he wouldn't ever speak of, no matter who asked, no matter the language. This was one. These people, they might try to know him. They might try to piece him together from the scraps at the bottom of the *Feroze*, but it wouldn't be enough as there were no words for some things. So they'd come to him and ask him, *tell us everything about you.*

When they did, he would be who they wanted him to be. They might try to make a monster out of him and he wouldn't help them.

"Horses," Philip said. "I saw them in your country, so don't look so surprised. They're not new to you."

Alamayou turned away as the echo of the whip filled him.

The coachman slowed the carriage to a trot. Soon the road fell away and they only saw the sky and the peak of the Round Tower. Behind, wisps of the morning fog tinseled the elms.

They came to a stop at the South Wing. A crowd of court handlers, servants in starched black and white, and midlevel royalty waited as the carriages emptied. Hundreds more lined the horseshoe drive to toss garlands of flowers. In front was Queen Victoria's second daughter, Louise.

Louise came forward to peer into the carriage. She wore a black dress of luminous quality that was scaly in appearance, its buttons hidden beneath folds of heron feathers. Her lace collar sealed her at the throat. About her left arm she wore the Garter, marking her among the St. George order.

She acknowledged Alamayou and Philip with a nod, then left. A group of court women smiled at her return as a child with curled ringlets played among the wide curtains of their dresses. She was draped in an elaborate white gown tailored to her still-boyish frame. She practiced a wedding march, her lace veil making a mystery of her face.

Alamayou stepped into the doorway of the carriage and instantly a wall of soldiers descended upon him, pulling him out onto the Walk. Philip pushed them away. The other soldiers came at him as white faces gathered.

"Let them be," Princess Louise said.

The soldiers complied. Alamayou and Philip stood shoulder to shoulder, waiting for what might come next.

"Are you Philip Layard?" Princess Louise asked. "The Abyssinian's servant?"

"I am, Your Highness. Philip Layard, that is. But no servant to the Abyssinian, Alamayou. We shipped together from Annesley Bay when the war was said and done. On account of our skin, you see."

"If not a servant," she said, "then what brought you to the Abyssinian campaign?"

"I was an assistant to the surgeon attached to the Second."

"You are English, I see. Well done for you. Tell me, how did this one come to attach himself to you in such a manner? Look at the both of you. Like two suits of the same cloth."

"I simply tried speaking to him," Philip said, "and not bringing harm or hate to him. A long voyage and only each other to spend the time."

"So you understand him?"

"Not as such. Not in language, but we gesture, point, and get by with a little luck."

"Clearly the Abyssinian has need of you. Are you both calmed?"

"Yes, Your Highness, and I'm sorry I wasn't ready for the guards taking hold of us. I shouldn't have behaved like that."

"Although it may be that a long sea voyage and a war explains it, be that as it may, you are English, and so for you at least, it was unacceptable to raise a hand to anyone here and we shall not witness it again."

"Yes, Your Highness. It won't happen again."

A small audience gathered to watch. Members of Parliament, of court, the hands upon the gears of England.

"Tell me, Mr. Layard," Princess Louise asked, "how did you come to meet the Abyssinian?"

"The first time I saw him, it was during the Easter attack, on top of a mountain. There was a fire and the doctor I assisted, White, found himself called to go. I went with but no good came of it. Alamayou's parents both burned to death."

"Dear Lord," one of the court women exclaimed.

"Mind who you're speaking to, boy," a gentleman of Parliament said.

"They died," Philip continued, "and he almost did, too. His hand burned."

"A remarkable experience for you," Princess Louise said. "One you were no doubt ill prepared to undertake."

"Nothing could prepare me for what I saw in the war, Your Highness."

The gentleman of Parliament spoke up. "If I may shed a bit of light, Your Highness. May I have the honor of presenting myself. John Hibbert Naismith, attaché to the Chancellor of the Exchequer, recently posted as ambassador to the newly installed governor and council of Abyssinia."

"May you fare better than the last diplomat, poor devil," another Parliamentarian said, shaking his head.

"Indeed," Naismith said. "On behalf of the Abyssinians now at work with our good governor there, I am tasked with accounting as to the health and well-being of their prince, this Alamayou. Alamayou's father was Tewedros, the despot. Theodore, as he is known here. You well know the history of this war. Theodore fancied himself a Christian, locked in a struggle with the Moslem countries surrounding Abyssinia on all sides. He sent word to England that he wished for diplomatic relations, and those were established. Then he asked for weaponry of all kinds and men to build and train his army so it could drive his enemies into the sea."

"The second coming of the Crusades, sounds like," another Parliamentarian remarked.

"Quite so. Her Majesty personally sent a diplomatic corps to express her regrets at not granting his request for weapons. He took that corps hostage."

"And Parliament intervened," the MP said. "Proud to say it was a unanimous vote to go to war. Sixty-two thousand men. Thirty thousand pack animals. An indeterminable number of Shoho retained locally through the tribes who saw in this expedition the end of Abyssinian rule under a tyrant. Seventy-five steamers, twenty sailing vessels, weapons. The most revolutionary of artillery. Rockets, fusillades, ordnance against which no rutted country could stand."

"The war itself?" Naismith said. "Over in a day. Our Easter of this year. As for Alamayou, his mother, the queen Tirroo Wirk, lived apart from Tewedros on a mountain called Amba Geshen. I've seen the reports. A small cottage. During the Easter attack, it was set afire with her inside. Our military believe Tewedros did it for reasons that only a doctor of the mind could understand. From what little we know, Tewedros saw the imminent defeat of his army, took Alamayou to Amba Geshen as his fortress collapsed, and intended to kill himself and his family there in a fire. He perished with the queen. Our men tell us Alamayou's own hand was pried free from his father's. We believe Tewedros was trying to drag his son into the fire with him."

Princess Louise's eyes glinted. "You were there, Layard. You saw this. How ghastly."

Philip wanted to answer her but held back. Naismith's account sounded right, the way *I saw Alamayou standing at the rail of the* Feroze sounded right. Right, but hollow. Something was missing from it that he couldn't quite grasp. It felt too vague and easily lost, like a dream that tattered into nothing when he woke up. All that was left was a feeling with nothing attached to it. No reason to be.

The feeling he'd had seeing Alamayou at the fire on Amba Geshen was the same one he'd had when he saw Alamayou at the rail the night before they landed at the Royal Victoria docks. Maybe there'd been another reason Alamayou was there, in both places and in both moments. Something not readily apparent. That was all he could name, but the feeling was enough to worry him.

He nodded dutifully at the ambassador's account of the fire even as doubt grew in him. It wasn't his place to say anything, especially if he himself couldn't be sure of what had just happened at that cottage. He wasn't going to give them a reason to look askance at Alamayou or him, royalty be damned. Still, what Naismith said felt off.

Maybe, he thought, *maybe he* didn't *see Alamayou's father pull his son into the flames enveloping him and Alamayou's mother. Maybe— he wasn't sure, but maybe—their hands weren't touching at all.*

"It was a terrible thing, the fire," Philip said to the princess. "See here, his hand."

She examined Alamayou's right palm. The scarring had healed only recently.

Alamayou pulled his hand away. Words he recognized, his own name, his father's, and one horrible sound, *fire*, flew between the white faces like birds roused violently into the air. They looked at him with such pity in their eyes. The woman who'd taken hold of his hand turned to her companions as if to say, *He's damaged. He's just another broken piece of Abyssinia.*

"A terrible act indeed," Princess Louise said. "And the Abyssinian witnessed them burn? His own parents? I cannot imagine the horrors he's endured. Or his mother, to belong to such a monster."

"One wonders how she survived as long as she did," Naismith said.

"We must never underestimate the indomitable spirit of a woman," Princess Louise said to the smiles of her audience. "And now the Abyssinian is safe, it seems. We will address your presence later, Mr. Layard. There is the Abyssinian's welfare, of which Her Majesty is interested. But I do wonder why it is that he's been brought here, of all places? There are homes elsewhere, where appropriate sponsors might be located for him. His story touched our mother's heart."

"Ah," the Parliamentarian said wryly. "A reclamation project, is he? Much like cleaning the Thames, this one."

"Begging your pardon," Naismith said, "but the Thames didn't take hostages and it didn't start a war."

"Nor did this young man," Princess Louise said. Naismith fell silent. "I expect all the more interest from the queen when she hears of his ordeal. For the moment, Philip, it seems that you serve a purpose. Companionship. Do you agree?"

"I do if you tell me I do."

Chuckling, the royals and their entourages walked off to the vast lawns of Windsor. The grounds had been prepared by legions of keepers who had uprooted trees, wrapped them in canvas, and carried them off to the far corners of the palace grounds. Paved walkways had been covered in polished wood planking. Seats had been placed across the lawn as far as could be seen, on either side of a massive structure that spanned the length of the field, some one hundred meters and as tall as the Long Walk elms. Struts and timber formed a skeleton that held its weight upright. Its silhouette was jagged and irregular.

"You there."

A man wearing a dinner jacket with split tails, a stiff white shirt with small winged collars, and a centered bow tie, approached. "We have appropriate clothes for the two of you," he said.

Alamayou and Philip followed him into the South Wing where servants in the Upper Ward dyed laundry to a mournful shade. Gray whorls of smoke rose above the Norman Gate, filling the air with the aroma of roasting meat.

Arriving at the East Terrace Apartments, they paused in the threshold of an empty ballroom. Pale lace ribbons hung from its timber ceiling, ivory shoots of cloth that tumbled down to the parquet floor where a group of maids silently took to them with blades. Their work curled the cloth into springs.

After passing through a series of receiving rooms where they were inspected, measured, and talked about in disapproving tones, the man they followed—a butler of some sort, Philip thought, by the haughty airs he put on—led them into an apartment. Its mauve curtains were drawn almost to a close, obscuring the view of the gardens and field, but the portraits on the walls could be plainly seen. Henry VII's court circled them. Reliefs of inlaid marble adorned the ceiling.

They were told to undress by court tailors, who directed them to stand behind separate partitions of wood and abalone shell. The tailors pulled their sea-worn garments apart at the seams, took the boat shoes from their feet, and made them step out of their undergarments. When they stood naked, the tailors turned away in disgust.

Over the course of an hour they fashioned an Abyssinian *shamma* for Alamayou and hastily composed a suit for Philip of subdued brown tweed too warm for the weather, a collared shirt and wretched cravat, and pants cinched at the waist with a frayed belt.

After they were dressed, the butler returned and led them back to the empty ballroom.

At one end, a swatch of black curtain hung from suspended lines. A shield of copper plate, lined in opposing triangles by metal piping, rested against the fabric. Two feathered spears, their sabre blades crossed at the hilts, fashioned an imposing X across the shield. Cushions were placed together to form a seat.

There was a young Indian man of twenty tending to the display. He stood before a camera and motioned for Alamayou to sit on the cushions, then lit candles that had been arranged at the base of each linen strip. The candle stems were framed in small boxes of red glass. When ignited, they cast an ember glow upon the linen.

"He needs to sit," the Indian said. His voice was gentle. "I'll make this as painless as can be for a scared young man asked to sit still."

The photographer slipped free from the camera cloak. A white woman, dressed not of the city but rather in a colorful shawl. "You must be Philip, and this one Alamayou. Do you understand what Alamayou is to do? Can you help explain it to him?"

"Look at him," Philip said. "Do you think he understands?"

Alamayou brushed one of the streamers dangling against the shield, which was a fraud, in no way like the shield his father had made him use. This one was made of some light wood that felt full of air.

"What's the point of all this?" Philip asked. "What're these to be, fire falling 'round his head? You mean to pose him like that, fresh from a war?"

"My purpose," she said, her voice rising indignantly, "is two-fold. To do as the royal family asks, and to create an image so others can see the young prince of Abyssinia. Is that plain enough? There's a curiosity about him, don't you realize? For months we've read of this odd prince on the way here from war. He's more than a young man. He's the answer to the questions of a country. On orders from Her Majesty's emissaries, he will sit for this and you will make him understand."

Philip went to Alamayou. "Sit." He pointed to the pillows.

"No," Alamayou said. "Abat."

"You know bloody well I don't understand you—"

"No!"

Alamayou took the pillows and threw them across the room. He pulled down the shield and stood in the wreckage, proud and defiant.

"I don't know what 'abat' means," Philip told the photographer, "but I suggest you take what he's giving you while you can."

Muttering under her breath, the photographer stepped back under the camera cloak. Her assistant hung a colored sash across Alamayou's midsection and placed a necklace of lion's teeth and beads around his neck, all the while staring at him nervously.

Alamayou didn't stop him. His eyes lowered as he sent his thoughts away.

Under the camera cloak came the whirring of a mechanism. Alamayou didn't understand what it was, only that he had no choices and needed to be careful. Still, he wouldn't sit on a throne of pillows as his abat had in front of a shield meant to evoke the ones carried by all the Abyssinian dead.

The Indian knelt to him. "Are you well?"

He understood enough to return the Indian's gaze.

"One day," the Indian said to Philip, "he'll look at this picture and remember his first moments here. I hope that will be a good thing."

The Indian and the photographer finished. They crated the moment that they had stilled and took it away.

§

THE BUTLER RETURNED. OUTSIDE, he said, was a gathering they needed to be a part of. "This is what he must say." He handed Philip a note. "See to it."

I was a stranger, it read, *yet you took me in.*

"It's in English," Philip said. "How's he supposed to read it or speak it? How do I even make him understand?"

"Find a way."

He brought them to a midpoint on the lawn, to face what looked like hundreds of white faces. Taking the note from Philip, he pressed it into Alamayou's hand. "If he knows what's good for him." He left them.

"May it please Your Majesties!" The master of ceremonies stood on a far platform. He spoke into a brass tube that sent his voice everywhere. "The young prince Alamayou, brought to you from the remotest corner of the world to this safe harbor by the friendship and affection of Her Majesty the queen, and all of England. We welcome this stranger to our country."

Alamayou stood in silence as the field filled with sights and sounds that mystified him. The dogs they'd seen from the carriage ride onto the castle grounds now raced each other in pursuit of some sort of pelt, pulled at top speed by one of the horses. Acrobats leapt over each other while juggling all manner of oddities. Rings, clubs, even swords. Men standing on wooden sticks towered above the audience. They danced an odd series of steps while below, little people no higher than his knee frolicked between their wooden legs.

Another horse walked slowly onto the field, led by a white soldier wearing a shamma. The horse was a deep brown chestnut with a white stripe across its flank. Its nose was scarred. Brightly colored ribbons dangled from its mane.

"An Abyssinian game played by the warrior class," the master of ceremonies announced.

As Alamayou watched confusedly, the soldier demonstrated *gugs*, the horseback game he'd grown up watching his father's army play. It was a warlike game where men charged at each other atop their horses, each man trying to knock the others off their mounts.

While he stared, the master of ceremonies called out, "Does the Abyssinian prince have something to say to us?"

"He doesn't understand what you want from him!" Philip shouted back. "Let me read it for him."

"Unacceptable. Look at him. He's not even paying attention."

From the box seats alongside them, a frail-looking figure stood. Using his cane, he steadied himself, waving off the servants who came to his aid. He was as young as they, perhaps seventeen, with a boy's wispy moustache and carelessly combed hair that the insistent sun plastered to his pale brow.

"He must recite by himself," the young man said, leaning forward to be heard. He pointed the silver tip of his cane at Alamayou. "There are eyes on him."

"I've told too many to count," Philip shouted, "he can't speak English. And I can't just give him the words, can I? I don't know how. I don't know how to talk to him and I don't know why you all think I do!"

The man turned to speak to the others in the box.

Alamayou's robes billowed in the wind. He held the paper out to Philip and pointed at the soldier atop his horse. "Gugs."

"I think he wants to play," the soldier laughed. He brought his horse alongside Alamayou and looked down at him. "If it pleases Your Majesties, since this Abyssinian can't speak, may we see if he can ride?"

The audience clapped expectantly. In a moment, a similarly decorated horse was brought to Alamayou. Ignoring the reins, Alamayou leapt atop its back and took the blunted pole from the soldier. They rode to opposite ends of the field, then turned their horses to face each other hundreds of meters apart.

"Come then!" the soldier shouted at him, to the delight of the audience. "Let's have a good old-fashioned English joust!"

"Leave him alone!" Philip shouted. "He's a human being, not a damned trained monkey! Is this what you brought him here for, to make a joke of him?"

Alamayou didn't know what they wanted from him. He could see that Philip was upset, maybe at the thought that he could get hurt. He wanted to tell him, *I know this game. It's a game of war. Men die for it. My father knew war and nothing else. I played my father at it once, with his words in my head*—ride, don't stop until one of us is dead—*and his gun in my hand. Yes, I know this game.*

His father had taught him gugs on the same day that he'd spoken of his own life before becoming emperor. It was the only time Alamayou recalled his father ever saying anything about himself that wasn't *doomfata*, the boasting of soldiers that they were brave, that they couldn't die.

That day, his father said that as a boy on a farm at the foot of the Entoto hills, he'd grown up loving horses. Remembering made his father smile, revealing sparse, broken teeth. In his youth he'd played at gugs and dreamt of being a soldier, but as a man he'd seen too many battles. He was tired all the time. In his dreams he smelled blood.

That was the most words he'd ever spoken to Alamayou, and the happiest Alamayou had ever seen him.

"I'm your father and I demand it of you," Tewedros had said. "Learn gugs. Be a man for me."

He'd led Alamayou to a deep brown horse much like the one he sat on now in front of the English. After Alamayou had gotten on that horse, his father had handed him a heavy shield. "Gugs is a game of war," his father had said. "It takes lives."

"I've seen it at Debre Tabor," Alamayou told his father. "Men die for a game. There's nothing more pointless."

"Men live. They are glorified. It belongs to them, that they do not die where other men do. Even if they belong to another as you do to your father. The gugs always belongs to the man who lives."

He'd tried to find a comfortable position to hold the shield but felt tilted and precarious. When the horse twisted to see him, he'd sensed its resentment that the flight it was capable of couldn't be appreciated by a boy who'd rather be on the ground drawing and staring at vistas.

His father had ridden off, halting several hundred paces away. "Ride fast, lij, and knock me down."

"You think I won't."

It shamed Alamayou, the shaking in his voice. He'd tried to shut it away somewhere he didn't know, where things could go and die inside of him. Or live, but never be seen or heard again.

He hoped such a place existed in the drifting, sailing world.

"Ride to me a man!" his father had taunted and goaded. "Trample me! Then ride away. You are free. Tell my spirit what it is to be free! Do it, coward. Woman! You're too weak to be the son of an emperor. Come at me. Ride until one of us is dead!"

"Come on then!" the soldier screamed again across the English field. There, before the white faces, Alamayou kicked violently at his horse's flanks, sending it hurtling headlong toward the soldier in the shamma. His speed, the sheer recklessness of his assault, stunned the audience. The distance between them disappeared.

As they flew past each other, Alamayou swung his pole, knocking the soldier off of his horse.

Alamayou brought his own horse to a halt. Leaping down, he went to check on the soldier as other men came running. Gasps rolled through the crowd.

The young man gestured with his cane, and at his command the butler came with other servants in tow. Hands grabbed Philip roughly. Two servants, little more than hooligans under their oiled hair and perfectly centered cravats, pulled Alamayou away.

Alamayou's eyes pleaded with Philip for a reason.

"Leave him alone!" Philip said before being dragged away to Windsor's gates, where the servants put him out.

A low rumble like distant thunder rose from the castle grounds. From behind the gate's bars, Philip saw the audience stand at attention as soldiers wheeled a heavily laden wagon down the center of the lawn.

§

THE SERVANTS BROUGHT ALAMAYOU to another room. Paintings of men hung on the walls. Somehow, he knew they were long dead.

In the center of the room, there was a large bed atop a box platform, covered in a blanket that puffed as if filled with clouds. There was a bowl of strange and colorful fruit on a side table next to a pitcher of water, and a window easily as large as the door the servants had closed and locked.

He heard their voices outside. Minutes passed, and still he heard them.

They'd imprisoned him. The room was no better than *ansara*. A cell.

Outside the window, he saw how the English had mastered the land. Carpets of flowers grew in carefully cut rectangles and no farther. The lush green grass came to the walls of the castle and stopped in a perfect line. The trees were bagged and trimmed into shapes as spherical as the fruit in the bowl. Everything that lived wild in Abyssinia obeyed the English in this Windsor.

Memories came. The tame grass outside the apartment window became the wild blades that grew all across the plateau at Debre Tabor, beneath the tents of his father's army, the fires and families that dotted the visible earth as far as he could see. He closed his eyes and was among them, watching the soldiers wrestle and duel each other on horseback with spears and shields, playing at the violence that would kill them one day. The winds peeled away from the black shale cliffs encircling the amba and the plateau to fill the tents and set their loose flaps dancing.

He remembered his mother dancing in her own tent to the pounding pulse of the *negerit* and not once looking up to see him watching her.

The sound of wheels outside the room's windows brought him back. Far from the castle, men pushed a massive wagon. They rolled off the cannon chained to its flat back and slowly turned its muzzle around to aim at the immense wooden structure he'd seen earlier, an enormous model of his father's Meqdala fortress, surrounded by potted trees and figures of straw, dressed in shammas like his.

The stem of the cannon ignited. A flame burst out of its muzzle and the false Meqdala exploded into fists of jagged debris. Pillars of ash and cloud, black as jet, swelled into the air above the heads of the audience.

The twists of smoke called the English close to wander among the debris, picking at it and laughing at the way it burned. Cheers and gunshots rang out in celebration of what the English could do.

He couldn't watch Abyssinia torn into any more pieces, and he turned away. At the farthest possible point away from where the English Meqdala lay in ruins, he saw the elegant gates of the castle entrance he'd come through with Philip. A dark figure walked away from the bars of the gate, having turned away as well from the hat-tossing crowd.

Alamayou threw open the window and screamed. His voice was immediately lost in the fading thunder of the cannon. "Philip! *Layard!*"

He didn't know if Philip could see him from so far away. Still, he raised his hands and clasped them together. He wasn't sure of the words, whether they were right, but his world had been reduced to one room, the rest to dust, and before when Philip had allowed their hands to join on the *Feroze* deck, the words felt like they fit.

"Layard not a-*lone!*"

The figure paused, then continued onto the long road away from Windsor.

Chapter Three

THE COACHMAN WHO'D BROUGHT them past the hot-air balloon to Windsor pulled up alongside Philip on the Long Walk. Up close, Philip found him a diminutive sort in a coarse black tweed and ascot. There was a cumbersome iron frame around his left leg, down to his thick-soled boot, that Philip hadn't noticed before.

"I'll get ye home," he told Philip. "Where d'ye hail from?"

"Lambeth as a boy, but pray don't bother. It's no home for me anywheres."

"Yer people then?"

"Dead and gone to the last."

"Got t' stay somewhere," the coachman said. "I can see t'ye t'night. Won't be much as I'm bare, but ye'll make out tolerably well."

Philip climbed aboard the coachman's trap and they headed northwest. For an hour, the only sound he heard from the man was the moist suckling of the tobacco sprig he kept firmly tucked in his mouth. But the coachman hummed an old melody, and Philip thought it an agreeable way to watch the scenery pass. At least it allowed him to avoid the worry curling in his gut.

They arrived in Hertfordshire at the base of the Chilterns. The coachman's modest cottage was nestled in a cleft in the land between a stream of mountain runoff and a windmill that looked to be from Elizabeth's age.

"Ye can call me by my given name, Charles," the coachman said. "Ye may be kaffir but yer a child of God, leastwise I see it thus. Din't used to think such things, but ye come to loss, ye learn patience."

A woman emerged from the cottage with a dishcloth in her hands. She was large in comparison to Charles. Weak flaxen curls framed her ample, rosy face. She did a poor job concealing her shock.

"One night," she said, refusing to make eye contact with Philip. "He can sleep in the stable."

That evening she brought Philip a peasant's supper of bread, cheese, and tea to the stable after sorting a makeshift bed from straw and an old sheet. Charles came to see him after and told him that he'd inquire of servants about work elsewhere. He brought a lantern and an old, leather-bound book.

"D' ye read or write?" he asked Philip.

"I do."

"Learn at school, then?"

"No. From a man who took me in after my father passed. A doctor, White. He taught me."

"Take it. It's th' holy book, an' some writings I made. Thoughts an' such. What I come t' know. But I'm old an' don' seem t' need it now. Got no thoughts worth remembering. It'll see ye through th' night."

Outside the stable, Philip heard the sounds of chopping, the ignition of fire, of empty buckets chiming their way to water and the gleaming note of the bottle-jack in the flames.

Whatever she may think of me, he mused, *she thinks enough of Charles to make a home with him.*

"Ye been at war?"

"Abyssinia," Philip said. "With the Second. It's a year I've been gone and no home, nowhere to go. I may as well have died there."

"I was at war. The Lower Canada Rebellion. Came home in body only, and not all a'me." He patted his leg brace. "Took me years. Lost m'family. A good woman, that, but not m'first nor m'wife. She abides me, is all. At night sometimes, I wake and I'm beating 'er.

I don't know who she is, even. But I'm here. I'm breathin'. Plenty who ain't. This is it, all I know. Ye born, ye die. Between th' days, ye find someone t' abide ye. Maybe, remember ye."

He walked to the stable entrance. "I'll go in th' morning. Ask around for ye. Maybe there's work."

"I'm grateful to you."

After Charles left him, Philip sat in the open entry, watching Charles's woman work through the cottage window and thinking of where to start.

He sat awake thinking about what to do when morning came. He'd need work of some sort or he'd end up in an almshouse. He was knackered, but he didn't want to sleep because he'd dream of the war, and the plague that took his old life in Lambeth, his father and his neighbors, and left him homeless until Marcus Baker White. He didn't like nights because his thoughts didn't even sound like his own, but instead like violence in him that he never asked for. Violence, and thoughts he wished he could rid himself of.

Let me just once wake up and be in someone else's body. Someone bound for a good, normal life.

Charles seemed a decent sort. Gave him a ride, a Bible, and some time, all for a Negro he didn't know from Adam. That took a good sort. Still, he was glad the coachman left him alone when he did. Their conversation had taken a turn toward the quiet things, the silences men carried in their hearts. The wars. The returns. The troubles. He'd even spoken some of his own out loud, which wasn't like him at all.

Sitting in the barn, he regretted saying anything. Words only led people to try and climb inside him and have a look around. Why did you go to war? Why did you go to jail? What sort of man are you?

Once they came inside, once they saw for themselves, they left. They ran.

It was strange, the thing he found himself wondering about there in the coachman's barn. There was plenty to keep him awake. Finding work, eating, finding a place to stay. But instead, he wondered what the next day would bring for Alamayou.

He barely knew the Abyssinian, but felt—knew, somehow—that it was the same for him. He wished it were different for them, but it was worthless for someone like him to pine for what he couldn't have. Love, or home.

He supposed he'd set out in the morning, but as he closed his eyes, he couldn't see what the use was.

Late that night, heavy steps came through the stable entrance. Charles lit a lantern and brought it close to Philip, startling him awake.

"Ye been summoned back to th' castle," Charles told him. "The African needs t'be questioned."

§

AT THE ROUNDED END of the Long Walk, Charles brought his trap to a halt. Philip climbed out and was immediately met by the butler, who led him through the guests' entrance into the Upper Ward, to the first floor. The bleed of some hollow sound came intermittently through the plasterwork and the wood. Voices.

On the other side of an ornate room—an immense reception hall with lavish Rococo ceilings and Gobelins tapestries—there was a knot of men and women standing in the open doorway of an apartment. Some were servants by their dress. The men were jacketed in the custom of valets, the women in lace aprons with tied sheafs around their hair. Many of them stared uncomfortably at the floor.

There were proper ladies as well, and at least one gentleman Philip spotted between the bodies. The noise by then was assaultive.

"This is the other one," the butler said, parting the crowd. "Philip Layard."

Philip made his way to the front, where he saw Alamayou inside the apartment, standing at the far end of the room near a great window that looked out onto Windsor's grounds. He still wore his shamma from the day before and looked as if he hadn't slept.

"It's me." Philip took a tentative step inside the apartment. "You know me."

"Philip."

"Yes, Alamayou. Yes."

"It is as I told you yesterday on the field," someone said. "There are eyes upon him."

The young man they'd seen in the royal box now stood in the apartment doorway. He made use of a silver-headed cane. "What shall we do for such as the Abyssinian?" he asked wearily.

The butler brought a chair to the doorway. "Please, Highness. You exert yourself."

"I'm fine enough, Simon."

He sat with the cane resting across his lap. "I see wisdom dawning in your eyes, Mr. Layard. Let me make introductions. I am Prince Leopold, Her Majesty's eighth child. Now you know to whom you spoke yesterday. Of all the white men you could have chosen to insult, you chose me. Let's be done with it for the moment, as there are larger issues to attend to. Nothing need be said to me until I wish it said. Much, I suggest, needs to be said to the Abyssinian. Mr. Naismith, would you be so kind as to explain the state of play to Mr. Layard?"

"Yes, of course, Highness."

The man who had introduced himself as the ambassador to Abyssinia came to the door of the apartment. He was attired in fine grey trousers and waistcoat, yet he spoke with a quieted Cockney intonation that years of study hadn't erased completely.

"You," Naismith said curtly. "Layard. Can you communicate with him?"

"Crudely," Philip said. "We use our hands, is all. That and the stray word."

"Do you know the word for mother?" Naismith asked.

"A queer sort of question."

"One I suggest you answer," Prince Leopold said. His voice no longer belonged to a young man but to a royal used to being obeyed without question.

"I don't know that word," Philip said.

"There are discrepancies in Alamayou's account," the prince said.

"Alamayou hasn't accounted for anything," Philip said. "It's everyone else supposing what happened, Your Highness."

"Yourself included."

"Yes."

"And we'll of course look into your account," the ambassador said. "As we will the accounts of the soldiers and those Abyssinians our governor there will find, to get down to the truth of him."

"What sort of discrepancies?" Philip asked as the familiar doubt began to creep in.

"For now," Naismith told the prince, "we can perhaps attribute it to the confusion of war, the loss of his mother, and his father's consummate evil. There's much to learn about him, and the queen Tirroo Wirk. How she died. What he saw. What he did."

Alamayou came at the sound of his mother's name. He took a few steps away from the cool air at the window, but no farther. There was something in the eyes of the one who'd said his country's name the day before, and *fire*, that made him hesitate. The man's eyes were on him in the way that the eyes of the tribal chiefs, the *kagezmachs*, were when he sat alongside his father. As if being alive with his father's blood in his veins was reason enough to hate him.

"Are you accusing him of something?" Philip motioned for Alamayou to go back to the window.

Alamayou did. He saw worry on Philip's face, and something else. A rising anger. "Philip." He clasped his hands together.

The sight calmed Philip. "Yes, Alamayou." He clasped his own.

"It seems you communicate at least in a rudimentary way," Naismith said. "Meaning simple."

"I know what it means," Philip snapped. "He lost everything in the war. Your Highness, you can't believe he'd do something to his mother."

"I don't believe anyone is suggesting anything of the sort," the prince said. "Are they, Ambassador?"

"We should be clear, the provisional Abyssinian government is keen to learn how its queen died. If by Tewedros' hand, the matter is at an end."

"She was all that was left to him," Philip said.

"With Your Highness's permission," Naismith said, "matters must be stated clearly."

"See to it."

"Let me be blunt, then," Naismith said. "He is the son and heir to a tyrant, one hated even more in his own country than here. They would like nothing better than to see him punished for his father's crimes, and how do you think it will be if we learn the queen didn't have to die?"

"What's he to do with it?" Philip's anger rose. "Your own soldiers said what happened. I'm surprised you'd have trouble believing them."

"Careful, boy," Naismith said.

"So it's true, we all have a bit of savage in us," Prince Leopold said. "Let us all reason with one another now, shall we? Mr. Layard, it's to the ambassador to conduct a thorough investigation into the circumstances of this queen. He will overlook no possibility, isn't that so?"

"It is, Your Highness."

"I speak not of hostility now, but duty. Do you see the distinction, Mr. Layard?"

"I do, Your Highness."

"And for you, you must reach the Abyssinian by any means necessary. He must be made to understand. He needs to speak to this. If he knows nothing and his account is found to be credible, so be it."

The prince rose with assistance. "Yesterday was nothing but pageantry and pomp, Mr. Layard. The words he was to say for all of our edification? A ridiculous notion dreamt up by Her Majesty's secretary as a tribute to English benevolence or some such drivel. As if by virtue of standing on our lawn he would magically transform into a man with no fear and no feelings about what had befallen him, oh, and he could speak our language to boot. Idiotic. But now we stand under a very different sky, let me assure you. This matter of his mother worries me greatly. We have under our roof the son of the tyrant we just went to war with. It doesn't go over well with certain of our political opponents. It may surprise you to learn that our monarchy isn't universally loved. And so, it comes down to a simple task. He needs to learn words. The right words."

Tottering on his cane, he left. Soon the service disbanded as well, and Alamayou and Philip were alone in the apartment.

For the first time since their arrival, they truly beheld each other. Their broad noses and full lips that turned down, the hooded eyes, almost Oriental in their gently crescented rims. Their hair was unkempt and wiry. Closely cropped by their own hands at sea, their crude efforts at grooming had left their heads choppy and uneven as a landscape of irregular hills.

"Damfino," Philip sighed. "What the hell am I to do? What the bloody hell happened at the fire? He's asking about your *mother*, Alamayou, as if something was done to her."

Alamayou got up on the bed. He took up a thin throw pillow and set it across his lap, much the way the prince held his cane.

"Prince Leopold. Prince, like you. He's important. He could send us both away or worse."

Philip called upon the limited language of their hands, sweeping them through the air in hopes of getting at least that through

Alamayou's head. "Away. As in, nowhere to go. I got not a bloody farthing to my name nor a roof to crawl under. Away!"

"Philip." Alamayou's hands tried and failed to convey. *You're all that I know. What's happening?*

Atop the bed was a box. He held it up for Philip to see.

"Gift," Philip said wearily. "I guess they wanted to give you something to make you feel welcome. It's yours."

He took it from Alamayou and unwrapped it, then handed it back. "Yours."

Alamayou took out a stuffed cat and handed it to Philip with a quizzical expression. Philip turned the key in its side, creating a metallic sound that startled them both.

In motion the cat was a rickety, quivering thing, as spindly and ancient-seeming as any Vaucanson pipe and tabor player. Its eyes batted and its paws moved as if wading through water. Its purr carried the atonal whir of mechanics.

Alamayou seized the cat, turned it over and tore open its woolen coat, revealing screws and secret interlockings under its poorly stitched hide where the heart should be.

Breaking it open, he scattered its insides across the floor. Its tin heart lay on the cold wood, a slowly spinning saw wheel in its woodblock chest.

"Well," Philip said, "that ought to go over well. What'll they say when they see what you did to their welcoming gift, eh? You need to be smarter than this."

Alamayou turned away while Philip picked up the cat pieces and hid them under the long folds of the bed's covers. Opening the window to the warm, heavy air of summer, Alamayou took in the perfume of the night garden. The wilting bloom of the landscape lay beneath dustings of light rain and spent gunpowder that still tainted the breeze.

Philip came and together they took in the bleary remains of the fortress at Meqdala, now in ruins from the cannons. "Home."

Philip pointed at the shattered structure outside. "Do you see, Alamayou? Your home's gone."

Alamayou didn't respond.

"I was a stranger. Say it. Can we at least start with that much? 'I was a stranger and yet you took me in.' Just give them what they want."

"Not alone."

"You won't say it? All right, then. What about your mother?" Frustration set in. "Damn it all! What happened to her? You must, for both our sakes. You must speak!"

Alamayou pushed him away. He screamed in Amharic; he thought of the *Feroze* and the lights and voices of war. It all came too near.

Retreating to the bed, he rested his head against the wall while Philip stared out the window, helpless. "Abat," he said. "Abat."

He called the old Amharic out, again and again, and in his heart he held a lost child's hope of being found.

"*Ya T'afa,*" he told Philip, though Philip couldn't understand. He could repeat the word all night and it wouldn't matter. Ya T'afa. Everything is gone.

§

LATE IN THE NIGHT, Philip snapped awake. He'd fallen asleep in a chair and dreamt of being back aboard the *Feroze*. In the dream he'd been terrified as a storm tore the ship apart plank by plank. Soon the cabin floor split open. He could see the ocean churning beneath his feet, rising up to swallow him.

He rubbed his eyes and stretched the kinks out of his back, letting the fear dissipate into the warm air of the apartment.

Alamayou was back at the window.

"Can't sleep either? Strange places, they take getting used to."

Alamayou said nothing. He didn't turn.

Watching him, Philip thought of how he'd looked the first time they'd locked eyes. Was it already four months ago? Longer? The notion seemed impossible, that so much time had passed so swiftly since Amba Geshen and the fire.

At first he hadn't been able to see Alamayou clearly against the cottage and the flames. Just his dark silhouette. The fire's intensity stole the details of him. It was absolute chaos. Soldiers ran around searching for water, the terrible roar of the fire as it consumed the cottage, the cottage walls buckling and cracking like bones beneath a butcher's cleaver. In the middle of all that, there'd been a stillness to Alamayou that caught Philip's breath. It was as if the violence of the fire stopped at the outline of Alamayou. It made room for him.

Philip shook the image away. He needed sleep, a meal, and an answer to the question nagging at him for a second full day. What now?

"If you're awake, you can at least try to say something. 'I was a stranger.' Just say that much, would you?"

He joined Alamayou at the apartment window and saw what he'd been so intent on. There was someone on the lawn, sitting in a chair. In the bright moonlight Philip could make out that it was a woman wearing a vivid white gown and matching wrap. She sat before a blank square of paper propped on an easel.

"You can't be spying on her, here of all places."

The woman turned to face their ward. She was too far away, and Philip couldn't tell where she was looking, or whether she returned their gaze.

"Christ on the cross, that's Princess Louise. I told you not to stare. Come away from the window."

Philip wanted him to step back, but Alamayou didn't leave the window. He could tell the woman on the grass was one of the important people they'd met earlier. Not the dour ones at the entrance to the room, but the pretty one who had many flitting around her but still seemed alone in the crowd.

That was why he didn't want to stop looking at her. Her aloneness drew him. He wondered if she was as alone as she seemed, and if so, was it because she was hated?

Solitude never bothered him. The cottage on Amba Geshen where his father had sent him to live with his mother was isolated from everything except her and a guard. The thought that he was no bigger than an ant to anyone glimpsing the cottage from his father's fortress meant nothing to him. That he was sent there because the sight of him made his father sick, that cut so deeply it turned his solitude into sharp, shearing loneliness. A radiant thing in his chest that left him feeling like an orphan.

He sensed that if he could say those words, Philip would understand. Maybe this woman, as well. The world was far larger than he'd ever imagined, and full of people like him.

Like them.

He and Philip watched the woman cross the grounds until she disappeared into their ward.

In a few moments there was a soft knock at their apartment door. "I saw your lights on," Princess Louise said quietly. "May I come in?"

Philip opened the door tentatively. Up close, the princess was as the news of London made her out to be. Tall and beautiful, with a perfectly oval face and cascading tresses of chestnut hair. She didn't wear the mourning weaves the queen had imposed upon her family, staff, and even visitors. She dressed simply in pale lace.

"He seems much calmer than before," she said. "It's necessary, since he'll be here until it's decided what to do with him. You as well, Mr. Layard."

"Highness, I know I'm not fit to be here. I should probably go before I cause more strife for you all."

She joined Alamayou at the window and pointed to the grounds, then to herself. "Me. I'm the one you watched. Louise."

"Alamayou."

She had a kind face, Alamayou thought. An ease. Maybe she wasn't as alone as he imagined her to be. Maybe it was only him after all.

"On the grounds," the princess said to Philip, "you spoke to my brother quite aggressively."

"I didn't know he was a royal, Your Highness. I've grown up never seeing any of you. I'm a bloody fool."

"Royal or commoner, he and the entire audience were white. Never do that again for your own sake. It's not your place."

"I understand."

"He probably deserved it. He can be quite good at the cutting word. Just not from you. There will be consequences for you, for as long as you're here."

"Your Highness, how long will that be?"

"Alamayou may become a ward of the court, so it may be different for him. He's an orphan of war. As long as he's found fit, this may be his life. As for you, that's not for me to say. He's a guest of the queen, but you? I suppose you're a guest of Alamayou. So my advice to you both is to watch yourselves, learn, and don't get too attached to anything."

Her reflection hovered in the windowpane. "One never knows when one's last moment in a place is until it comes. Then nothing of it belongs to you anymore. Only the memories. So watch, listen, and remember. This is a most unusual place, Philip. One we aren't meant to have forever. That's reserved for the queen only."

She traced shapes on the window glass with her finger. "I walked these halls as a child. Restless as a girl. I still am. At night, I see all that I used to see. Now tell me, what do you hear out there?"

"Voices. Footfalls. Horses out somewhere. The night birds."

"I hear the stories in this castle. I hear the Master of the Horse outside, preparing the coach to take me to see the prince at first light, as his health suffers. Do you hear the chiming? Brass buckles along the reins, with circles of some stamped metal that jingle when they grow loose. He's never changed out those reins and he'll tell you it's because as a girl I said how much I loved the chiming. The low whine of aged wheels. Do you hear it beneath these floorboards? The chambermaids bringing fresh linen to the ward, to the Grace and Favour apartments. Beneath the wheels, the kitchen's clamor. I can smell orange zest and clove because I know it's there. There will be a young girl, new to the kitchen. There always is. She'll take bread or a bit of gristle and she'll bring it home to someone. She'll make a secret of taking it. The sound of her walking will be different. Remember that, Philip. The sound of secrets is always different."

She was so lost, Philip thought.

"Of all the music you'd hear," she said, "I assure you, none is as loud as the sound of the queen's absence. It's almost as deafening as her words."

She stepped away from the window. Outside it was a perfect world at near dawn.

"Thank you," Philip said.

"For what? Saying too much, perhaps."

"For a look at your home that I'd never seen. I'll never forget it. I hope one day he and I'll understand each other. I'll tell it all, I swear."

"We shall see."

"Your Highness, why's it matter what happens to us?"

She smiled. It was a kind thing, Alamayou thought. He hoped she had children who saw it.

"The life that's taken hold of you now," she said. "Not what you thought it would be. And the war. All of it. You're not free. Either of you."

"Likes of us," Philip said, "we're not allowed thoughts of what life should be. Speaking for myself, I've come to a place where I just don't think about it. Does no good to dwell on what can't be for me."

"We differ then only in this one way. You may speak of it."

Louise opened the door. "You're both at the end of your endurance. A brief warning and I'll leave you. It's a different language, the words that come quietly at night. Don't mistake what we've talked about for something we can speak about in daylight. Only night truly belongs to you, him, or me. Especially here."

After she left, and in response to Alamayou's questioning eyes, Philip extinguished the lamp and settled into his chair. The events of the day spun and he craved quiet.

Soon Alamayou's restlessness stopped. He slept atop the bed. He kicked, sweeping the covers as a swimmer would. Shifting, he spread his fingers as if clasping hands.

The morning would bring round another day full of things Philip couldn't possibly predict. He hoped there'd be food, but didn't know if it would be brought to them or if they'd have go in search of it. And where would they wander? In what clothes? How many fine silks would it take to make two wayward Negroes look like they rightfully belonged at Windsor?

He decided that, at the least, he could keep trying to get Alamayou to say the words. For whatever reason, it mattered. They would give the royals what they wanted. In return, perhaps the royals would give them something. A chance to wipe the past clean.

Settling back into his chair as the war and the voyage finally overtook him, his last waking moment was the sight of a figure in one of the palace's upper windows across from their apartment. Another wing, another ward. He could see the outline of a person as the wind blew the curtains in around them.

Gone. The wind died, the curtains fell, and they were gone.

It was as if they never were.

It was 5:20 a.m. Princess Louise had left them. Left him to consider Alamayou's turnings, and his own.

Chapter Four

L ITTLE BRITAIN WAS A cluster of streets and broken old homes that once mattered. Christchurch and St. Bartholomew's to the west, Smithfield and Long Lane, Aldersgate, Butcher Lane, Paternoster Row, Amen Corner, Ave Maria. Above it all, the blight on the sky that was the dome of St. Paul's.

He stood with the rabbi before a derelict flat. Its original occupant, Marcus Baker White, was dead and gone, beginning a succession of low-rent occupants that ended a year or so ago. The place had been vacant since. Number Twenty-Nine Frith Street was available.

He opened the door, then lingered in the entryway, taking in the hymnal breathing of the flat. It was in a considerable state of disrepair, so much so that he worried it might crumble around them both the moment they stepped inside. Still, it presented just what he needed.

Rabbi Ariel went in and put his valise down in the sitting room. Near the sooted windows there was a chaise, neatly brocaded and covered in withered lace. The rabbi sat there, breathing laboredly.

"I'll fetch you something to drink, rebbe. There's a pub not far."

"A good port would be lovely."

He didn't like the old man's color. "Let me just take the measure of this place and I'll go quickly. In the meantime, lie down."

"I'll be fine. Do what's needed, Philip. No need to keep a deathwatch on me just yet. There's still so much for me to hear about."

"There's one errand I need to do. I'll be quick."

"Stop fussing."

He left the rabbi for the adjacent room. Atop the end table in there, he found dusty old books on manners and domesticity. The first portrayed in loving detail the ideal expectant wife. That she should avoid crowded rooms. Her mind must remain an oasis of calm. Nothing disorders the milk such as the passions, the violent actions of the female humors. Fitful temperaments are injurious. Calm, placid dispositions raise the woman's worth.

If it turned out that his stay lasted beyond the next day—a difficult thing for him to imagine—he'd consider keeping the flat decorated in the reassuring manner proper European ladies expected. Flowers of silk and wire, ornamental ceramics, Oriental lamps, curtains patterned in wedding weave and then covered again in heavy chintz to close out the world. There was a cozy fireplace with a torn fabric over the mantel that he could mend, and on top of it some hideous knickknacks.

The lone ode to Dr. White's life in the bottom rungs of medicine was a painting on the wall, "Old Schoolfellows." It was as if the doctor only just departed for a walk, one lasting thirty years.

He returned to the sitting room and found Rabbi Ariel uncomfortably curled up on a settee, asleep. His breathing was even and soft as a child's. He removed the rabbi's black hat and set it alongside him. Before departing, he unbuttoned the rabbi's heavy coat and lifted the *tzitzit* dangling from his side, so that the strands wouldn't sweep the dusty floor.

Opening the front door, he found that he couldn't simply leave. Everything was more complicated than he imagined.

He conjured the flat as it would have been decades before, with the women coming to its door in secret to see Dr. White.

He closed the door and set off. Briefly, he considered going back to write a note for the rabbi, so the old man wouldn't think he'd awakened to yet another disappearance by his friend Philip. But he couldn't go back, now that his feet were making their solitary sounds on London's walkways. He needed air and movement more than anything.

§

AT THE LATE HOUR, Frith Street was empty. Tilting tenements still showed signs of craftsmen's work across their facades. The maple carvings of mythic creatures he saw along the streets would have been right at home on a church roof. An omnibus passed him, its upper level seats filled with silent men in grimy dusted coats, smoking and reading while around them London's spires loomed in the bright fog. Below, the women and their restless children clung to the frames of the compartment's closed windows.

He crossed the lane as two-seat hansom cabs filled the avenues, weaving between carriages. Men and women stepped down from curbs onto the street, umbrellas raised to hail cabs in hopes of escaping the bitter cold. Intersections were crowded and tight, even at the late hour. Baked potato men, oyster sellers, sheep's trotters stalls on wheels, stewing eels and roasting apples, milkmaids with enormous silver canisters from their shoulders, all fought for a breath's worth of room on London's many paths.

The city thrilled and terrified him all at once. He found it nearly impossible to believe that he was really back.

He went round to the Honourable Society of the Inner Temple, to the south of Fleet Street. The Society sat atop three identical two-story sarcophagi of sepia-toned brick crowned with a conical of hammered iron sheets, opal inlays, and a dome of limestone. The dome was crowned with thorny scaffolding encircling a statue in mid-erection to its pinnacle. A man, a torch, the search for knowledge. Or some such.

Envelope in hand, he waited beneath the scaffold's webbing. It was nearly midnight and the evening's festivities were concluding. Drinks and cigars following a presentation on the emergence and spread of typhus in London's poorest pockets some fifty years before. Its origins, its toll, its eventual decomposition, and the legalities of forced segregation of the sick.

Now London stood at the edge of the century's passing and the dawn of a new age. Those who crossed into the future would see many things, but none would see anything like the miasma, the pall, the red flags marking tenements as occupied by the dead and the soon-to-be.

In time the solicitors emerged, heads bowed in sober— and for a few, drunken—contemplation. One of them spoke to a colleague, lingered in the doorway examining a pocket watch, then motioned for him to follow.

On the other side of the building, the old solicitor turned to face him. "I am Lord Grant. And you, you are the author of this correspondence?" He held up a letter. "Philip Layard?"

"I am."

"I instruct you to take care in addressing me, Mr. Layard."

He knew the tone well. His skin brought the same reaction in all fine white gentlemen.

Only the rabbi, he thought guiltily, *didn't despise me on sight.*

"Though I don't recall you much beyond a vague notion that one such as you was there, Mr. Layard, I well remember the case of the Abyssinian, Alamayou. You were involved, you say?"

"Yes. I helped him understand."

"Ah, I do remember you better now. Cheeky fellow, as I recall."

"I see you remember me well, in fact."

"And then, if my research since receiving your letter from Paris serves, you simply vanished."

"I did."

"Which makes you a fugitive, if you did something wrong."

"Why would you think I did something wrong?"

"Why indeed. The secrecy of your reaching out to me, for one thing. This clandestine meeting, for another. Explain, sir, why I am not turning you over to the authorities. Or Parliament. Or the queen herself."

"Because tomorrow, Lord Grant, I'll do it for you."

He handed Lord Grant the envelope. The solicitor opened it, running his fingers along the thick stack of pound notes inside.

"What is this? Some sort of bribe?"

"A retainer. You helped Her Majesty once, sir. You advised her, and your advice was, as I recall, to send the Abyssinian back."

"Now look here. I don't know what your purpose is, but I have a clear conscience."

"She, however, does not. Nor do I. I need your help."

"What do you want from me, Layard?"

"By this time tomorrow, I'll have need of your services. The day's events will make it plain. I will be facing charges. A friend, a rabbi in fact, will reach out to you. I beg you, come to me when he calls on you. This is all the money I have."

He turned and left the solicitor staring at the envelope. "This is highly suspicious," Lord Grant called after him. "Why should I help you? What charges?"

He kept walking. It wouldn't have helped matters to respond. His journey would end before it began if he'd answered the solicitor's question. *Charges? My dear Lord Grant, why would a nobody like me ever need a high-born, influential barrister like you?*

Murder, of course.

§

IT WAS NEARLY THREE in the morning. The sky bled shades of crimson and mauve. The long day's travels were done at last, and yet he wasn't nearly ready to sleep.

He'd purchased a bottle of port and two glasses, some food for a late supper, and some trinkets for the rabbi. But he didn't want to return to the flat on Frith yet.

To Cooke's Menagerie.

A sarcastic billing. It was no Wombwell's. There were no elephants, no gorillas, ocelots, or rhinos. No colorful signs for children to pass with adorable drawings of mythical creatures. He remembered seeing such a sign at Her Majesty's zoo. It depicted a rhino, and next to it the proclamation *the unicorn of faerie tale come to true life!*

How to live a true life? he wondered. *I never did figure that one out for myself.*

He'd become intimately acquainted with Cooke's when it passed through Paris ten years before. He'd found it on a chance visit, on a sunny afternoon with nothing to do. He couldn't count the number of times he'd returned to it if he tried.

It was past closing. He walked quietly by tents that were home to the dwarf, the bearded lady, the legless, the armless, the torsos on pedestals like Grecian busts. He knew their names. The Fat Boy of Isfahan preferred to be called Raj, the better to recall his home in Ceylon. Li Jun was known popularly as Poor Yoo Hoo, a boy of Oriental ancestry who was unintelligible to anyone who heard him speak. No one came to listen to him. They went to stare at his loins, at the "infernal birth" dangling there, so it was billed. A bulbous mass, like the crown of a baby's skull, hanging from his sex like a fleshy pendulum.

He learned. Freaks in public, in daylight, tried their best to please. They were no better than well-trained dogs that knew what was expected of them. Like those dogs, they went to great lengths to hide their suffering when eyes were upon them.

One night as he'd slipped through the menagerie outside Paris, he'd heard Yoo Hoo crying because he missed Nanking.

Everywhere at the menagerie, the borders of science and medicine crossed. The Python-Armed Girl was a mere child with unchecked elephantiasis. Yoo Hoo's condition was really a tumor of the scrotum left to run riot. It had lain dormant for most of his life, but one day he'd surely awake to find that it too was awake, and taking him.

He was a doctor, no matter the contempt of others, and so he'd offered to help them. They all refused, every last one. To be better was to starve; they would never be whole and so would never live the way others did. To be the way they were gave them a way to earn money, to stay with the menagerie. To live.

He understood them more than the self-made men he saw around him. The Grants of the world. *We're all freaks, they and I. We're not be prepared for the life we lead, but we're certainly not prepared to hope for more and fail.*

At least up until now, he thought.

There were only a few customers lingering around the grounds. He went to the last tent. It was separate from the others, built from saplings and fronds of painted paper to resemble the sort of hut Europeans thought were everywhere in Africa. Its occupant performed as Anchala, queen of a cannibal tribe. She'd done that for a long time.

It was dark, and he stayed far away so he wouldn't be spotted. Over the years, the others had seen and even spoken to him, but they didn't know him from Adam. Anchala was different.

He watched her remove her headdress. Time and labor had rounded her shoulders, and he couldn't tell from the dim light of the tent opening if her wiry hair had gone gray or if her eyes were moated with puffy sacs and lines.

There was a drawing above her bed, of her. It had been done long ago. She'd said that she wanted to be beautiful, and that no one had made her feel that way before. So he painted her to be beautiful.

She stood in the doorway, regarding the night. She faced in his direction but he was too far and too dark to be seen.

A queer sensibility filled him, making light of his fingers. In Paris, the first time he'd seen her, he'd wanted to go to her. He didn't know her well in their briefly shared time at Windsor, but she was there, and the fact of her being in the same city after so long felt important. He imagined what it would be like to approach her and say something. "It's me, Seely. Do you remember? You helped us talk to each other. I painted that for you."

What he imagined was her remembering him, then screaming his name as he ran.

He left the menagerie as pieces of his past peeled free to fall around him like burnt leaves. He knew he wouldn't sleep soon. But for the old man waiting, and no doubt worrying, he felt as if he could walk alone all night long and not care. It would be dawn or nearly so and the light would find him still walking, still remembering.

§

WHEN HE OPENED THE door, quiet as a common cat, he found the rabbi was awake.

"I hope you weren't worried, rebbe." He closed the front door behind him.

The rabbi was in the cramped kitchenette, staring haplessly at the iron back stone and the logs below it that refused to kindle.

"I'd hoped to make you oat cakes." The rabbi sighed in frustration. "I see I'm still the same old chef I always was, sadly for you."

"I brought you food and the port you asked for."

"I ate already. I found that pub you mentioned, on Aldersgate. Good chops and they seemed mightily entertained by me. Lively conversation these past few hours. The widow who keeps room and board there struck up a conversation with me at the flowerman's. Charming lady, and she liked me."

"Her patience must be the stuff of legend."

Rabbi Ariel smiled, all angles and yellow, crooked incisors beneath the silver thorns of his beard. "A port, you say? Join me, Philip."

He poured the rabbi a glass and one for himself. In the sitting room he fell into a chair, weary at last, and yet his heart still pulsed with anxiety.

Across from him, the rabbi struggled to thread a needle.

"And what are you doing now?"

"I have holes," Rabbi Ariel explained with a shrug.

He slickened the thread with candle wax and stabbed at a needle in his thimble hand. On his ample lap was a black sock, rent open at the toe.

"Let me help. Here, I found this and thought of you."

He gave the rabbi an églomisé souvenir tray, upon which a chromolithograph of the cathedral at St. Paul's appeared. Taking the thread and needle from the rabbi's trembling hands, he found the needle's eye in the low light and slipped the thread through.

"It's wondrous, Philip. Thank you. Where did you find such a thing?"

"There are vendors everywhere if you walk far enough."

"Indeed there are. I found one on my own long walk." He muttered over his port, then sipped it contentedly. "Join me in the prayer for this fine drink, will you?"

"I think not, rebbe." He knew some of the Jews' words, but it still felt wrong to say a language that wasn't his.

He smiled at the irony.

They were quiet for a while. Around them, the flat filled with dusty colors of the dawning light seeping in.

"Was she a friend, Philip? The queen?"

"For a while."

"I'm sorry she's sick. A terrible thing, getting old. But tell me, how will you see her? I don't imagine you can simply knock at her door."

"There's a procession at the castle tomorrow. The Order of the Garter, to honor her. I thought maybe I'd go, see if I could perhaps…I don't know, just see her somehow, I guess."

"Now that I'd like to see very much. A black and a Jew attending a procession. May I come with you?"

"I don't think that's a good idea, rebbe."

"We'll talk about it in the morning. It's late, and you must be spent. But I have questions, Philip."

"I know you do."

"How did you meet her?"

"The first time? It was late at night. Quiet. Just her, alone."

"Remarkable. And the war? How did you end up in Abyssinia? Of all the far-flung places, and a war. Terrible."

"There were moments of beauty even in the middle of war. You'd be surprised. They came at the most unexpected times. Like a gorge I saw, between two mountains. One was called Meqdala, where the emperor's fortress was. The other was called Amba Geshen, where there was nothing but a small cottage. Two people, living alone."

He closed his eyes and let it all come back to him.

"I sat at the very edge of that gorge and from below me, white clouds rose as if they were boiling over the lip of a kettle. They were filled with gray and with light. They swelled higher and higher until they covered the space between Amba Geshen and Meqdala. Lightning flashed inside them. The air smelled like burning metal and the skin on my arms tingled. Then a raindrop struck my face, and another. But the rain wasn't falling. It was flying up. The wind swept it up from far below, in the gorge. It swept everything upward. The rain, the lightning, all flew upward, past me and into the sky."

He felt it. The rain, the uprushing winds.

"She called it the 'white dream,'" he said. "That's just what it was."

"Who?" the rabbi asked.

"The queen, Tirroo. She loved it so much. She said, 'Whatever happens to us, think of us here where we'll always be happy. They'll call but they won't find us unless they look for us here. The clouds take everything away, even pain. May they take us soon, because we don't belong anywhere in the world.'"

"Us, Philip?"

"She said those words to her son."

"Alamayou."

The room deepened with color. Mauves, pinks, warm and hazy with dust motes rising into the light. The rabbi was staring at him with that smile that he never felt deserving of.

Where have I been, he thought, *that I didn't feel the night moving all around us? I wish I commanded the ability to go there. The place where forgetting resides.*

"Philip."

"Yes. I'm still awake."

"You're crying."

He touched his cheek. Dewy with wetness. "I am. Didn't even realize."

The rabbi began to whisper.

"What are you muttering?"

"A prayer for you. That you find peace and reason in whatever lies ahead for you."

"Don't pray for me tonight, rebbe. Pray for me tomorrow."

"I don't understand."

"No good man could."

"You're tired," the rabbi said. "A bit of sleep and in the morning, this won't be so bad. Look, I told you I came across a souvenir seller. I bought something for you. Maybe it will bring back good memories."

The rabbi held out a small case for *cartes de visites*. Silverleaf and raised impressions of Buckingham Palace decorated the front.

The rabbi opened it. There was a picture inside.

"Is it him?" the rabbi asked. "The Abyssinian?"

The shield. The necklace. Hints of the dangling linen, the falling evoked by that photographer and her Indian.

The eyes. How they looked left, away from the camera to the only one he knew after his world had ended.

"Yes," he said. "It's Alamayou."

"So young to be taken from his home that way. To Windsor and the queen of England, no less."

The rabbi led him to the couch and told him to lie down. He placed the carte de visite on the table beside, then completed his prayer. The rabbi's eyes closed as his hands hovered over his heart.

"Amen," he said at last. "Would you like to know what I said?"

"I know you'll tell me."

"'Grant me light, so I do not sleep the sleep of death.'"

The rabbi arranged a thin blanket over him.

"Alamayou wasn't alone," the rabbi said. "He had you. Remember that."

"I'll try, rebbe. It's late and you must be tired. Try to sleep. Here, take the couch. I prefer the chair."

After a token bit of resistance, Rabbi Ariel took him up on his offer of the couch. Soon the old man fell into a weary, deep sleep. His chest rose and fell rhythmically. A light snore escaped his lips.

Philip brought the chair to the window so he could watch the gas lamps lift Frith up out of the shadows.

Grant me light, he thought, *and don't let me sleep the sleep of death anymore.*

There'd be no sleep for him. Not until the next day was done with. He wondered where he'd be by that time, what sort of roof he'd be under.

Not alone. Remember that.

I do remember, he thought. *I remember everything.*

Chapter Five

C ARTS TOOK THE LAST of the mock fortress down a bridle path in pieces, out of Windsor and to the raging bonfires of London. After the splintered mountains and the plaster bodies were finally swept away, gardeners trimmed the lawns and clipped the old copse of trees in order to plant bays, corks, oaks, and evergreens that would stay green and defy the seasons. Life surged forward.

On that same bright morning, Princess Louise walked across the greens in the company of a man with a satchel on his back. In time they stopped. The man unpacked two easels and spread their legs while the princess stood with her hands on her hips, surveying the scene before her. Something in the light, or in the weave of the far, bare trees against the clear autumn sky, caught her painterly attention.

The man arranged some brushes and erected two large canvases of stretched white. He set them on the open easels, one beside the other.

Alamayou watched them from the open apartment window. The smells of fine, savory food perfumed the air—bacon, breads baked to mellowness, and something sweetened with warmed brown sugar—but he was captivated by the painter and the princess, too much so to take notice of his grumbling stomach. He recognized the painter from the day of his arrival, the one who found peace in the middle of all the activity that day.

He envied that man, then and now. In the center of such a place, he had somehow earned the right to be left alone.

Soon, maids came to the apartment. They escorted Alamayou and Philip through the halls near St. George to a terrace overlooking the gardens. Their table soon filled with pastries, fruit, and strong tea with milk. The sun lengthened and warmed away the morning dew.

"Stranger," Philip said. "Say it, please. Start with just the word. The rest will come and it'll be done. The first step toward whatever life they've got planned for you. At least try. That's what we do. We try."

Alamayou's eyes wandered from Philip to the lawn.

"Stranger, Alamayou. Come on now. Stop being so stubborn."

Paying Philip no mind, Alamayou pointed to the painter and the princess.

"Painter," Philip said, resigning himself to another failure. "He is called a painter."

Alamayou made a canvas of the air, a brush of his finger. "Painter." He touched his chest, hoping Philip would understand. *It's a simple thing*, he thought. A word. But Philip, all of them, was still too far away for him to reach. Something had to bridge the space between them.

"You?" Philip said. "You can paint?"

Alamayou smiled. "Painter."

"Come, Alamayou. We have to tell the princess."

They ran together from the veranda overlooking Windsor's color bursting gardens to the lawn, where they approached Princess Louise. "Forgive the intrusion, Your Highness," Philip said. "But Alamayou's just now told me something! He watched you hawk-like. He says he can paint."

"Says?" Princess Louise asked.

"Well, not in words. But he did say 'painter' and pointed to himself."

"Indeed? We must explore."

She turned to her companion. "He's from Abyssinia. A prince, now orphaned. Doubtless you've heard about him. This is Edward Corbould. He's an instructor of art here at Windsor, and a dear friend."

Corbould was thin and gangly at the joints but graceful in the movements of his hands. His auburn hair protruded from under a sun hat, and his beard and moustache were wild and untended. He wore loose trousers and an outsize smock that, in its freely flowing length, reminded Alamayou of his ceremonial shamma.

Corbould put out his hand for Alamayou to take, but Alamayou reached past it for the nearest paintbrush.

Corbould opened his satchel and withdrew a pad of many clean sheets. He took the brush from Alamayou and replaced it with a cylinder of coal chalk, then showed Alamayou his own canvas, where he'd begun painting the tower standing against a gauzy sky of orange, sienna, and gold.

"Tower." Corbould pointed first to the building itself, then to the drawing. "You." He took Alamayou's hand and together they made one soft line on the tablet's first empty page.

Alamayou sat on the grass and set to work. It was not the tower he tried to make, but a high place and a ragged structure.

Corbould knelt beside him. "Tower?"

Alamayou shook his head. There was no way to explain what he wanted to draw, only to finish it and let them see.

Philip will know, he thought, *and who can say what we might be able to tell each other by then.*

"Perhaps the young man would like to visit us again," the princess said. "He shows progress. It would appear that the tower put him in mind of something else. I know it does that to me. Reminds me of being a little girl here, climbing up the motte and kicking up a cloud of chalk dust while I was at it. Good memories."

"That I'm most pleased to paint for you," Corbould said.

"There's no one else I'd rather have do it for me." The princess smiled and turned away, her cheeks red.

Philip shifted uncomfortably. He wanted to take Alamayou and leave the princess and Corbould alone. Their conversation carried an intimacy.

"I'd like to see what Alamayou ends up creating," Princess Louise said. "If only the other words came to him as easily as 'painter' did. Philip, are you familiar with the notion of action, consequence?"

Philip shook his head.

"It's a simple thing. To my mind, there are no right or wrong decisions in life. Be it a small matter, where to take supper or where to invade, there's only the act and its consequences. If those consequences are acceptable, then by all means. If they aren't, refrain."

"A perfectly applicable theory," Corbould complimented her.

"I've seen some of those consequences," Philip said. "So has he. It's not my place, I know, but standing here, it's hard to understand how the consequences made it worth the blood."

"Perhaps you answer your own question. As a consequence of war, Alamayou and you find yourselves standing here. But let us think now about painting, and Alamayou's pressing task of learning our language. Now, Alamayou, pay attention. 'Stranger.' Alamayou, say it for me."

She took the coal stick away when Alamayou didn't answer her. "Please don't think that I'm being cruel to him for no good reason. There are things he must do to secure himself here."

"True of us all," Corbould said. "If he complies, we shall be here again tomorrow. If it pleases Her Majesty."

Princess Louise took the pad next. "Stranger," she said to Alamayou. "You say it now."

Alamayou stared longingly at the pad.

The princess moved the pad behind her back. Its corners protruded tantalizingly for Alamayou to see.

She turned and left.

Alamayou didn't move. "*Layard,*" he said angrily. "Layard, Layard, Layard—"

"Wait," Philip said. "What an idiot I am. He doesn't understand we want him to repeat it. He needs to be shown."

He drew close to the princess. "Stranger," he said slowly, then held out his hands. Princess Louise gave him the pad. He returned it to her and they repeated it with the coal.

Alamayou stood. He approached the princess. "I…stranger…" Alamayou said.

Princess Louise gave him back his tablet and chalk. "I was a stranger," the princess said slowly, nodding her encouragement before returning to her own painting there on the lawn beside him. She pointed at the Round Tower. "I'm going to give it a go. It won't be anything to rival Edward, but when has that stopped me?"

"Never in all the time I've known you," Corbould said.

She began to paint alongside Alamayou. Bent over the tablet, Alamayou never looked up at the tower. All that he needed to see lived on in his mind, if no longer in the world.

"Stranger," he muttered, smiling at Philip as Princess Louise nodded encouragingly. "I was."

§

OVER THE NEXT SEVERAL weeks, Alamayou gave them more words. *Easel. Brush.* Even, *ochre.* Simple questions and phrases. *I hungry. I thirsty. I no want to. I paint. I tell.* The more he gave them, the more freedom he and Philip were granted, and soon they were exploring the halls of Windsor.

One October evening, they walked down corridors they'd never visited before. No longer in their ward, they passed chambers instead of apartments.

When they saw none of the familiar servants, Philip knew they'd come too far. "Enough wandering for today. We should go back."

Alamayou found an immense hall that captured his attention. The room was ornately paneled in dark woods that crosshatched

at the ceiling in patterns of timber beams. The drawn curtains
bathed the room in unnatural shadow. What was striking about
the space was simply that the room held so little. A loveseat near
the cold hearth, a simple chair at the grand window nearest the
door, a table with a candelabra and tapers sweating long-dried wax
tears. An enormous painting hung on the wall above the fireplace.

It was the painting that Alamayou had to see. Entering the
room, he crossed the empty space and sat down on the floor by
the hearth to stare up at the portrait hanging on the wall above.
His eyes were full of questions.

Philip recognized it at once. All the royal family had been
assembled in the painting: Helena, Vicky, Bertie, Arthur, Beatrice,
Her Majesty the queen, Affie, Alice, the princess Louise, and the
frail prince, Leopold. They were gathered around their Albert,
Prince Consort, husband and father, whose death shrouded
Windsor every bit as much as the shadows shrouded that hall.

"Family," he told Alamayou. He pointed to the prince
Consort. "Father."

"Father? Abat?" Alamayou pointed at the painted man.
"Abat. Father."

"So that's what abat means. He was abat of Louise and Leopold,
Alamayou. He was a prince like you."

Philip fashioned a crown of his fingers, then rested them
atop Alamayou's head. Directing Alamayou's attention to Albert's
crown, he said, "Father, prince. A prince like you."

"Lij," Alamayou said, patting his chest. "Prince, is lij."

Philip pointed next to the queen. "Mother."

"Mother is anat."

"Anat. Alamayou, anat, yours." He touched Alamayou's
shoulder. "Abat, anat. I'm sorry." He raised his hands to show
Alamayou how empty they were. "Gone."

Alamayou was quiet then. His own hands fell silent.

He left the room, soon to return.

§

IN ALL, ALAMAYOU MADE the journey three times to the portrait room and back again to the apartment before night fell. Each time he returned, he added to the painting he'd started out on the lawn. Philip soon grew tired of him turning the canvas away so it couldn't be seen. He settled back into his chair while Alamayou worked. After a few hours spent reading, he fell asleep.

The distant sounds of storms woke him with a start. "Alamayou, what—"

Alamayou lay on the floor at the foot of his canvas, staring at the rain-spotted window. The painting was complete.

He turned it so Philip could see.

"Bloody Christ."

It was Tewedros' fortress at Meqdala, perched against pillar-like mountains, and a gorge at its base. There was a white space within the gorge, a sea of pure cloud. Across the gorge was another mountain peak with a small cottage on it. The cottage was intact and undamaged, the fortress whole. It was as if there'd never been a war.

Two figures occupied the lower left corner of the canvas. They walked together toward the bottom left corner of the painting, leaving the stone fortress and the clouds behind them.

Alamayou propped himself against the unmade bed and smiled, a crooked and proud thing.

"I was a stranger," he said, "yet you took me in. You, Philip."

§

PHILIP FOUND SIMON AND told him to send word. He asked for food. "Something sweet," as if he and Alamayou belonged.

"Uppity, aren't we," the Lord Steward muttered. Still, the service brought sweet cakes and puree of orange, which they gorged on.

In an hour, Princess Louise arrived.

"I was a stranger," Alamayou said in her presence, "yet you took me in."

"Remarkable," the princess said. "He's come a long way already. Well done, Philip."

"Thank you, Highness. But this you need to see."

He turned the canvas to face her.

She traced the dry lines of the figures in Alamayou's painting.

"I saw him, too," Philip told her.

Alamayou sat up straight. Wary.

"We wish her to hear the words," she said. "Perhaps, to see this. I'm not sure how she'll take it."

She looked at Alamayou. "It is a strange and beautiful thing you've done. I wonder if you even know."

§

AT MIDNIGHT THEY WALKED hurriedly past the Royal Library behind five silent housemaids who kept them moving at a brisk pace. The faint light of the torchières reflected the crimson damask hanging from the library walls, cordoning off wooden shelves of books and the stone chimneypiece. There was a sameness to all the rooms. The Private Dining Room, the Chapel between St. George's and the Crimson Drawing Room, the Red and the Green Drawing Rooms; they all lay behind shrouds of dark-hued curtains.

The circuitous route ended at the Blue Room on the south wall.

The oldest of the maids that brought them was spindle-thin. Her hair was pulled severely and separated at the scalp by a comb of abalone. She alone approached the Blue Room and knocked softly. In a moment she entered and closed the door.

Before it shut completely, Philip saw more blue damask suspended on golden cord from a ceiling of angels and a votive candle on a stand near the window at the far end.

They waited a long time, but no sound emerged. The other maids stood perfectly still, as if afraid even to stir the air.

Finally the door opened, revealing in full a room that existed out of time.

There were two beds, adjoined and identical, on either side of a small window, with a chair next to each. A carpet of gold and reddened copper shades covered the floor. A swatch of it lay at the foot of a burning fire in the hearth. Fresh flowers had been arranged in a crystal vase on a desk near the far, wide window. The sheets had been turned down. Clothes were laid across the nearest bed, a man's dress uniform with epaulettes and gold brocade.

There was a plate on the other bed. On it sat a fresh orange studded with cloves of cinnamon. A tray beside it held a razor and brush. The scent of persimmon and cream perfumed the air.

The scrawny maid stood near a screen of wood and taut bone embroidered with scenes from a hounds' hunt. A terrified fox, mounted huntsmen, the copse, and the fields. There was yet another window behind it, one which reflected that corner of the room partitioned fro view. In the glass they saw an image of a gently rocking chair and a woman's hand resting atop it. Her veined, bony arm was bare of jewelry. She was older. The rest of her was hidden, as if she knew precisely where to sit to remain unseen in the glass.

The maid nodded to Alamayou. "Come forward."

Philip touched his own lips lightly. "Stranger," he whispered to Alamayou, then pointed at him.

Alamayou filled with fear. He couldn't understand why he was there to pronounce words to the quiet room. Only that it mattered. It was in the eyes of all of them. The princess, the maids, Philip, especially. That it mattered to Philip made it matter to him.

For you, he thought, *because we've come so far.*

"I was a stranger," he said carefully, "and yet you took me in."

He waited as the reflected bit of chair rocked soundlessly.

"Prince." He patted his chest. "Lij."

The reflected chair came to a stop. That aged hand rose from the armrest, fingers spread, remaining in air.

"We welcome you," a quivering voice said. It was a woman's voice, full of weariness. "Lij."

Alamayou turned to have her words explained. He looked for Philip's hands to transform her voice into language.

Philip held his arms out, embracing him. "Welcome."

As they were led away, the faintest of smiles came to Alamayou's face. *I'll know that word always*, he thought. *The one that brought Philip's arms around me. "Welcome."*

§

PHILIP SETTLED HIMSELF IN for the night with a book of fanciful myths and a pot of piping tea. Outside, the maids departed the corridor having finished their work, the turning of sheets and the lighting of tapers.

"Philip."

Alamayou held the painting. Carrying it, he went to the door.

"We shouldn't," Philip said, but Alamayou was already gone.

Philip followed him through the halls, back to the portrait room. A bit of light danced under the closed door. Alamayou turned the knob and pushed it open, spilling a hazy glow into the corridor. He slipped inside.

The glow emanated from a fire in the hearth at the far end. It fashioned a lovely lit path down the polished floor. All else fell into shadow.

Alamayou carried his painting to the hearth. There he rested it against the wall, beneath the portrait of the royal family. A gift.

Behind them, the push of a chair. They weren't alone.

In the dark they watched a silhouetted figure pass from window to window. In moments, the light of the fire found her. She wore a simple black robe. Her hair was pinned loosely. She wore no makeup, no ribbon or jewel. No crown.

Philip felt frozen. He couldn't speak or bow. For a commoner like him to be there with her was unheard of. A Negro of no status who'd never laid eyes on the queen before. To see her emerge like a wraith from the shadows of the room was stunning, as was the realization that this was her night world they stood in.

She went to Alamayou's painting.

Alamayou pointed to the figures he'd added. First the smaller, dark-skinned one. "Prince," he told the queen, and patted his chest. "Lij."

Then to the taller figure. White, male, with beard and his dress uniform, its epaulettes and golden braid. Alamayou pointed to her husband, rendered next to him in his painting. "Prince," he said. "Lij."

She held a hand out to Alamayou. He took it and helped her to her knees. She wanted to be close, to see.

"Gone," she said, and touched the figure of her husband. She opened her hand like a bloom to the air. "Gone."

In the hearth, the logs collapsed in an upward draft of sparks. Seams of flame threaded them.

"Your father," she said.

"Your abat is gone."

Alamayou nodded. "Abat, gone."

"Yes."

She gazed at her children.

"Mother," Alamayou said. "You. Mother."

"Yes, Alamayou."

Alamayou knew before she did it, before she pointed at him, what she wanted from him. It was clear now, he had to find the words to give them the fire and the war, but not all of it. He didn't know what it would mean for him when they understood that he had no one left. But he knew he couldn't tell them the reason why.

"Mother," she said to him.

"Mother. Anat." He knelt next to her. "Father, abat. Gone." He pointed to the fire, then through the window where night clouds passed over Windsor.

Philip brought her a chair from the far end of the room and helped her into it, there by the dying hearth. He left the two of them and retreated to the far corner, where he sat against the wall and watched.

Their shadows turned with the fire. Occasionally, one of their hands made shapes against the light. If words were spoken, he didn't hear them.

He couldn't know how it would be when they saw the queen next. There probably would be many more people around her. Servants and dignitaries and pomp, and they would be who they were expected to be.

The two of them, he thought. *This is the first time they've seen each other. The first words to pass between them, and what they give to each other is their loss. Their mourning.*

The sight of Alamayou and the queen jarred something loose in him. The *Feroze* felt like a lifetime ago, the last night at the ship's rail longer still, but Alamayou *had* been on deck, staring at the waves, and that feeling Philip had while watching him was the one he'd fleetingly felt at the cottage fire, and now it was here in the room with them. A strange feeling that if he'd left Alamayou alone, just a bit longer, something would have happened. He wouldn't have left the fire, or the rail. He would have stayed.

Jesus, Philip thought. *Maybe he wanted to burn. Maybe he would have jumped.*

It was her presence that enabled Philip to put a name to the sensation he'd been carrying since Naismith's account on their first day at Windsor. Watching Alamayou with the queen, Philip wondered if the queen carried it, too. The room of portraits might be where she went to commune with the dead. To touch the idea of ending.

He knew it was true. That's what Alamayou was doing. Turning the idea of killing himself over in his hands like the mechanical cat. Seeing how it might work.

Why didn't he?

He sat back as the realization settled in. There would be questions, more and more of them as Alamayou learned to speak. But bloody Christ, the more he thought about it, the more he felt that he was right. They wanted Alamayou to learn English so he could present himself as a grateful foreigner. What they'd find, Philip feared, was just how alone he was, and how badly their invasion had broken him. Then what would they do with him? Not exactly the grateful prince come to embrace England's cause, is he?

It was all a jumble of chaos, blood, smoke, screams, silences, but as he thought harder, he couldn't say that Alamayou's hand was in that fire by force, or that his father had hold of him. Watching him by the glowing hearth with the queen, thinking of all the questions yet to come, it felt like Alamayou had been there at the fire, his hand beginning to shrivel and burn, by choice.

The moment you give them words, he thought, *they're going to pull your insides out. I know what I'm talking about. May you be smart enough to stay silent.*

Only at night, Alamayou, can you let anyone see. And only to me. I'll keep it all safe, I swear.

He watched Alamayou with the queen, as if he belonged. With a word she could banish him anywhere in the world. She could send him back. And if he was alone, somewhere far away from anyone, he might find himself facing another fire. Another rail with no one there and no reason to remain. His hands outstretched, ready to embrace the fall.

They remained in the portrait room together, deep into the night. As exhausted and worried as he was, Philip couldn't close his eyes. He couldn't miss so simple a thing as two people who'd lost, alone and silent, speaking a night language only they understood.

Chapter Six

THE RABBI FELL ILL during the night.

Stupid is what it was, he'd tried to tell the stubborn fool. An old man walking the heart of the city in search of dinner, conversation, and souvenirs, and expending far too much energy in the bargain. The body, like an old engine, needed time and tending to return to operation, and here Ariel was already exhausted from the Channel crossing.

The rabbi lay quietly in the bed he'd purchased to make the flat more comfortable. A thin blanket covered him to his belly. He'd been working on a translation of the Talmud. His scrawlings littered the floor.

Looking at the old man, Philip realized that he'd never seen the rabbi without his religious garb, his hat and his heavy black overcoat. Propped there against a stout pillow, the rabbi wore a nightshirt alone. He was smaller than he usually appeared, a striking thing. They'd known each other all these years, and the rabbi was smaller than he ever knew. *From this day forward*, he thought, *I won't think of him and see the same man.*

Shadows swelled on Frith. He took a chair to the window, where he sat and listened to the incantations of the street. Horses' hooves on broken cobblestone, the bit-muffled protests of the laboring animals, the chimes of St. Paul and Dunston ringing together across the dark skies.

It was nearly six in the morning, and the procession at Windsor was still a good while away. Even at the early hour, London lived. The sun was still missing from Little Britain, but soon the fortunetellers on Howsten would emerge to promise husbands for the wayward girls. Men with powder keg cameras would manipulate the smoke to fool the gullible into seeing their own souls on glass. Boys with pranks to play would break into the oldest houses, where they'd light candles and start rumors of hauntings that would cross the still waters of Bull and Mouth.

It reminded him of his arrondissement in the Marais. There above Ha Kehilot, he spent so much time caring for the elderly, ill Jews sent to him by the rabbi. He helped with births, and later with the common bouts of childhood. He practiced the medicine of life. No one among their odd little community in the Marais had many choices. All they had was each other. They closed their circle tight.

I'll miss that most of all, he thought. *Belonging somewhere. I feel as I did the day I saw the queen at Villefranche, near the sea. As if everything is falling away from me. It falls and I'm falling with it.*

He left to change his clothes, returning to the front room in a good suit and a face shaved clean. The letter he always kept close was tucked safely in his breast pocket, next to the carte de visite.

He thought he would simply leave them by the sleeping rabbi's side, but upon entering the room he discovered the rabbi awake and dressing.

"So," the rabbi asked as the first morning light blossomed across the flat's walls, "what will you do with yourself after I'm dead?"

"Dear God, don't be so morbid."

"Morbid is to admire death. I'm enjoying myself in life far too much for that. But I must know what you'll do. That's why I came, if you'll recall. To exercise my considerable power to secure your future."

"Well, this much I can see. You're better and you won't listen to me."

"I heard you. The body fights what it doesn't understand. Did I get that right?"

"You did, to my great surprise."

"That must be why you're always fighting me."

"In a few days, you'll be back to dining with widows and shopping for all the trinkets you can carry back to Paris."

"Return to Paris with me, then. You can convert. Become a black Jew."

"Anything but that."

The rabbi labored to put on his heavy black coat.

"Rebbe, I don't want you there with me."

"What harm could a sick old rebbe cause you?"

"It's not a joke. I'm not asking your permission. I'm going alone."

"Did you take notice of all my work?" He gestured to the papers covering much of the room's flat surfaces. "It's the Talmud. Holy writings. I'm translating them to French and English. You may not realize it, but to some, I'm something of a noteworthy man. Eisenmenger translated the Talmud to German, and Chiarin— an Italian no less!—translated it to French but that was a blasphemy, intended to turn the Jews away from its influence. Horrible. A colleague, Rebbe Pinner, and I are taking on the task and we'll see it through properly. I'm telling you this because last night I came across something you might be interested in. It seems that the Talmud has a word for confession of a crime. It means 'silence,' Philip."

"I know I've told you so little about myself, it's a wonder you've put up with me all these years. There's a reason for it. There always has been. I don't want to lose you. You're the only friend I have in the world."

Bells. Church towers across the city proclaimed the commencement of the procession at Windsor. Among them there would be the gentle bells of a small, forgotten chapel, so modest that it could be taken for a potter's shed. No one visited its untended cemetery as he recalled. A few headstones scattered across a tiny enclosure of overgrown grass. No one of importance lay beneath its soil.

He wanted to be at Windsor, now. He wanted to walk its halls, find the stone steps that led up to the top of the Round Tower, go to one of its parapets and see everything from up there. The chapel, the villages nestled against the far rolling hills, the paths winding away from the castle to other towns, other lives.

He'd have just enough time if he left immediately.

"Listen to me, rebbe. Something is going to happen today if I'm able to do what I came here for. I need to see her. The queen. But it's more than that. You'll learn of it sooner or later, but I don't want you there. I don't want to see you when you hate me."

"Philip, are you going to hurt someone?"

"She's dying. What more can I do to hurt her? I'm hoping to take her pain away."

"At some cost to you."

He didn't answer.

"There's the man I know," Rabbi Ariel said. He put on his broad brim hat. "Come. Let's get one of those English hansoms. I'm in the mood for royalty."

"In that case, there's somewhere I need to go to first."

§

UPON SIZING THEM UP, the chapel's caretaker assumed they were vagabonds looking for somewhere to get away from the insistent winter.

"I'll not let you in," she said. She was short but barreled about her waist and hips. She carried a spade and wore the dirt of the churchyard like a badge of honor.

"I've nowhere to go to say my prayers," he told her. "Isn't it obvious that's the case? Look at me, for God's sake."

"Ignore my friend," the rabbi said. "Synagogues have much to learn from churches in terms of sublime beauty. If we could just go inside for a moment, just to see it, I know we'd find it inspiring. And I'd like to offer a prayer for Her Majesty's sake. It would be a mitzvah. A kindness."

She relented when he smiled. Opening the chapel door, she stood aside for them. "Rest assured I'll be right here," she told them.

It's changed, he thought as they wandered inside the chapel's tight space. The chancel was where it had once been, in the eastern corner where the altar stood, but it had been raised a few steps and a worn-looking sanctuary built around it. The stained glass looked foggy and untouched by a duster. He wondered what it was the caretaker actually did.

He could feel the gruff woman's eyes on him, so he bowed his head and muttered to himself. The rabbi did the same, though his were real words of prayer.

"Who rests here?" Rabbi Ariel whispered.

He got up to show the rabbi the brick wall where a brass tablet was affixed. The rabbi followed him.

Approaching it, he traced the inscription for the first time while Rabbi Ariel watched him, his body bending ever so slightly forward and back. "Davening," the rabbi had called it. Submitting oneself to God's power.

He'd only ever seen a blurred photograph in the *Journal*, long ago. But this:

Born 23 April 1854. Left us 9 January 1869.

He was a stranger no more.

"I'm so sorry, Philip. I'm understanding more each day. I never wanted to ask you what happened to him since you told me you knew these people. But I suspected. He was your friend, I see that in you."

"Rebbe, you don't know what you see."

"Let me say a prayer for him, and for you."

The colored glass above them was growing lighter. The bells across London swelled and twinned. It was getting late and he wanted to leave. He needed to do what he'd come to do.

"No more prayers," he said.

§

HE STOOD WITH THE rabbi outside the castle gates, next to the bars, and watched the goings-on as the crowd around and behind them swelled in size. Windsor was draped in somber bunting. An air of contemplative quiet settled over the grounds, the arrivals, and those members of the court visible in the castle doorways. Many in the crowd wept.

Signs of the queen's imminent death were everywhere.

He shifted restlessly, waiting for the right moment. His stomach lurched and fear dewed his forehead, making him feel sickeningly dizzy. It was worse than being at sea.

Carriages pulled up to Windsor's gates before a throng at St. George's Chapel for the Garter Service. A chamber quartet played a lilting, melancholy piece from Handel as the carriages came to gentle stops under the porte cochere. Coachmen stepped down to hand out the elite of London: Honorable Members, dukes, earls, lords, esteemed patrons of the arts and the artists themselves. They wandered onto the drive to await instruction on where and how to walk and how to bow properly. In due time they'd walk the path to the chapel. If there were to be initiates this day, the inductees would don the velvet and ultramarine mantle, the heraldic shield of St. George's Cross encircled by the Garter, the surcoat and Tudor bonnet, and the collar—some thirty troy ounces of gold.

The onlookers would rain good wishes on the newly chivalrous member. *Honi soit qui mal y pense.* Evil to him who thinks evil.

But not today, he thought.

"Who should go to such lengths just to have white hair?" Rabbi Ariel asked as he watched the coachmen. He stroked his beard.

"Solicitors, for one."

"How do they get their wigs to look like that?"

He told the rabbi of a day he'd spent in the warm kitchen of the castle. While cooks prepared the luncheon, Charles, the castle coachman, got ready for his formal duties that evening: the driving of distinguished guests from a celebration on Temple Street to a grand Windsor dinner. He dressed in his livery, a white shirt as hard and unyielding as the planks of a barn, and stockings of equally intense white beneath silver buckled pumps and knee breeches of a dark, lush blue. A swallow-tailed coat the color of blood topped it all off.

For his duties, Charles had to wear a wig. He'd watched the coachman wet it with water and rub a mild soap into it, after which he used a fanned puff to apply generous dollops of powder. By the time he'd finished, Charles looked as if he'd stepped out of a painting in the halls of Parliament into a world he no longer belonged to.

"Better they should pretend to have young men's hair," the rabbi said.

"They're wearing the colors of mourning."

"I know, Philip."

The rabbi was trying to cheer him up. It had been that way all morning. Mild jokes, terrible puns, casual observations of others, and questions about trivia. All for nothing.

"Philip—"

"Wait. It's starting."

Sextons held open the Chapel doors for Princess Louise, who emerged alone. She remained the most beautiful of the queen's daughters, all the more so for her isolation. It wasn't mourning as with her mother, her lost brother Leopold, or the lovelessness of her marriage. She'd chosen the roads she walked that took her so far away from duty and country.

He admired that about her. Once he'd faced the moment when it was clear, he had no choice but to leave everything behind. All that he'd left, he stared at now.

Reaching into his pocket, he took out the yellowed letter and pressed it into Rabbi Ariel's hands. "Rebbe, I want you to take this."

He caught a glimpse of the Blue Room window, and he knew the queen was in there. When the glass was open to allow even a sliver of chill winter wind inside, the curtains swayed inward, shaping themselves in twists of dark fabric before the air paused and the curtains fell. It reminded him of the simple beauty of watching a loved one breathe.

It is perfectly her, he thought. *She's here and not here.*

He moved closer to the stone pillar of the gate.

Rabbi Ariel stared at the letter. "What are you doing?"

Beyond the bars, children played atop the mound. They chased each other in a game of needle's eye gone to anarchy. Their two lines were ragged, their teams fluid. Three of them collided and they tumbled to the soft ground, laughing as they sang a childish rhyme in exuberant, breathless tones.

The needle's eye that doth supply
The thread that runs so true
I stump my toe and down I go
All for want of you

They didn't fear the world, he thought. *The world awaits them. Money and station would accomplish a lot for them, and yet they'd still learn that some things burned themselves onto the skin, so they're never lost. They'd learn that there were so many kinds of memories. The things they'd remember until life pulled them somewhere else, no matter how many promises they would make, that they'd always recall the moment.*

We should try harder than we do to hold on to such things, he thought at the gate, *but matters come over the course of the years to push them away.*

Then there are the other memories, which never leave us even when we beg them to. They lie with us every night. I suppose those children

*will eventually collect some of those, too. If they're lucky enough to have
and lose something so rare.*

"You're my dearest friend," he told Rabbi Ariel above the
growing din of the crowd.

The rabbi put a hand on his arm. "I'm not letting you go."

The crowd erupted in cheers as others emerged behind
Princess Louise. There were officers of some military branches.
The insignias of the Irregular Horse, the Dragoons, the long-ago
Abyssinian Second.

They marched in unison past the waiting dignitaries to the
Middle Ward and the long shadow of the Round Tower. Seeing
them, the boys and girls fled to the motte. Up its chalk hide they
went to the keep. There they held out their arms and pretended to be
dirigible pilots, cloud-hopping falcons, pirates sailing the high seas.

In a moment, the Lord Steward approached the children
and admonished them to keep their clothes tidy. Simon had
aged considerably and was all but bald. The skin on his head was
a spectacle of sunspots and scabbing wounds.

It was time.

Grabbing hold of the bars, he began to climb. Those closest
to him screamed.

"Stop!" Rabbi Ariel yelled. "What are you doing? Get down
before they see you acting like a madman. They'll arrest you!"

He pulled himself to the top and paused there. He only had
moments, but this was once the view from the castle that, however
brief in his life, belonged to him.

Up so high, the cold wind stunned him. Past the surging
soldiers and the staff of the Middle Ward, and the men in the
crowd below him trying to pull him down, Windsor lay out for
him to see. Its towers, spires, parks, and the palace, its paths and its
people. The sun struggled to burn patchy holes through a wintry
fog, opening a glimpse at the wing he once lived in, the spinal span
of the Norman Gate, masts of smoke as fragile and spindly in the
wind as the smallest whorls on his finger. Below him was the chaos

and rage he'd started by doing what he was doing, but up high the world felt eerily quiet and it was easy to imagine that there were many roads available to him, not just the one he was about to take.

Somewhere beyond sight, the one he thought of in all the moments of his days and the hot hours of his nights saw him. Right now, he saw everything, even if no one else could. A ridiculous, childish hope. But the heart had more rooms than Windsor. There was no end to what it could hold.

He let himself fall to the ground on the other side of the gate, in the ward. Soldiers surrounded him and ordered him to put his hands up.

The rabbi screamed his name, but he was intent on the distant open window of the Blue Room. "Your Majesty," he shouted, "I must speak to you!"

"Get on your knees!" the yeoman of the queen's body guard ordered, pointing a halberd at his chest. The soldier was no more than a meter away. The other yeomen stood around him in a semicircle, leveling their own blades at him.

"Your Majesty," he screamed again, "please! Let me speak to you. Someone let me see her!"

One of the yeomen pushed him to the ground, then placed a knee against his neck. Dirt and frost filled his mouth.

"Please don't hurt him," he heard Rabbi Ariel plead from across the ward. "He's sick. He's not himself—"

The yeomen pulled him to his feet. They bound his hands at the wrists.

Princess Louise stood in the chapel doorway, watching him. He saw her fear and that made sense. A madman, a Negro, invading her sacred home and screaming for the queen.

But he saw something else in the princess. The way she stared at him. At his hands. She knew who he was.

She didn't turn away fast enough to hide it from him.

Rabbi Ariel pressed himself against the bars of the gate, begging for his friend's life while the yeomen held their blades to his throat. The stunned crowd, Simon, the now-silent children on the motte, the princess, they all watched him and whispered to each other.

He held his bound hands high. His right palm. Princess Louise gasped.

The Blue Room curtains blew gently apart.

"Please tell them you're sorry," Rabbi Ariel called to him. "They'll throw you in a cell or worse. Tell them, Philip—"

"*I'm not Philip!*"

It was as if the world stopped. He felt an overwhelming need to turn away from the rabbi's pale, shocked expression, from his eyes that the distance made black and full of pity and anger.

He'll hate me, starting right now. The both of us, friends and yet worlds apart, and the moment finds us thinking the same thing about me. That's not the man I've known all these years.

A razor-sharp and merciless feeling settled in him. *I said it too soon. I'm not ready. I want the words back. The years. I can't come back from this. I can't beg or lie my way back from this and I'd give anything to run.*

You said once, we could run. I'd give it all to have listened to you, Philip.

"I'm not Philip," he said, his voice cracking. "I need to see the queen. Please, she can't die without at least seeing me. I'm begging you. At least tell her, there's no reason to punish herself any longer. She didn't kill me."

"Who are you?" Princess Louise shouted at him from a safe distance.

"I'm Alamayou," he said, loud enough for all of them to hear.

TWO

Chapter Seven

29 December 1900

RABBI ARIEL SAT ON an uncomfortable, rickety stool alongside Lord Grant. The deafening cries of Newgate's prisoners echoed through the dank corridors. Many of the jailed men he'd passed on his way inside the prison were hard at menial labor, weaving, mopping, picking akum apart and separating the strands to make new rope as the tar covered their trembling arms.

The men who objected, Lord Grant explained, or who talked, or in any way acted out, were dragged into a separate wing and beaten nearly to death.

"That's what you're hearing," Lord Grant told Rabbi Ariel. "The lullaby of the Old Bailey."

The cells themselves wept mold and stank of unwashed, miserable men. Their doors were fastened by rusted slip bolts to stones of two- and three-tons' weight. A cold and unforgiving wind swept through the prison's halls, bitter and hard. It rattled anything loose.

"I tried to bring you a blanket from the flat," Rabbi Ariel said through the cell bars, "but the guards confiscated it from me."

"I appreciate it, rebbe. You didn't have to do that. You could've gotten into trouble."

"I don't know what to call you anymore." The rabbi began to weep.

"Stop it," Lord Grant admonished him. "Don't draw attention or they'll put us out. The fact we're seeing him at all is a minor miracle and a testament to my influence, if you want to know the truth. In any event, it's one visit we may never get again, so control yourself."

"Call me by my name, rebbe."

Alamayou sat on his cot a few feet from the rabbi. He was separated from his friend by thick iron bars. A tin of soupy porridge lay on the stone floor inside his cell, untouched by all but the rats.

"We have very little time," Lord Grant said. "Nor will your retainer last forever. What you face, whoever you are, is both serious and unprecedented in my years. If you're truly the Abyssinian, those charges brought against you thirty years ago were beyond anything I've ever argued at bar. War crimes. Deviancy."

"Deviancy?" Rabbi Ariel snapped.

"Let him finish, rebbe. Can these charges still be brought against me after all this time?"

"I'll have to research the applicable statute of limitations, but that will matter only as far as your being formally accused of a violation of law from the past. Let's not lose sight of the fact that you violated the law not a week ago, leaping the gate onto Her Majesty's grounds."

"I don't understand any of this." Angry, the rabbi wrapped his woolen coat tightly about himself and shivered miserably.

"He means, rebbe, that they don't need to charge me to do what they meant to do the first time. Send me back to Abyssinia."

"If you're Alamayou," Lord Grant continued, "you are correct. The punishment will no doubt hearken back to Parliament's original decree. If you're the other one? Philip Layard? In that case, you're no better off. The charges are trespassing, endangering the health and welfare of the royal family, and fraud. You'll never see the outside of these walls again just on those bases, I'm afraid."

"I'll die in here or in Abyssinia, is what you're saying. So be it. Just find me a way to get word to the queen and I'll die with my name. I'm Alamayou."

The rabbi stood abruptly. "I can't listen to this."

"Listen to *me*, then, Ariel."

Staring balefully at Alamayou, the rabbi returned to his seat.

"There aren't many left who know me," Alamayou said, "or knew me. Prince Leopold is gone. The queen is gravely ill and I don't expect her to get into a landau and come to Newgate Prison to see me no matter what she believes. Princess Louise is the only choice I have to get word to the queen. If I can get to her."

He handed Lord Grant a letter. "Last night, I wrote this in hopes that it might reach the princess."

Immediately, a guard came and took the letter away. After several minutes, he returned to Alamayou's cell and handed it back without a word. Lord Grant took it and read it over.

"They didn't cut it to pieces," the rabbi said.

"Consider yourself fortunate indeed." Lord Grant gave it to the rabbi.

28 December 1900

Your Highness,

I've held too many secrets for far too long. Rest assured, I've paid a high price for that. But I can't make a secret of myself any longer. Not after the day at the Exposition in Paris when I heard the queen cry my name. I know what it is to carry such a burden as hers. I beg you now, let me give her the peace she deserves, before it's too late. As one who knows what it is to bear responsibility for a death, it's not something you can let her take to her grave. Let me end it.

Alamayou

"And now I see why they didn't destroy this," Lord Grant said. "It reads like a confession of a crime."

"Like the Talmud says." He smiled at the rabbi but received a turned back. "Will you see to it that the princess gets this?"

Lord Grant shook his head. "I'm not comfortable with this. As a solicitor who has advised the family, the queen herself, it's not appropriate—"

"I'll do it."

Rabbi Ariel stood. He took the paper from Lord Grant's outstretched hand. "I'll do what I can in the name of the friendship I had up until a week ago. But I need to speak to you privately. Lord Grant, will you give us a moment?"

Somewhere down one of the prison's many arteries, a man cried out for God while his fellow inmates screamed at him to be quiet. One told him to kill himself.

"Don't be long," Lord Grant said, the unease plain on his face, "or I'll leave you here with the lot of them."

"Is it true?" Rabbi Ariel asked Alamayou when Lord Grant was a safe distance away.

"Yes."

"Then why do what you've done? You were safe. You had a life in Paris. You had a friend."

"Do I still?"

"I don't know."

"She's dying, rebbe. She's old and ill, and she's lost like we've all lost if we live long enough. But when I saw her collapse at that Human Zoo, when I heard her cry my name, I knew one of the things killing her, killing her all these years, was living with what she thought she did to me. She thinks she sent me away to die. I can't let her die now, still believing that."

"And Philip?" the rabbi asked. "What of him? Or should I say, you?"

"Philip can't help me now. But I miss him every day."

"Damn you. I don't understand anything that's happened to my life this past week. It's like you've torn it open."

"Devorah, rebbe."

"My wife? Why are you bringing her up? What right do you have? She has nothing to do with this. I don't understand what you're trying to tell me."

"I heard you cry her name at night for years. I heard how much it hurt you. You miss her. You ache with it, still."

"Yes."

"Then you do understand what I'm telling you."

Rabbi Ariel held Alamayou's letter to the princess in his hand. "I never opened the other one. The old one you gave me at the gate. I won't, not ever. Is it from him?"

"Yes."

"God Almighty."

"Do this one last thing for me, rebbe. Deliver what I wrote to Princess Louise. I don't know if you can reach her, but try. And then you can be done with me. I hope you'll forgive me, in time. You're my only friend and I've never needed another. You're the best man I know."

"You're lying again. There was another."

"Yes."

"Who you loved," the rabbi said.

"Yes."

The rabbi touched the fringe of his *tallit* and began to whisper the prayer for the dead. "*Yit'gadal v'yit'kadash sh'mei raba…*"

Alamayou sat back on his cot with his head resting against the hard stone wall. He was so terribly tired. It was his ordeal, but, too, the sheer gathering of the past pressing down on him.

The rabbi's hands trembled, and Alamayou saw that he held both letters. His to the princess, and Philip's to him.

"Rebbe—"

"I'll go now, to the castle. I'll do what I can, and I'll think on all of this. There's nothing left to say tonight. A life that I didn't really know the way I thought, and now a prayer to carry it away from here. Let it all leave with me."

Rabbi Ariel came close to the bars. In the gloom of the prison corridor, Alamayou thought he could be taken for young.

The rabbi's hand slipped through the bars. Before the guard saw, Alamayou came over and let the rabbi touch his cheek. "I see it now," the rabbi said. "In that photograph."

"What?"

"Your story."

Alamayou watched him cross the corridor and disappear around a corner.

After a while, the prison settled in on itself. The sounds of breathing men deep in sleep rose and fell like a church hymn.

He said the rabbi's prayer. *Grant me light. I know I'm speaking to empty air. I'm not a believer, never have been. Not in his god or anyone else's.*

It's just that I don't want to die in here. Not yet.

I miss you.

§

UPON HIS ARRIVAL AT Lord Grant's home, Rabbi Ariel was ushered into a well-appointed study by a silent young maid. The residence featured warm woods and bookshelves that spoke to Lord Grant's interest in the origins of law, his refined taste in literature, and his passion for religious thought and scholarship.

"Perhaps we have some common interests," the rabbi said, then thought better of it given the expression on the solicitor's face.

"Quite the opposite," Lord Grant said curtly. "I was this very moment musing on what's become of me. Representing a renegade Negro at bar, and now a man in my home, quite visibly a Jew."

"We live in interesting times, do we not?"

"Indeed we do."

Lord Grant's wife entered the study ahead of the maid who carried a delicate pot, cups and saucers, and a plate of shortbreads. She set them down and poured the tea.

Rabbi Ariel nodded in gratitude to the maid. He saw the surprise briefly register on her face at being acknowledged.

Such a place, he thought.

"You knew him before?" he asked Lord Grant.

"No. I have been fortunate to be considered a trustworthy solicitor to Her Majesty over the years. On the matter of the Abyssinian, I was asked by her to offer my opinion."

"Which was?"

"That he presented great risk. That's what I remember of him. Of the other, I don't remember anything at all, other than a cheeky, angry colored who had great difficulty keeping to his place."

"Philip. His name is Philip Layard."

"Is. Was. No matter now, eh?"

Rabbi Ariel set down his cup. "I don't know what to do."

"Nor can I help you decide. I will defend this man despite my trepidation because, candidly, I've been paid. The moment that his case in any way conflicts with the interests of Her Majesty or the royal family, I will withdraw and return his retainer. To you, I imagine. Money can't help him where he is, or may go."

"He gave me a note to deliver to the princess somehow. Do you agree that's what's left to do? Is it even wise?"

"None of this is wise, Rabbi. We're far from wise remaining at the Negro's side. For what it may be worth to you, I do recall the princess being sympathetic to the Abyssinian's cause. As was the queen."

"Then why did she send him away?"

Lord Grant turned to his wife. "Give us privacy, my dear."

"I'll be near, should you require anything." She rose and left them alone in the study, sparing the rabbi a disapproving shake of her head.

"She suspects me of something?"

"It's not that. Your appearance, I suppose. You're quite foreign. But we speak of Alamayou now. In the end, the queen didn't send him away. She fought for him until she could no longer. She reached the only decision left to her and her monarchy. Don't fight for him anymore. Don't stake the prestige and the political capitol of the Crown on such as the Abyssinian. I give you the same advice, Rabbi. If he is whom he says, he is the son of a murderous tyrant who caused a war. He may be a deviant man. I ask you as a man of God, is he worth saving?"

"As a man of God, that's not my decision to make, nor is it anyone's."

"So be it." Lord Grant stood. "I'll see you out."

They walked to the door under the watchful eye of Lord Grant's wife. "There was a servant in the castle," Lord Grant said quietly. "The Lord Steward, Simon. Get the letter to him. Beg if you have to. I don't know of any other way to reach the princess. I will reach out as well. That's all I can do until we are before legal argument."

"Thank you."

"I cannot say I understand your concern for a man such as him," Lord Grant said before he closed the door, "but I suppose any man's last words are worth something."

§

AFTER PAYING THE HANSOM driver, Rabbi Ariel walked to Windsor's gate and peered in. The grounds were empty of all but the occasional servant, bundled against the biting cold as they crossed from ward to ward in the lengthening shadow of the Round Tower. Above him was the spot where Philip had climbed over, setting everything into motion.

Philip. Alamayou. His head swam with it all.

The change purse he carried felt heavy. He still had much of the money he'd brought from Paris.

I could leave, he thought.

It stunned him, how simple a thought it was, how easy to hold and just look at, as if it meant nothing. He had enough to cross the Channel and return to the Marais. By now his congregation was no doubt wondering what had happened to him. He could go home, make tea, and then close the wooden sign that directed his congregants to other synagogues. The sign Philip made for him, a simple and lovely piece of carved wood. That was a kindness.

Then he could preside over services, retire to his *appartamente*, and cry for Devorah.

Everything he thought he knew, he realized he didn't. As he stood at the gate in the very spot where they'd stood together just a week before, he wondered whether he'd ever had the friend he thought. Who was he? What was he?

His Torah had a name for it. *Mishkav zachar*. It was forbidden. It was punishable by death.

There was another word, *ahavah*. Love, spoken as "give." In the years he'd known the man as Philip, that's all he'd seen: Philip giving medical services and comfort to Jews he owed nothing to. He'd given friendship to an old rebbe. Now, for wanting to give a dying queen comfort and peace, he sat in a cold cell, awaiting a fate he couldn't escape because of who he loved as a son and who he loved as a companion. All of them, now lost.

Devorah. You miss her.

You understand me, rebbe.

He took the letter from his coat pocket.

There was a boy racing across the grounds. Eleven or twelve, Rabbi Ariel guessed, and too shabbily dressed to be a royal. The offspring of a servant, more likely. There was no shine on the boy's shoe buckles and his clothes were out of date.

He'd do. He was on the right side of the gate. "Won't you come see what I have for you?" he called out.

The boy eyed him suspiciously. *Good lad*, the rabbi thought. "There's a servant of Her Majesty, the Lord Steward. You'd know him by the scabs on his head. Yes?"

The boy hesitated. Rabbi Ariel shook his purse, letting him hear the chime of coins.

"Simon," the boy said warily.

"Well done! Simon, yes, that's it. If you deliver this to him," and he held the envelope for the boy to see, "then you may have this." The purse.

The boy extended his hands, expecting both to be handed over.

"You seem a trustworthy sort. To be sure, that's important. You understand, I need some proof you've done as I ask. Tell Simon to come to this gate with the envelope. When I see such a thing, the money is yours to spend as you like. Do we have an agreement?"

He let the boy peek inside the purse. It held more than enough for a good meal of meat, broth, and beer at an Irish ordinary.

The boy took the envelope and left Rabbi Ariel at the gate. It didn't take long for Simon to come, in the company of three yeomen.

Simon thrust the letter back to Rabbi Ariel, but he refused it and kept his hands warm in the folds of his meager topcoat.

"You've got the time it takes to walk away," Simon told him, "unless you're eager to sit with your friend in Newgate."

"Would you just let the princess read it for herself?"

"Why should I do that? So you can carry on your companion's work upsetting the royals? Isn't it enough they're on a bloody deathwatch? Now she's got the likes of you and him, trying to force your way inside? No, old man. I'll not show this to her. Take it and go."

"I don't know how long he has. I suppose they'll send him back, or hang him. But between now and then, I'll come back every day if I have to."

"For what? What do you want?"

"A word. That's all. He mattered to her once, didn't he?"

"Bloody crazy, the Jews are."

Simon stuffed the letter into his pocket. He and the yeomen left the rabbi huddled against the cold stone.

The wintry winds picked up, and before long a dark pall stretched across the sky, bathing Windsor in deep gray. Behind the rabbi, as far as his eyes could see, fog wrapped everything in clouds. He felt the bitter, unforgiving cold overtake him and despair that he'd failed.

Hours passed. He shivered uncontrollably but he refused to leave. Servants passed through the grounds, glancing at him and shaking their heads.

Finally he saw a light rise in a doorway. Simon came out, followed by Princess Louise. She was veiled in ermine against the cold and held a steaming mug of tea. At the gate, she gave it to him.

He took the mug gratefully and let its warmth burrow into his palms. He couldn't feel where his skin ended and the porcelain began.

"If you remain any longer, you'll freeze to death." The princess stepped back from the bars. "You must go."

"Did you read it?"

"Yes. I don't know that it's true, or not true. It's just words on a page."

"He's risked everything, Your Highness. Given up everything, simply to say those words to you and to your mother."

She unfolded the letter and stared at it as if it were on fire. "Are you a part of this? This extraordinary claim?"

"For thirty years, no. As of a week ago, I suppose I am."

"Do you believe him?"

Rabbi Ariel sipped his tea. The winter had leeched it of its warmth. "I believe him, Your Highness."

"Why?"

"I suppose it's because it's insane, what he's done. Who ever put so much at risk for a lie? Only the truth does this to men. At least to the man I've known."

"Then I suppose it's to me. Wait here."

She turned and went back. "My carriage," she told Simon as she walked briskly. "I need to bring a few items. And find a suitable coat for the stubborn old man who won't leave our gate."

§

"WE WISH TO BE alone with the prisoner," Princess Louise said.

At her command, the prison guards stepped away from Alamayou's cell to be replaced by her yeomen. They took up positions all along the corridor, which had been plunged into darkness at Simon's insistence. Only when every last torchière was snuffed out did the princess slip inside Newgate unseen, followed by a regiment of armed men.

She sat on the other side of the bars from Alamayou. A small table had been set before her. A large case rested on the floor at her feet.

Rabbi Ariel and Lord Grant stood to either side of her, watching intently.

"Is it really you?" she asked. "In the courtyard, when the guards took you, I saw your hand."

Alamayou held up his right palm for her to examine up close. "It's not enough proof for you, Your Highness. I can see it."

"No. It isn't. But your eyes are familiar to me."

"As are yours. You were so kind to me, Your Highness. To us."

"You and Philip."

"I still remember it was you who opened the door to my being able to paint. Do you recall? Action, consequence. A word for a brush, an easel."

"I do."

"It was while I was painting in Villefranche that I saw you and the queen after all this time. A funny thing."

"What you claim is hard to understand. Your death was confirmed. But what you ask, to speak to the queen after all these years, and especially at this dark hour, is to upend everything she's learned to live with. And that is impossible."

"I'd give anything for someone to say those words to me." He rose and took hold of the bars. "I would die for the chance to hear, 'You don't have to live with it anymore. He's not dead.' Happily so. Don't you think she might feel the same?"

"You presume to know how she feels? The queen?"

"No, Your Highness. But I knew her heart, once. I listened as she told me what it was to see a bright hot star, and then see it go out."

She fell silent.

"Your Highness," Rabbi Ariel said, "what can be done?"

Princess Louise opened the case. "You may be who you say you are. You may be Philip Layard. Or no one at all. Just an insane man who wants to see the queen."

"Why would he do that?" the rabbi asked.

"There was a man, Edward Oxford. He fired two pistol shots at the queen sixty years ago, while she was pregnant with my sister. He did it because he was insane. There was the Boy Jones, who wanted to be near her. Fenian separatists in Ireland want to blow her to hell and back to be rid of her. There are as many reasons as men to act on them. Now, why would you? Because you hate her. You feel colonized. You hate her skin and her wealth. You feel poverty crushing you each time you think of where we live and how we live. Or you feel nothing. Just a whim. It doesn't matter why."

She removed the contents of the case and placed them on the table, one at a time.

"Do you know what these are?" she asked.

"Forgive me, Your Highness," Rabbi Ariel said. "Is this some sort of test? His life is at stake."

"It's all right, rebbe," Alamayou said. "She should know in her heart that what I'm saying is the truth before she allows me anywhere near her mother."

He gazed at his palm, at the old fire scars there. "These wounds aren't enough. Philip had one too, in the end. Though you wouldn't have known that, Your Highness."

He pulled his cot close to the bars. Were it any other setting—a private tea, perhaps, and a fire built by the princess's service against the insistent winter outside—they might have shared a smile at the old memories stirred by the items arrayed on the table.

An orange, studded with cloves of cinnamon. A stethescope. An antique gun, smashed to uselessness.

"At least you didn't bring the whip," he said, taking a moment to watch the shock register in her eyes. "I see you remember that, once, there was a table very much like this one set out before your mother and me. There was a whip. Evidently, your family finds value in these challenges. Very well, then. Let me tell you of our time at Windsor. You, me, the queen, Philip. The memories are all I have of him. Soon, the same will be true of the queen, for both of us."

He studied her. She was listening intently, and remembering just as fiercely.

"Shall I begin with the orange?" he asked.

Chapter Eight

O N A MORNING OF low mist and rain, Alamayou and Philip sat beneath a canopy, eating breakfast on the covered veranda overlooking the Round Tower and the surrounding land. A deep chill settled over them despite the fire burning in a nearby brass pit. Light flurries of the coming winter's first snow had fallen overnight, and the grounds were dusted with a thin powder cover that the morning sun melted. Pinpoints of reflected sunlight burst from the damp grass.

Alamayou watched as a maidservant peeled the last orange in a generous bowl of fruit, then disappeared inside the ward. After her departure, he took up the fruit and drew on it with a stick of pitch coal.

"That's rude," Philip said. "People here don't act like that."

He tried to take it away but Alamayou was too fast. He held the finished product up for Philip to see. "Why?" he asked.

The cloves, Philip realized. Alamayou was trying to make the orange look like the one they'd seen in Her Majesty's Blue Room, atop a tray and studded with fresh cloves of cinnamon.

"I don't know," Philip said, "and she's not around to ask, is she?"

In the weeks since their night in the portrait room, they hadn't glimpsed the queen again, though they did see the army of servants attending her. Her court employed personal physicians from all fields, as well as a secretary, innumerable ladies-in-waiting and of the bedchamber, chefs who prepared her meals from a menu years in the planning, and young maids-of-all-work who swept, mopped, hauled water, and carried out slops, all while the scullery girls stood three bodies thick around the kitchen maids and cooks, hoping to learn and move up in rank. The housemaids could at least leave the lower floors of the castle to strip and make up beds, light fires, open windows, and prepare rooms for meals.

Philip begged pardon of a passing maid. "Alamayou wants to know why Her Majesty's got an orange with cloves in it."

"It's not for me to ask," she said curtly. "Nor for either of you."

She picked up their dishes and took them away.

They left the veranda for their apartment and some coats, then met Corbould for Alamayou's painting session. After setting up an easel and helping him choose a range of colors, Corbould tried to encourage Alamayou's study of an oak leaf, the veins and the way the light made them appear translucent, in preparation for a still life. Alamayou complied at first, but soon it was obvious that he wasn't painting the leaf at all. He coated the canvas in black, and on top of it brushed out a circle of orange.

"What is this?" Corbould asked.

"Her Majesty's odd orange," Philip said.

"I've heard of no such thing."

"It's on a tray, just a piece of fruit by itself, as if for decoration. The rind's dotted with cloves. She keeps it in the Blue Room."

"Something to do with him, I suppose."

"Prince Albert? What's an orange to do with him?"

"That room's a museum to him. I'm sure you've noticed if you saw it, and if you did, you're among a select few. Nothing's been touched since his death. The princess told me about it once. The prince's clothes are lain out as if he stepped away for a stroll. It's been that way since eighteen sixty-one. If she's ever seen in public, it's only on travels to Balmoral for extended stays, or maybe the walk from one ward to another here at Windsor. Nothing more, really. She clings to what she knows."

"I heard tell, but didn't understand how bad it is until I came here. Everything's black or gray or purple. Curtains all closed, the women in their weeps. All these years, you say? We saw her once, at night. It was a bloody shock to the senses... I mean, it was surprising."

"Don't worry yourself with grammar. You're not among royalty at the moment. I'm a rank commoner. You should consider yourselves fortunate, both to glimpse her and to not glimpse her again. She's a difficult one, as I hear no shortage of from the princess. A distant and troubled soul even before Albert died, and ever since she's plunged into mourning, it's as if the sun went out around here. All the time. At least she's a prolific writer. Notes are all that her children know of her. Imagine an entire life together, built more on quiet, soundless words than spoken ones."

"You make her sound like a cousin to Alamayou."

"Perhaps they're not so different, though I'll deny ever speaking such a thing aloud if asked."

"I did ask one of the maids about the orange. She was short with me."

"They learn not to speak of her," Corbould said, "or else find themselves place-hunting. Never again in their lives should they see such as Windsor."

"I suppose it's difficult to leave this place once you've been inside."

"For many, I suppose that's true."

"But not for you?"

Corbould sat on the grass. Spreading a cloth, he opened jars of paints and poured them into dishes. He dipped a spoon into each, washing it in between, and built a palette of hues.

"It's not life here," he said.

He set up a canvas of his own next to Alamayou's. "What I paint, it exists in the world, does it not? Yet it's different. It's done. If I paint a tree, that tree will remain forever as I made it, while the real life subject is free to grow lush or wither and die.

That's what it's like to be among them. It's as if you're made by them. All the possibilities are theirs. Yours are done."

Alamayou added another dab of color to his canvas. It was riddled through with black. The color of mourning, like everything at Windsor.

"My words," Corbould said. "They lack. Why I paint, I suppose."

He added to the painting of the Round Tower. A bit of yellow that brightened the sun.

"For the princess." He smiled wistfully.

"It makes her happy to see you painting it. I remember the look on her face the day we met you."

"It does, doesn't it? I'm glad others can see it, even fleetingly. Makes it real, you see."

The same sense Philip had that first day returned. Listening to Corbould speak of Princess Louise, even watching him paint the vista she loved, carried echoes of other, quieter conversations, and of wants not spoken.

"How long have you been among them?" Philip asked.

"These last three years. And I'm only now learning my way around without having to think. But what of you? How long will you remain here?"

"I don't know. This is all unexpected, to say the least."

"May it stay that way," Corbould said. "Makes for a far more interesting life, don't you think?"

"But I don't know anything about royalty, let alone how to live with them."

"It seems to me you're doing well with the prince right next to you." Corbould smiled at Alamayou. "The care and feeding of royalty is, in the end, relatively simple. Give them what they want."

§

"YOUR HIGHNESSES, I PRESENT at your request, the Abyssinian and his valet."

"Bastard," Philip muttered under his breath. He and Alamayou waited in the open doorway of an enormous room filled with light. Over Simon's shoulder he saw Princess Louise and Prince Leopold at a long wooden table. They stood close to each other, intently studying the papers strewn before them.

Prince Leopold looked up at Simon's announcement. He gestured for Alamayou and Philip to enter.

"Don't forget to bow," Simon remarked as they passed.

"I'm not his valet."

"Kaffir to a kaffir is what I see and what you are."

"Is there a problem?"

They snapped to attention at Prince Leopold's voice. It was angry and agitated. The princess placed a hand on his arm, calming him.

Alamayou bowed first, followed by Philip. He looked at the prince with concern. Leopold's skin was pale and glistening with sweat. He seemed unsteady on his feet.

"Leave us," Princess Louise told Simon. "Close the doors. Alamayou, Philip, come to us."

She wore a broadly fanned gown of muted grey. The henna wisps in her hair shone in the light, but there was none of the warmth or the assuredness they'd grown accustomed to. She stood uneasily next to her brother, who glowered at them.

"We're experiencing difficulties," she began, "and in rather odd places. It may be related to Alamayou."

"There's no question who it's related to," Prince Leopold interrupted. "How much does he understand?"

"He's better every day," Philip said. "He's trying his best, Your Highness, and just yesterday he spoke a new phrase."

"It's not enough," the prince snapped.

"Please, brother. You exert yourself."

"Our monarchy," Prince Leopold said, ignoring his sister's plea, "exists because the people believe it should. They see us as the best of England. We stand for what they wish all of England to stand for. We may have the occasional difference of opinion with Parliament or our subjects, but we cannot be questioned on the wisdom of our decisions or our moral standing to make them. Our mother cannot be questioned as to the fitness of her ability to rule. That's especially true of an act of charity. Of all things."

He put a hand on the table to steady himself. At first Philip thought he was selecting one of the documents, but then he saw the prince sway in place. He shot a confused look to the princess.

She'd seen it, too, but her brother's anger cowed her into keeping quiet.

"We asked for a translator," the prince continued. "Surely someone from the Second could speak a few words of Amharic, at least. We thought it would be a benefit to him and an easy enough request for Parliament to approve. We were proven quite wrong."

They were all staring at Alamayou. Their eyes were upon him, the lovely one and the angry, sick one. Only Philip didn't look at him. Alamayou didn't know what was being said, but he knew it was about him, and if Philip wouldn't look at him, it was bad. Because if it were something good, as it had been when he'd said their words to the old queen, Philip would turn to him and smile, be the man he'd seen at the fire. He'd be safe.

"They delayed, and then they refused." Prince Leopold felt behind him for a chair. "Inquiries were made and we have now learned that concerns have been raised to Ambassador Naismith and to Parliament, in secret. Now we are in a most awkward position. Because of you."

The prince pointed at Alamayou.

"Your Highness," Philip said, "he doesn't understand."

"*Make* him understand, Layard. Or else what in God's name are you good for? What further purpose do you serve us, being here?"

"Appreciate our position," Princess Louise said as she guided her brother to the chair. He sat, his gaze fixed on Alamayou. "The translator's but one part, and on that we're looking at other options. But we've now learned there's to be a banquet here at Windsor in a week's time. It's for the living veterans of foreign wars. Crimea, Sepoy, and yours. There will be members of Parliament here. Soldiers from the campaign in Abyssinia. The Abyssinian ambassador. They'll all be here, in these halls, with some sort of secret that causes them to oppose us on the matter of Alamayou. We don't know what's happening. The queen, who relies on us, doesn't know. This castle will be filled with men we honor for bravery in a war fought against Alamayou and his father. Do you see the difficulty?"

"What we need to know," Prince Leopold said, "is simple. What is the truth of Alamayou?" His breathing was heavy and hoarse. The color rapidly faded from his cheeks.

"Leo," the princess said urgently, "what's happening? You're ill."

"Leave me alone. I'm fine…"

The prince slid off his chair and crumpled to the floor. His arms wrapped around his leg as if trying to hold it together.

"Take me to my apartment," he said through gritted teeth.

"You need a doctor—"

"No!" He pushed his sister away as Alamayou and Philip reached his side. "The court doctors owe everything to her, nothing to me. They'll tell her and then I'll be confined to my bed. Again. I'll go mad. No. Say nothing, do you hear me?"

The first thing Alamayou noticed was the smell. Rot, copper, warm and bitter. He gently rolled Prince Leopold to one side and found blood freely flowing down his leg.

"Oh my god, he'll die." Princess Louise twisted his pant leg tightly, trying to make a tourniquet of the material and staunch the flow of blood.

"Do as I tell you," Leopold said between gritted teeth. "Lift me up and get me away from here before Simon and the others come."

After checking the corridor, Alamayou and Philip carried the bleeding prince to his apartment in the Middle Ward. There they gently lay him on a couch.

The apartment's receiving room resembled a cottage interior, with a narrow wood-paneled entry and a thread of shelves below spaced candelabras on mounts. Some figurines more appropriate for a child than a prince populated the shelves, along with enough books for a student of the world.

Princess Louise took a seat in a high-backed rosewood chair. There were tears in her eyes as she watched her brother roll his pant leg up. His face was so pale. Purpling spots appeared on the surface of his skin.

Leopold lay back and took deep gulps of air. "You all stare at me."

"What happened to you, Leo?"

"I fell."

"My god, Leo, why didn't you tell anyone? We have to stop the blood."

"I said no doctors."

"I'll do it," Philip said.

"You?" The prince raised himself up from the couch. "Someone like you touching a prince, Layard?"

"I apprenticed to a doctor," Philip said. "I know what I'm doing, and I know what I'm seeing."

"And just what is it you think you see?" Prince Leopold asked him.

"Hemophilia, Your Highness. If we don't stop that bleeding, you'll die."

"You need to understand," the princess said, "no one outside of court knows. This could destroy us if our own subjects in their usual rashness conclude that the royal bloodline is afflicted with disease."

More secrets, Philip thought. "What instruments do you have? Something to cauterize, something for the pain? We need those at least."

"You'll not touch me!"

"Let him, Leo. For God's sake, what choice is there?"

She took her brother's hand and laid him back on the couch. "Do it," she told Philip.

The prince's breath came in time to the pulse of blood leaving a small cut on his ankle. *It was like watching the beat of a heart*, Alamayou thought. That regular rhythmic bleeding.

The prince had a medical kit in the apartment. Inside the bag there was cotton, a flat iron, and a sealed ampule of chloral. Philip asked the princess to put the iron to the hearth. Alamayou lit kindle, and soon the metal grew red.

Philip doused the cotton with chloral and pressed it to the prince's nose and mouth.

"Deeply now," Louise told her brother.

The prince did as he was told. In a moment his breathing slowed. His eyes rolled over white. Philip gently closed them.

The sight of his eyes was too much for Alamayou to bear. "No. No *mamot*," he said. "No mamot!"

They didn't understand. None of them understood him, and Alamayou wanted to tear down every last wall cutting him off from everyone else, all the time. Grabbing one of the prince's figurines from the shelf, he set it next to the fire and the flatiron reddening against the wood. "Abat, anat, mamot." He held the figurines closer. *See me, Philip. Like you did before.*

Philip didn't understand what Alamayou was doing, and he didn't have time to puzzle it out. The prince was bleeding inexorably to death. Even taking the effects of the chloral into account, he had little time. The prince's veins were emptying. That was the worst of it, the awful grace of being near when a man died. That ancient, leaving light that you didn't realize was there until it went out.

He placed his secret with us, Philip thought as he wrapped the pant leg tighter. *I don't know what it means, but it won't add up to a damn thing if he dies. If he dies it'll be because I failed to help him. They'll say I killed him. A bloody prince. My black hands killed him.*

Reaching around Alamayou, he took hold of the flatiron with a bundled corner of his shirt and pulled it out of the fire.

"Philip, see."

"I can't, Alamayou."

But he did. He met Alamayou's eyes. The fire burned in the hearth behind him. Alamayou's head and shoulders glowed against it. It made a shadow of him, except his eyes. One hand held the figurine. A soldier, it looked like. Alamayou raised it over the fire. His other hand, his ruined hand, reached for Philip.

For just a moment, Philip felt the wind and smelled the sulphuric cloud of rockets and war, and they were back in front of the burning cottage on Amba Geshen, with Alamayou straddling the space between life with Philip and death with his parents.

My parents. Anat, abat. Mamot. Mamot, Philip.

Die.

His fist knocked the figurine over. "Mamot. Abat, Albert—"

"Die," Philip said. "He means die. Mamot."

"Die," Alamayou repeated. He pointed to the prince. "No die."

"No, no die."

Philip took a stethescope from the prince's medical satchel and laid its circle upon the prince's chest atop his heart. He showed Alamayou how to slip the buds into his ears, then set Alamayou's hand just above the prince's mouth to feel his breath, soft as silk.

Alamayou listened to the steady pulse of the prince's blood.

"Life," Philip told him. "No death. No mamot. Not him, or you, or me. His heart wants life, not death."

Philip pressed the iron to the prince's wound, cauterizing it. It was all that could be done for him and would be ungodly painful when he woke.

A royal, Philip thought, *scalded by a Negro. It might be funny if it wasn't me.*

Outside, the light dipped and the grounds crackled with kindled gas lamps. Night, at last.

He and Alamayou sewed and cleansed together, saying not a word. It was more blood than Alamayou had seen since Abyssinia.

When he finally woke, Philip gave the prince laudanum and he descended back into a drugged sleep. His burn leaked from beneath fresh linen and iodine swab. Philip changed his dressing, letting Alamayou help.

"Will he be all right?" Princess Louise asked.

"The bleeding's stopped and the wound ought to stay shut. I hope he can be more careful, Your Highness, or this could happen again."

Princess Louise closed her brother's medical bag and gave it to Philip. "It *will* happen again. He's right about this much: anyone who finds out how dangerous his situation is will tell the queen. He has dreams of going to Oxford, courting a girl, marrying. I know the chance he'll live long enough to see any of it is near none. He knows it as well, what's worse. We don't talk about it. That's what he needs. Not to talk about it. Just live."

"We'll hold our tongues," Philip said. He tried to hand the medical bag back to the princess, but she gently pushed it to him again.

"In case he has need of someone," she said, "let it be you."

"What about his clothes? The bloody sheets?"

"We can't let the service see them, or my mother will hear of another bout on him so soon and she'll confine him. He'll be miserable. We must dispose of them."

"We'll do it," Philip said, and looked around for a sack to put the prince's blood-soaked clothes into. While he searched, the princess left her brother a note.

Your secret remains safe with me, and it's safe with them. For this, we must thank them with our belief, our support, and someone to help Alamayou be heard.

§

AT WINDSOR, ALAMAYOU AND Philip crossed the grounds alone in a strong cool wind that felt bracing. To their right were the black rectangles of the windows. One burned with curtained light and when the wind found it, the curtains fluttered mightily.

In a patch of soft ground behind the Lower Ward where no light found them, they dug deep and buried the prince's clothes. When they were done, Alamayou put a hand on the patted earth. He said words from his faraway country, too softly to be heard by anyone.

The sound of wagon wheels rolling atop the Long Walk broke the stillness. Servants, coming to the castle for their duties, or leaving for a visit home. The comings and goings of lives beyond the gates.

They continued to the apartment, and to silence again.

Philip found a place under the bed's long, loose covers to hide the medical satchel. Before retiring, he wrote a note to the queen.

The prince Alamayou delivers Your Royal Highness his regards and affections, and begs to ask, if it is not too presumptuous a question: what does the orange with cinnamon cloves stand for?

Most humbly, Philip Layard

After a few moments spent wandering the corridor, he found a startled Simon, who grudgingly agreed to deliver the note to the Blue Room if Philip would simply remove himself from sight.

He returned to the apartment. "Alamayou, the mystery of the cinnamon cloves'll soon be solved—"

Alamayou had fallen asleep with the stethescope to his chest, where he had located the beat of his heart.

Chapter Nine

5 November 1868

As Windsor prepared for the banquet honoring England's soldiers, a winter storm swept whirlwinds of snow across London. The light took on a shimmering and enduring quality, turning the castle woods into watercolors. Hennas and golds that had burst in the elms disappeared, leaving bare branches and dangling icicles. Beneath the chandeliered trees, gardeners crossed Windsor's grounds with mufflers across their faces to collect holly and ivy, which the castle service used to decorate every balcony, staircase, and fixture. Soon the halls resembled a forest. The castle filled with the delicious smells of cooking meats, browning pastries, and fermenting jams.

On the morning of the banquet, an editorial appeared in the *Telegraph*. It openly questioned the Crown's involvement with the heir to Abyssinia's tyrant. By that afternoon, soldiers appeared at Windsor's gates. Only a few, crippled by injury or sickness from the arduous voyage back after the war. They silently protested Alamayou's presence while onlookers gathered in support.

Most of the castle service saw them through Windsor's many windows. So many had sons who went to one campaign or another. They turned from Alamayou in disgust when he passed them by.

As the afternoon light faded, carriages pulled up to Windsor. Others queued up on the Long Walk. Veterans who'd lived through the empire's many wars climbed out and walked into a castle they'd never seen the inside of. By eight, Windsor's constellation of ballrooms teemed with veterans freely mingling with Parliament members and the royals. Only the queen was absent.

At the princess's request, Alamayou and Philip remained in their apartment, resigned to having their dinner alone, with only the faint sounds of the chamber orchestra reminding them of the feast they weren't invited to.

Near nine o'clock, there was a swift knocking at the apartment door. Alamayou opened it and found Simon waiting impatiently, dressed in the uniform of a Crimean veteran. "Your presence is required in the State Dining Room."

He sent in valets to redress them both in black waistcoats, shawl collars, false cuffs, and woolen trousers. Then he led them the back way, through the servants' kitchen and scullery to a room gilded in gold and lit by a vaulted lantern. The banquet was in full swing two rooms over.

Beneath the flickering lights, the princess sat with Prince Leopold and the Abyssinian ambassador at a long table of freshly stained oak.

"We have been assured this won't take long," Princess Louise said. "As you can plainly see, we have guests. This entire evening is for them, Ambassador. Not for this, whatever this may be."

"An excellent segue," Prince Leopold said. "What exactly is this?"

"As ambassador," Naismith began, "it's my responsibility to provide updates and assurances to the governing council of Abyssinia on the well-being and status of their prince. In my correspondences, though, I'm hearing rumors. Allegations. There's growing concern in Abyssinia, and I'm afraid it's been conveyed here."

"So we've seen," Prince Leopold said. "We too appear to be on notice of growing concerns, though no one's seen fit to do us the courtesy of corresponding with us in the normal course. No, we get our news through declination of a request for assistance, and then in an editorial. A strange way to communicate concerns, would you agree?"

"I wasn't involved."

"These concerns have been conveyed in the refusal of a translator to assist the one who, we assume, you have concerns about."

"Your Highness, if you'll permit me to ask some questions, I'm optimistic we can clear matters up straightaway. That was my intent for tonight. Nothing more."

"One presumes your questions might best be answered with, say, a translator assisting," Princess Louise said.

"Point taken. But you understand me, don't you, Mr. Layard?"

"So far," Philip said.

"Then tell me about the fire on Amba Geshen."

A small bloom of dread opened in Philip's stomach, spreading its petals slowly outward. "What of it?"

"What did you see? Why were you there? I'd like the account to be as full as you can possibly make it."

"In a war where I saw men die, there was a fire where I saw two more die."

"I'm going to suggest that someone impress upon you the importance of this." Naismith pushed himself away from the table. He motioned for Simon. "A brandy, warmed."

Before her brother could say a word, Princess Louise took Philip by the arm and led him away from Alamayou's questioning expression, and from the ambassador's wary gaze, to the opposite side of the room.

"May I remind you of our previous talk?" she said.

"I don't like him."

"You've no right to any feelings whatsoever. There are royals in this room. A foreign prince. The ambassador to Abyssinia. A servant. And then, you. In that order. Am I clear?"

"Very, Your Highness."

"For what it's worth, I don't like him either. But I know enough to distinguish between who I like and who I must deal with."

"I understand."

"Unless I'm very much mistaken, you're Alamayou's only friend. Don't do something that will destroy him."

But that's exactly the point, Philip wanted to say, and for a moment he thought of saying it. *I saw Alamayou come this close to death twice, and the only reason he's here is because whatever secrets he lives with, he swallowed them back. He's that strong. We can't let this man pull those secrets out of him. We may not want to see them in the light.*

He thought better of saying anything. Those were night words.

"I want what's best for Alamayou," he said.

"Good. I see that you do." She was looking at him as if she'd come across him for the first time. It made him squirm, the way she appraised him, so he stepped away from her and sat back down to resume his response to Naismith.

"I was assisting Dr. Marcus Baker White," he said, "in the camp of the Second Regiment, on the Falah Saddle."

Naismith sipped his brandy, set the glass on Simon's silver tray, and returned to the table across from Philip.

Falah. Alamayou sat up straight. He knew he was being watched closely. In Abyssinia, at his father's capital at Debre Tabor before he trekked with his mother across the country to the fortress at Meqdala, he'd sat in his father's tent surrounded by tribal leaders. They all hated his father. He'd brought the English army to their shores in search of a war.

They hated him, too. He was his father's son.

His father knew their resentment and rage at him. He basked in it. A man, he told Alamayou, looks at everyone or no one. If a man is afraid, he looks at everyone in search of the biggest threat. If he's brave, he looks at no one, because no one deserves his gaze.

Philip had said Falah. *That was where the English camp stood, across from the fortress. Philip's going to talk about the war. And that means he's going to talk about me.*

He and Philip had been trying to understand each other for months, and after all that time he still wasn't sure what

Philip thought or knew of him. He wanted to know those things. It took him by surprise how much he wanted that.

"Go on," Naismith told Philip.

Philip cleared his throat. It felt as parched as it had in the war.

"We got a report in camp of a fire on the next peak over from the fortress. Small, unimportant, but scouts saw figures leaving Meqdala and heading in that direction, to Amba Geshen. They sent a small party to intercept. Dr. White was told he had to go because of the possibility of troop casualties. And if he went, I went.

"By the time we reached Amba Geshen and the cottage, it was already collapsing. It was engulfed on one side. The walls were buckling and the roof had fallen in partway. The fire was everywhere. Even the door. It split in so many places, and each crack was filled with fire, like veins.

"The first thing I saw was Alamayou. He was standing in the cottage doorway. I think he'd gotten it open somehow and the flames were swelling through, toward him. Behind him, there were two people. They were leaning against each other, on their knees."

"Tewedros and the queen," Naismith said.

"You couldn't tell who or what they were. I only saw them for a moment."

"Then him. Alamayou."

"Yes."

"How close was he to his parents when you saw him?"

"The flames covered everything. The heat made it hard to see. The whole cottage, even the air around him, it was all shimmering."

"You didn't answer me."

"I can't say for sure."

"Close enough to touch?"

"It's possible."

"To be held there by one of them?"

"The angle I was at. I can't say whether they were in arm's reach or not. There was too much chaos."

"I don't understand why you're asking all these questions," Princess Louise said.

"I need you to be certain," Naismith continued.

"I can't be certain," Philip told him. "Everything happened at once. I was just trying to get him away from there."

"Because his hand was burning." Naismith leaned forward. "Is that true?"

"Yes. It was in the fire."

"It was in the fire."

"Yes. Or it had been. I don't know."

"Can it be possible that he burned his hand earlier?"

"Maybe moments. The wound was fresh, open, and still smoking."

"Could it be that Alamayou burned his hand because he was forcing someone to remain inside?"

"What?" Philip cried.

"If you can't be sure what you saw, then you can't be sure of him, can you? Can any of us?"

The prince held up a hand, silencing Philip before he said anything more. "I need to understand what's being said, Ambassador."

Naismith sat back in his chair. A slight smile played about his face. "The Abyssinian council advises of witnesses who saw figures leaving the fortress as it fell."

"Yes," Princess Louise said. "He just told you that."

"The figures were the emperor, Tewedros, and Alamayou. These witnesses say Alamayou brought his father to the cottage where his mother was. There was apparently a system in place between the two structures. The fortress at Meqdala and the cottage, owing to the fact that the queen and Alamayou lived there. Some sort of surveillance involving signals sent to each other by lamplight. This was how Tewedros kept watch over his wife. Perhaps Alamayou, as well. Or perhaps the son was just a younger brute like his father."

"I don't know anything about that," Philip said. "Neither do you."

"Speculation and innuendo," Princess Louise said. "A son brings his father to a place of presumed safety during a war. And? What of it? The country was falling around their ears. You paint him as a cunning deviant, not a terrified young man trying to save the lives of his mother and father."

"He brings his father to the cottage," Naismith continued, "where, shortly after they arrive, a fire breaks out. There was no fire before they arrived at that cottage. After, there is, and it kills the emperor and queen. But not him."

"This is outrageous." The princess's face reddened with anger. "Who are these witnesses? Abyssinians who hated the emperor and his bloodline? That would be the entire country, Ambassador."

"There's more to it."

"Philip?" Alamayou asked, alarmed. He wanted Philip to look at him, because everyone was saying words he knew—Falah, Amba Geshen, Tewedros—and the more they talked, the harder Philip stared at the table, as if it were on fire. The prince and princess watched him and he could hear his father's voice ringing out across the plateau, louder than the English rockets. *God did not make you like me.*

"I know." Philip put his hand next to Alamayou's on the table. "Just be quiet."

"Those Abyssinians I mentioned saw evidence of beatings," Naismith said. "Bruises, whip marks, especially on the body of the queen. When she was summoned to the fortress, they were plain on her."

"Tewedros was a monster," Philip said, knowing full well he was out of place. "Everyone knows that."

"*Fresh* marks, on the queen as she came from Amba Geshen, where Tewedros banished her and her son to."

"Are you suggesting Alamayou took a whip to his own mother?" The princess stood. "My God, what sort of man are you?

You come to our home and accuse him of the most heinous acts, and on what basis? He whipped his own mother? He murdered his parents in cold blood, burning them alive? How could he? How could he hold two people inside a burning cottage without burning alive himself? It defies common sense and you, an ambassador on behalf of our country, think it wise to hurl slanderous accusations before exploring—"

"His father was wounded in the bombardment, Your Highness. And his mother *couldn't* have escaped. The queen's body was found later, charred beyond humanity, curled up against what was left of the cottage wall. There was a manacle around her ankle."

"Oh my God." The princess turned away.

"Did you know this?" Naismith asked Philip.

"No! We left Amba Geshen with him. The fire was spreading and the whole cottage was collapsing. No one could get close."

"Did anyone try? Or were you, in particular, only interested in Alamayou? This young man?"

Philip's fists curled.

"You make him out to be a far greater monster than his father," Prince Leopold said.

"I'm not making him out to be anything, Your Highness. I'm merely doing what I was appointed and asked to do. My job. Which at the moment is trying to understand just who is living among the royal family. That applies to his companion, Philip Layard, just as much, if not more."

"I've had quite enough of this," the princess said. "He is a ward of the queen. *Your* queen."

"You'll forgive me, Your Highness, but there are men being honored tonight, men who saw war in the queen's name, and while many returned home, some didn't because of his father. The men here tonight know who he is. They know he gets to live here in luxury. To come here tonight and see Tewedros' son and heir isn't easy for them. They haven't met the queen. He has."

"It strikes me," the prince said, "the similarities between what you say and the recent editorial in the *Telegraph*."

"I had nothing to do with it, Your Highness. As I said. But I confess to sympathizing with it."

"You'd better hope your investigation supports your brazen attack on the reputation of a foreign prince and our reputation for exercising good judgment," Prince Leopold said coldly. "For now, we find ourselves at odds, clearly. That makes you unwelcome. Do what you must. Simon, see this man out."

After Naismith left, the prince sat down heavily. He daubed at his brow with a linen napkin while his sister watched from the entryway.

"He's gone," she said.

She wasn't coming back into the room. Alamayou studied her, the way her shoulders were turned away, her head tilted as if the sounds of the guests in the far ballrooms, the music and the clinking of crystal and porcelain, were suddenly and terribly important.

Her eyes, though. They kept darting to the corners of their room, to her brother and to them.

"Don't look at her," Prince Leopold said. "Look at me, both of you. Simon, see to it that no one comes near."

Simon bowed and went to clear the next room of any stray guests.

"I'm grateful for what you did," Prince Leopold said when they were alone. "Without you I might well be dead now in a pool of my own blood. I'm grateful for your discretion and your silence in the days since. But don't for a moment think we'll tolerate lies, or the sort of monstrosities we just heard about. Naismith wouldn't simply weave such stories out of thin air. Maybe they're the stuff of rumor and malicious retaliation against the son of Tewedros, as my sister would believe. Or maybe we truly don't know who we've invited into our home, before all of England. Call me cynical, but this needs to get sorted. Now. It's already moved past us, into newspapers. Into the bloody halls of Parliament, for God's sake."

"What do we do?" Princess Louise asked plaintively.

"Nothing tonight. But beginning tomorrow, we hear the truth or we send you away. Both of you. You and your secrets, Layard, don't matter. You're expendable and you have somewhere to go or you don't. But he's a different story entirely. He sits at the center of a war and a peace we're trying to forge. We took him in, and to cast him right back out again would be extraordinary. It would be fraught with problems."

"Cast him out where?" Philip asked.

"Abyssinia, in all likelihood."

"I'm stepping over bounds, I know, Your Highness, but I can't believe he's what that man says he is."

"Why can't you believe it, Layard?"

"Yes," Princess Louise said. "What do you know that could help him, or yourself?"

"I'm no one, Your Highnesses. I don't matter. He does. I don't know any more about what happened, but I've seen him for months now. He's a good man. At the fire, on the *Feroze*, all I've seen is good, and pain. Not hate and not cruelty."

"And so, for reasons I'm not clear about, Alamayou has one witness against Abyssinians, soldiers, God knows who else." The prince shook his head dismally. "Poor odds. You are who you are. Is there something of you, Layard, yet to come out?"

Philip fell silent.

"Bloody hell. Both of you leave us. We've much to discuss."

"Let us make no mistake, brother." The princess came to Leopold's side. "He dies if we send him back to Abyssinia. They hated his father. That much we can be sure of. He's his father's son."

"He may well be. More than we know."

§

SITTING AT THE WINDOW of the apartment, Alamayou painted the trees across the grounds. His mind was thousands of miles away, back on Amba Geshen.

Since the fire, he sometimes imagined that he never really left. That everything around him now was a dream. The reality was the fire, and it was a reality he'd never left. He'd never escaped it. He'd gone in, in the end, and died there. At this moment he was dying and this, everything he saw, was where his heart took him to be as far away as possible from the agony of burning. Any moment he'd wake up to see the last of himself melt and go to ash, like his parents.

It was with him every day. It clung to him as they'd crossed Abyssinia to Annesley Bay and the waiting English ships. It covered him the whole way across the sea, and each day since. He'd grown used to it. He told himself that it was a measure of his good fortune to have lived through so much. Some might call the sensation gratitude.

But he didn't like the sensation now. As he watched Philip get up and go to the door, the sensation felt like loss.

"Did you hear footsteps?" Philip asked. He opened the door and peered into the hall. Simon was at the far end, turning a corner.

An envelope lay at his feet.

Returning to the chair, Philip opened it and unfolded the stationary.

> *5 November 1868*
>
> *From the Desk of Her Majesty*
>
> *First, we have been successful in locating a translator for Alamayou despite what appear to be certain obstacles. We instruct you go to the docks at Wapping tomorrow, for the auction of Abyssinian items, which will take place. You will meet the translator there. This may seem a hardship to Alamayou but he shall*

not have another glimpse of his once-life. Perhaps he shall see something he desires. We expect you to set an example for Alamayou on grace above all. We ask that you explain this to him in your inimitable, silent way.

Discretion is key. Speak of this not at all.

And this, to answer Alamayou's question: each clove of cinnamon represents our children. The orange represents the late Prince Albert. We find it a more pleasant way to remember him than what life has left us.

"That's it, then."

Philip folded the letter and left it on the bed. "They've seen to it. One way or the other, you'll talk. I wish to God we could talk first. If I knew what the truth was, I could tell you you're safe, or not. It's us and it's them, Alamayou. The way it always is."

He went to the window to see what Alamayou was painting. The bare elms, a night sky. Just the world outside.

"No stars?" He dotted the air with a finger, then pointed to the sky.

Alamayou gestured to the painting, because Philip wanted stars but the English night's sky wasn't what he wanted to portray. He wanted clouds. "See?"

Philip looked closer. The black had pigments of gray in it. "Clouds. You and bloody clouds."

Alamayou waited for the slight smile to come to Philip, the one he'd come to know. It made him want to work harder, learn the words, and hear what snide, funny thing Philip said to bring that smile out.

Philip wasn't smiling. He looked afraid. "Alamayou, listen to me now."

Alamayou put down his paintbrush, more than ever feeling the sick anxiety that his dream was closing like a door, and in a moment the fire would be all over him.

"Ah, but I wish to hell you understood me," Philip said. "They're going to talk to you. Ask you about things. I told them you didn't do what that man Naismith says. You couldn't. I don't believe it, but I think he does. What the royals believe, I don't know. But I'm worried for you. I told them what I know." He paused. "I didn't tell them what I felt."

Alamayou's brow furrowed. He was trying to understand, to piece it all together, but Philip's hands weren't making anything. They just rose and fell with his words.

"I'm no help to you," Philip said tiredly. In the ballroom, he'd held back. From the expression on the princess's face, she knew he was keeping something secret. She might ask him. Certainly, she'd ask *about* him. So would Naismith. His tone made it sound as if he'd already done so.

They would ask and they'd find out about him. His life before Abyssinia. They'd learn where he'd met Marcus Baker White and why he was there at Newgate in the first place.

In the ballroom, before royalty, he'd objected to Naismith's allegations against Alamayou without thinking how stupid, how childish it must have seemed. He knew nothing of Alamayou before the fire. He wasn't anywhere near Alamayou until that moment. Why should anyone believe him? He was nothing but a kaffir, a colored sticking up for the only other colored in a castle that didn't want him. That's what they all saw. And when they learned more about him, well, it would be clear.

His very presence endangered Alamayou.

"Someone's coming who speaks your language. Then you tell them you didn't do those things. Even if you did. You get through this and take the life they're offering you, right? No more thinking of it. No standing at fires or rails, thinking of dying. You hear me? No mamot."

"No mamot, Philip."

"I don't matter. You do. Not because you're a bloody Abyssinian prince. I forget about that, isn't it funny? It's easy, being here with the lot of them, to forget who you are. They're always going to matter more than us."

At the fire, Philip thought, *there was the moment before I saw you, and the moment after. All they want is what happened, were you held or were you holding someone in it. Chains, whips, bloody hell, I only remember you, the fire around you, your good hand out to me.*

"Philip, eyes."

"I know. Be quiet, would you?"

He wiped his tears, then took Alamayou's brush and a fresh sheet of drawing paper. "This is going to look like shit."

When he finished, Philip turned the crude image so Alamayou could see. A square, bars, a tiny, smaller square, more bars. "Prison," Philip told Alamayou.

Alamayou studied it. It reminded him of the cages in his father's fortress, where he kept his prisoners chained to the stone walls.

"Ansara," he told Philip.

"Maybe you understand more than you let on. I want you to know me, Alamayou. Because I won't always be here. I won't always be with you."

He pointed to the image, then to himself. "I was there. Prison. Ansara."

It came back in a flood, the rusted bars, the trembling cot and the cold stone beneath his bare feet, the fetid smell in the prison corridors and the cell across from his where a drunken old white man passed the time talking loudly of medical procedures he'd done, legal and not. One day the old man introduced himself as Marcus Baker White and told the only man he could see that he was getting out at last thanks to a wartime need for doctors of all stripes. All he had to do was give up a year of his life to go to Abyssinia.

He said he needed an assistant. "Just so I know," he'd asked Philip through the bars, "you're no spring-heeled Jack, are you? What did you do?"

"Why ansara?" Alamayou asked him.

"Because there's something wrong with me that'll keep me alone all my life. It's ugly. It's not love. I wish I were different. And when they find out, I'll drag you down. So I'm talking to you about me, because I want you to remember me."

He spoke for a long time, about nothing Alamayou could understand, but he still listened as Philip spoke of ansara. Philip had been in a cage, he understood, or he was going to be, or they were both going to be. Because of the man they called Naismith, probably. The princess seemed good, and the prince seemed sick, and the queen, she'd known his heart for one brief moment, one night. She'd seen two princes, one lost and one who still could be saved. She'd understood him.

Whether Philip's words were good or bad, safe or dangerous, Alamayou just wanted to stay where he was and listen. After a while, when theirs was the only lit apartment in the ward and Philip had run out of words, Alamayou took his turn. He began to talk, and Philip listened to the Amharic words, about how beautiful Abyssinia was before the war. How Alamayou woke to thunder one day. It was on the morning he and his mother were sent away to Amba Geshen. The day was warm and the blue water of the sky was filled with clouds and birdsong, and the soldiers in his father's camp, some forty thousand strong, scuttled over the plains below the lip of the cliff to take up spears, muskets, and maces, tie their possessions to their pack animals, and swing themselves atop their mounts. Their grass huts already crackled with the fires they had set to their own homes. It was what his father demanded of his army when he called them to war. Burn where you come from. You're never coming back. The field should burn, the ashes should turn in the wind and settle to make the soil fertile, and a new crop would grow, and new boys would grow into men who would build new huts until the day they marched off to die, leaving fires in their wake.

He told Philip that his father expected him to be one of those men, but he was too unskilled and too terrified.

"Only my father and mother knew that about me," Alamayou told him. "Now you hear those words. They hated me for being what I am. I hope you don't. Because I feel like maybe you know it, too."

They sat together most of the night. First one, then the other, they took turns listening to the other's words, sifting the melodies of their voices and the shapes their hands made for meaning, searching for each other in a language they were beginning to understand.

Chapter Ten

6 November 1868

THE CASTLE COACH BROUGHT Alamayou and Philip to the docks at Wapping for the auction of Abyssinian treasures. By the time they arrived there was a line stretching past the shops, down to the street.

The water turned below them as they entered from the Thames at Shadwell. A high wall surrounded the auction site, thirty-five hectares in all and nearly four kilometers of it quay and jetty. Warehouses lined the docks. Stone plinths carved from top to bottom in ammonites and other castoffs from the sea decorated their walls.

The courts, alleys, and the low-lodging houses of London's waterside poor shone in the new light. Ramshackle storefronts studded the path from Shadwell. Every one of them catered to the sailors and the ships that took them away. Their windows brimmed with quadrants, brass sextons, chronometers, and compasses. Meat was tinned and men were in waistcoats, with canvas trousers and black dreadnaughts. They came from everywhere, down to the slowly rolling sea.

A forest of masts rose in the distance. Tall ship chimneys belched coal smoke clouds that drifted over the many-colored flags of nations. Men with painted faces mixed with fine English gentlemen and ladies, with flaxen-haired Germans and Negroes in a pungent haze of tobacco, spice, coffee, and sweat. Around the perimeter of the queues, benches filled with women and children preparing themselves for voyages away from their husbands and fathers, having been found out as immigrants unwelcome in London.

To live in the city, Alamayou thought, *is to risk being sent away.*

They made their apologies as they moved between bodies to the front of the queue, where they presented a letter of introduction from Her Majesty to the nearest uniformed man. Then they were escorted through the rest of the line, to the annoyance of the lords and ladies at two Negroes given priority.

Ahead of them was an enormous stage at the edge of the dock, filled from one end to the other with Abyssinian antiquities. A placard soared above it, some forty feet long and at least as high, showing maps of the landscapes, roads, bridges, and rails England had built from Annesley to Meqdala to find its way through the country.

Alamayou recognized a photograph of Sooroo Pass. He and his mother had trekked it on their weeklong journey from Debre Tabor to Meqdala. Over the course of three long days, they ran out of paths and had to cross the Sooroo over ridges of scrap rock so narrow that they were forced to walk in a single snaking line, with thousand-foot drops on either side of them.

As he walked beneath the image, Alamayou felt the whipping winds all over again, the thorny branches of unyielding trees, the stunned peels of pack animals tumbling over craggy cliffs and down through oceans of cloud to die on the hard earth, amid the pale flowering lichen and stone-splitting tendrils that grew from the cracks toward the sun.

At the sign's bottom was a broad and stunning panoramic photo from the war of the encamped invasion force at Zoola. A vast and terrible landscape of equipment, weaponry, tents, animals, and people sprinkled throughout like rye seeds.

The photograph presented a stilled moment of impending violence to him, and he turned from it to approach one of the displays of Abyssinian artifacts. Beneath his feet, the dock undulated in time with the sea as it wove into the piers and shuddered the anchored ships in the bay.

He found a crown lying under a sack of broken pottery. It was fashioned from gold and alloys of silver and copper. The cresting waves along its surface were vaguely Arabic and delicately pigmented with glass beads and gilded metals as red as Windsor's autumn leaves.

His fingers traced the carvings. It had been so long since he'd seen it. His father had removed it from his own head on the day he'd sent Alamayou and Tirroo away, and he'd never put it on again.

"Abat," he told Philip.

His mother's things were laid out on rugs. Shawls, silver bracelets, anklets, rings, amulet necklaces of amber and leather, filial pins, and Galla chains. Alamayou touched what was within his reach, the hem of a shamma, then climbed onto the stage with them.

Some men gathered to watch him. "A monkey must climb," one of them remarked to his fellows' amusement.

Alamayou retrieved some frayed pillows from behind piles of primitive weaponry that his father had collected, the spears and shields and old rifles that had served no good purpose in the war. He made a base of the pillows, then another on top of the first one.

"But what's it supposed to be?" one man asked.

"A throne," Philip said. "His father sat atop it at Meqdala."

"Here, now, I know who you are, the both of you."

Men came from everywhere, gathering round in anticipation of a fight.

"Let me tell you," the man said to Philip, "those pillows shouldn't fetch a cent for him. Not when there's men coming home with little to show but scars and a paltry wage. He doesn't deserve anything. Nor do you."

The other men cheered and applauded. Beneath them, the boards of the docks keened.

Philip's anger rose like a heat, but before he could do anything, Alamayou touched his arm. "No."

He was grateful for Alamayou's calm. Two Negroes standing in the shadow of the built world hadn't a chance.

"Don't let your orphan's days at Windsor convince you of value you don't possess," the man said. "You stumbled into a man's war. And this one's a spoil of that war. In a different time you'd both be auctioned off, along with the pillows and trinkets."

Behind them, above the veil of cheering men, the auction of Abyssinia commenced. It took on the air of a festival. The first item bid upon was a musket.

Philip guided Alamayou away from the voice of the auctioneer asking for barter over the carcass of Abyssinia. "I hope you don't understand any of this. The raised cards, the bidding for pieces of your life. Yet I fear you do, somehow."

Alamayou watched as a man standing on the stage reeled words off with the speed of gunshots, his father's musket raised triumphantly over his head. The audience surged forward, hands waving, calling out words of their own, while onstage the man pointed at them and wrote on a pad. Soon, man by man, their voices fell away to a few, then to one.

The man onstage handed that last remaining fellow the musket. Others made a circle around him as he cried out Tewedros' name.

"You there!" he yelled, parting the men walling him off from the rest of the dock. They all turned to regard Alamayou and Philip. "Pay close attention now, you kaffirs, you vermin. This is what's thought of you. Here, come now and see what you're worth."

He brought the musket down against the seaworn boards of the dock, again and again until the musket barrel bent and the wooden stock shattered with a dull crack that traveled the air, spoke over the sea and the men, and found Alamayou where he stood.

"Here, then," the man said as perspiration beaded his brow. He picked up handfuls of the battered musket and handed them up to the stage. "More of Abyssinia to auction off."

"Don't look," Philip said. "Come away before they set their sights on you."

Alamayou followed him away from the auction and farther out to the pier and the sea. He wondered if it would be far enough.

§

SEVERAL SHIPS WERE ANCHORED in the bay. Small rowers shuttled to the dock, bringing casks, kegs, gifts, and sailors while walking women and the wives left behind waited.

It was there that they met Jonathan, the man Her Majesty's letter instructed them to find. A mate from the ship *Keally Star*, he was older, with sun-worn skin and lines around his eyes like the tines of a fork.

"You the translator?" Philip asked him.

"Not me." Jonathan wandered over to the end of the pier. In the distance, the tall-masted ships gently listed from side to side. "Wait here," he told Philip. "I have what you came for."

Alamayou was confused. "Philip?"

"Give me a moment, Alamayou. Just to be sure of what's happening. Stay here, would you?"

There at the edge of London, Alamayou watched the sea and the small boats bobbing on it. Behind Philip and the sailor that he spoke to so warily was the auction, the photographs of war, and the city. The work of men.

The sea ebbed and made gentle music beneath him, and the men of the dock who'd broken his father's musket now that his father was safely dead, they didn't know what he'd come through. *The sea looked at me*, he thought. *The war, England, they look at me still. And I look back.*

He wasn't afraid, to his surprise. He knew the sort of hate that men held for other men. All his life he'd known it. A man looks at everyone, or he looks at no one.

He opened his arms wide to the sea that had brought him where he was. "No sad," he said, his English words turning Philip around to face him. The new words carried what needed to be said. Philip would understand. "No sad," he said. "This, enough."

Remnant echoes of the ships listing into the far docks rose, blending with the call and response of the auction. It all came to them like the water came.

Jonathan walked out to the edge of a stone jetty, holding out his hands for a rope tossed from a small rowboat pulling alongside him. He secured the line around a large boulder and took the hand of a girl climbing out of the boat onto land. The boat returned to its ship while the girl Jonathan helped ashore fell down. He picked her up with little care, and she walked unsteadily behind him as if she'd been at sea too long.

She was dark like them. Young, in her early womanhood, with hair as wiry as a cook's scrub brush despite efforts to tame it with oil and a band of cotton. She wore a simple English frock in a threadbare nosegay pattern. She was small, spindly, and afraid.

Jonathan brought her to the end of the pier, where Alamayou and Philip gawked at her. He stepped aside while they all regarded each other.

"Tell them," Jonathan ordered her. "You're here for the Abyssinian."

"Servant," she said. "*Wazadar.*"

"She speaks Amharic?" Philip asked.

"Isn't that why you've come?" Jonathan asked impatiently. "To get this one a translator?"

Alamayou touched his chest. "*Abisinya.*"

She shook her head. "*Katanga.*"

"She came from the Congo," Jonathan said. "But she's been traded many times over. She picks up words, this one. She'll be of some use. She has been."

The girl dropped her gaze.

"Traded? How did you come by her?"

"As I said. From the ship out there."

"You know what I'm asking you."

"You're calling me a blackbirder, then. Is that how you came to be here, Layard? From the net to the hold?"

"Look in my pockets and here's what you'll find. Papers saying I'm free and papers saying I'm on queen's business. Unless you've got papers of your own that trump me, you'll be answering to a Negro, like it or not. Now, speak to it. What's happening here?"

"What's happening here," Jonathan said, his face reddening, "is that I'm meeting the task put before me by people the likes of which I never see. All'a them, those prats, they don't show their faces, do they? They do their business through layer on layer of go-betweens. I can tell you who she is. She's a black who could see a lot worse if you send her back to that ship out there and you ought to know that better than most, free man or no. She was seized en route from Dahomey, bound for the Indies and the Americas after. The Royal Navy took her under the Act when the ship crossed into our waters. Enough for you?"

The girl spoke up. "Please. I am not go America. Servant. *Wazadar*. I do for you."

"Her kin?" Philip asked. "Who're you taking her away from?"

"Who can say with them?"

"No family," the girl said. "Me."

"What's it to be, then?" Jonthan asked.

"Does the queen know she was meant for slavery? That this is what's delivered in response to a royal request?"

Jonathan's eyes dropped. "I got what I could," he said. "I was told to be quiet about it and I was."

Philip knew they had two choices. He could turn the girl away, and that would send her back to the slave fields, the lash, rape, and death in childbirth if she could count among the fortunate, followed by burial in a potters' field. Or take her, and understand Alamayou's words for the first true time.

"She'll make a good belly warmer for you both." Jonathan left them.

"Seely." She pointed to herself.

"Philip. This is Alamayou. Tell him you're here to help him speak to us."

So much needed to be said, Philip thought. They had this girl
now, however legal it was, and through her they could learn
something of each other at last. The months aboard the *Feroze*
felt suddenly close. Aboard ship, it became so clear how simple
and yet miraculous words were when only their hands could speak
the crude, basic bits of life. *Eat, drink, sleep, shit,* and, beneath it
all, *we're alone. You're all there is.*

So many words to give each other, but one thing first.
In the center of their lives now, holding them still the way the
photographer's plates and chemicals held Alamayou still on glass,
was the fire.

"Anat, Alamayou," Philip said. "Abat."

"Mamot, Philip. Fire."

"Yes. Seely, listen carefully and tell him every word I say.
Tell him I'm so sorry, and that I know he had nothing to do with
their deaths."

She translated, and Alamayou stared at Philip in utter
confusion. He pointed to himself, eyes wide and disbelieving.

Good, Philip thought. *He understands he's being accused.*

"The man at the banquet. Naismith."

"Naismith," Alamayou said, his expression falling further.

"He's going to ask you questions about the fire and what
happened there. He said you were seen by someone, taking your
father to the cottage on Amba Geshen, before the fire started.
Before I found you there. He said your mother was whipped.
That she was chained to the wall."

Alamayou watched as Philip spoke. In Philip's kind face, he
saw the way the dream of his life now would end, hurtling him
back to the fire. The end would come in language.

"I'm a monster," he told Philip. "I don't belong anywhere in
the world. My father said so. My mother died saying it. But I didn't
kill them. I shamed them."

Seely translated his Amharic words to English, and with each
word Alamayou felt the new world he lived in unlock and open wide

to take him in. That was hard to be brave in the face of. He didn't know how to be brave, only how to look at Philip and not look away.

"I don't believe you did anything," Philip said. "I never will, no matter who saw it. Because I know you."

"It's good to hear your words."

"And yours, Alamayou."

They smiled at each other, while Seely caught up with her translation.

"Let me tell you where it is we live now," Philip said. "Who these people are and how important they are to your future."

Philip told Alamayou about Windsor, the royals, and of the growing calls for him to speak or leave.

"Are you royal?" Alamayou asked him.

"That's ridiculous. I'm nothing at all." He smiled slightly.

I missed that, Alamayou thought. "Are you African?"

"No."

"But you're black."

"I was born here in London."

"You know medicine."

"Hardly."

"I saw you. You're a doctor."

"There's so much to say, Alamayou. I'm at a loss."

They looked at each other and for a moment neither could think of anything to tell the other. It wasn't for lack of things, but rather because there was far too much.

Alamayou wanted to know one thing that held everything inside of it. But he couldn't bring himself to ask. *Can I hope? Is the worst over?*

Instead, he asked about the last thing that he'd painted.

"The fruit," he said.

"You're hungry?" Philip asked.

Seely translated. Alamayou shook his head and dotted the air with his fingers.

"Orange," Seely said.

"Oh-ranj," Alamayou said.

"Yes. With cinnamon cloves." Philip made the dotting. "Tell him each clove represents one of the queen's children."

"Clove?"

"The black marks."

Seely looked almost proud, hearing that. They were, after all, three black marks upon the Victoria docks.

"What will happen to us?" Alamayou asked.

Philip thought about how to answer him. With a translator there, he was no longer needed. He knew leaving was the best thing for the both of them.

"Just tell them you're innocent, and a new life awaits you."

He didn't say anything about himself, Alamayou thought. "Will they send you away? " he asked Philip. "Where will you go? Will you still be near?"

"Don't worry about me. You're the one they need to hear from."

"If they send me back to Abyssinia, I'll be killed. I'm hated like my father."

"But you're not like him."

"No."

"Tell them so. Tell them what they need to hear, that you did nothing wrong. Clear yourself and stay."

Seely drew back when Alamayou spoke. "He say he should go back and die."

"No. Listen to me, Alamayou. It's a terrible thing that's happened and it's useless to try and make sense of it. We can't do anything about our lives these past months, maybe ever again. Our pasts don't matter. What you were, a prince, it's gone. You're here now and you need to make the best of it. We both have to. Think of all you've lost, every damn day if you want. You can think of me as your friend if you like. I hope for that, but never say that you don't want to live even if you truly wish it. Even if you're alone. You mustn't.

"I've learned not to expect anything. I've no right to think I can live how I want or give voice to what I feel like other men. I'm not like other men and I've accepted my lot. That's further than I ever thought I'd be.

"I remember White working over one of your countrymen in the war. He opened that man even further than his wounds had. There was smoke and scraps of hot metal inside, and he took out all that he could find. But before he could sew the man up again, he died. White saw the look on my face. I'd seen the dead before, mind you, but all the blood, and the way that man fought just to hang onto what little life he had left. I'd never seen the knowing up close like that.

"White told me the body had a rule. If it hurts bad enough, leave. The heart gets wise and stops.

"I've thought about that a lot. There've been times for me, for what I know I am, and I wake up and I can't believe I'm this. I feel this. I want this. And I've wondered, is this the line? Over here, live with what I am. Over there, decide it hurts bad enough to leave. I'm not saying it right and that's on purpose, Alamayou. Whether you understand me or not, I won't admit it out loud, that I've thought about dying as something to choose, not something that happens. I'll never give in to it no matter how hard this life becomes because I'm a stubborn son of a bitch. No one takes what's mine. Maybe no one gives me anything, but I'll be Goddamned if anyone takes. The world's a furnace and I'll not tell you otherwise. But there are reasons to live if you just look. The best reason? Spite them all. Tell him."

In her patchwork Amharic, she did the best she could to make Alamayou know those words.

"Do you believe what you say to me, Philip?"

"I'm trying."

"Believe it for you, not me. You don't know me."

"You said you didn't kill them."

"I didn't."

"Then what is it?"

Alamayou walked away, following the edge of the waterline. Anchored ships keened to and fro in the bay. The sway of their masts put him in mind of the winds at sea, and how much more violent they were than on land.

By then the crowd at Wapping had dispersed. The stage was empty, the auction over. Wheelbarrows full of Abyssinian trinkets trundled by to waiting coaches.

"Gone," Alamayou said. "So much is gone, Philip."

"Yes. I know."

Men labored to dismantle all that had been built upon the dock. The great sign that greeted visitors with the Sooroo Pass, the Devil's Staircase, had already been cut into sections and tossed onto piles of refuse.

"There's something I need to know," Philip said. "I want to know why you were at the rail that night on the *Feroze*. Were you going to jump, Alamayou?"

"I don't know. I thought I saw things. Heard things. The fever… I don't know what I wanted to do. Live, die. Jump. Maybe I was thinking about it."

"And the fire—"

"I'd started to burn. I wanted to."

"Bloody Christ. Why?"

"Because there's no home for me anywhere."

"Why didn't you, then, if that's what you think? Why take my hand?"

Philip's words were heated and furious. They surprised even him. *Why come back with me? Why take me this far only to tell me you'd rather die?*

Alamayou didn't know what might happen when they got back to Windsor, or with Naismith, or with any of them. Right now, he only knew that he could finally hear Philip's words, hear them inside of himself, and make them a part of him. He didn't have to imagine anymore.

The sound of them made him smile.

The world wasn't promised to any of them. It could slip away or be taken by force at any time. He'd learned that. *All I have*, he thought, *is what I felt, and I want to give it to Philip. I think he needs it as much as I do.*

"Because at the rail," he said to Philip, "I saw you and I thought, what if I'm wrong?"

§

ON THE WALK TO the carriage that would take them back to Windsor, Alamayou spoke. "I want to know all that's happened since Abyssinia. What happened in the war and at sea. What people say. Louise. Leopold. The queen. All of it."

"You were *there* for all of it," Philip told him. "You don't need to hear such things again. To look so closely at it doesn't do a bit of good."

"I want to hear you say the words. What it means, the things I didn't see or didn't know. The things you think about."

"For what? It's gone. Remember, Alamayou? Remember the room at night, your painting, the queen? You said it yourself. Gone."

"One thing, remember? You told me on the ship to take one thing."

"Yes."

Alamayou held out what he'd stolen from the auction stage while building the pillow throne. Smashed beyond recognition, his father's pistol resembled a twisted metal sculpture.

"Some things remain," Alamayou said. "Not everything's gone."

Seely translated while Alamayou spoke. "My father had slaves. The first thing he said to them was, 'You have no family. No home. No past. You have no name. No life before me. Only this, the chain.' There was one slave, the same age as us. My father killed him twice. He took away his name, all he had, and then he strangled him. After the slave was dead, my father told me, 'This is how you kill a man. Take away who he is and make it yours.' But I knew the slave. I knew his name. I remember him. We need to give each other everything we can. Our names and our lives. Then we need to keep it all safe. We need to remember."

From the direction of the sea, a whistle came, followed by a groan so loud and elemental that Philip would have believed it if one of the seamen told him it was the voice of the water itself, or a god stirring to life just offshore.

The *Keally Star* pulled up its anchor, sending another groan trembling through its hull.

"I don't even know where to start," Philip said. "But I'll try to tell you everything I know."

Waves washing in from the wake of the *Keally Star* lapped at the shoreline. Seely's once-home set sail and soon dwindled to a shadow at the horizon.

For hours they remained at Wapping, speaking the past back into existence. Three dark figures, considering what the sea could do.

Chapter Eleven

THEY ENJOYED A QUIET dinner together in the apartment. Seely wore a new frock, blue and heavy. She glanced around her surroundings while anxiously pushing her food around her plate.

Alamayou and Philip were both spent from telling each other all that had happened, all they'd thought and felt, beginning aboard the *Feroze* and continuing through the very moment they stood on the docks at Wapping.

Philip left any further talk of the fire alone. It had been enough to see how stricken Alamayou was that anyone could think he'd held his own parents in the flames. He didn't want to press the issue, though he felt he had enough to back up his insistence that Alamayou had done nothing wrong. He could tell the royals now, I was right and Naismith was wrong. "When I say I believe him because I've been with him and I know him, you ought to listen."

The idea that Alamayou was a killer seemed far-fetched from the start, but Alamayou had confirmed his suspicions about the fire and the rail. Whatever darkness Alamayou communed with, it wasn't the murderous kind Naismith suspected, but a darker impulse to look out at the world and see no reason to live in it.

He hoped Alamayou was past that feeling now that he had a place in the world. Now that he had a friend.

He put down his fork. "I'm too bloody knackered to speak, and what strength I've got left I'll spend on this good food. But of everything we gave each other today, hold onto this if nothing else. Be who they want you to be, and then live the life they give you."

"I will," Alamayou said. He was too exhausted to say any more, as well.

Over the remains of their meal—rabbit stew brimming with chunks of dark meat, carrots, and turnips—Seely described her own life. "I was a child, Egbado village. My people, attacked by Dahomian warriors. Homes on fire."

Alamayou looked up from his meal at a word he understood. Fire.

"Drums," Seely said. "Screams. Men fight but no, they fell to sword. Food, our flock, all gone. We walk before their spears. All night we walk. Women, babies. Some die. We leave, to Whydah. They sell us to Abomey, to Gezo. I too so many, so many years. Last time, sell to white man. Blackbird."

"Blackbirder," Philip told her. "A slave runner."

"He has ship. *HMS Seely.* He name me for ship. I cook and clean. Sew. I lay with him. Gave daughter but he throw her to sea."

She grew quiet.

"How old are you?" Alamayou asked her, and in Amharic she told him. Then she said it in English for Philip.

"Fifteen year."

"But you're free now," Philip assured her.

There was such confusion on her face. "Free," she said. "Go where? Be what? Free mean no place to stay. No food."

"True enough," Philip said.

Their dinner was done, the hall outside the apartment quiet. For a while, they were content to listen as the castle settled in on itself for the night. After an hour, a maid brought dresses that had been gathered for donation to missionaries, and Seely selected a few that reasonably fit her small frame. Simon found quarters for her among the service and provided a cot, a desk and chair, and an oil lamp which she was too afraid to operate.

She didn't want to be alone, so they brought her back to the apartment.

"Who will they make me lay with?" she asked.

"No one," Philip told her. "It's not like that."

"Always like that."

"All I've ever known," Alamayou said as she translated, "is people forced to be with others. No one chooses who they feel must be theirs. You were told who to be with. It was the same with my mother. They tried to force me once, and I said no. One of the only times I ever defied my father."

"Why did you say no?" Philip asked.

"I didn't love her." He thought of how to say it right, but realized it didn't matter. Philip understood.

"I couldn't love her," he finally added. "What about you?"

"Love is a thankless thing in my life," Philip said. "Better not to care."

"There are no words for some things," Alamayou said. "Or they're terrible words. Words that can kill us."

Us, Philip thought.

"But for some things, there aren't words to hold them. We try. That's all we can do. Try to find," and he smiled, "the language."

"A poet and a painter. I knew there was a reason I saved you."

They laughed together, an easy thing that had never come to them before. It was just a little simpler to imagine a path ahead.

Maybe I could stay awhile, Philip thought. *See where matters lead. Like the wise prince said, what if I'm wrong?*

Their laughter was interrupted by loud knocking at the apartment door. When Seely opened it, she found Simon there with a grim expression.

"She's set a month from today as the time for him to speak," he said. "I suggest you each cease your grinning and prepare."

§

SEELY AND PHILIP WORKED with Alamayou for hours upon hours, every day. Alamayou acquired words, then phrases, and by the seventh of December, 1868, Alamayou was able to find the meaning in far more sentences than any of them expected. He still relied on Seely, and when at a loss occasionally lapsed into their old language of hands, but he could carry on a rudimentary conversation with the service and follow Philip's instructions.

As a test, Philip told him that the day had come to speak to the queen, and that he ought to wear the suit hanging in their armoire. Alamayou rose from his chair and dressed.

"Well done," Philip said proudly.

Just past ten, they entered the Private Audience Room, a high-ceilinged chamber in the South Wing. The light dispensed shadows across the modest throne occupied by Queen Victoria. She wore the widow's weep. Blacks, coals, silk-and-bomberdine bodice, a matching grosgrain ample skirt. The crown was her only embellishment.

Princess Louise and Prince Leopold sat on either side of her. A table had been placed in the middle of the room, separating the royals from the summoned. A long black cloth covered it, but Alamayou noticed the outlines of something beneath.

"Thank you," Alamayou began, "for—"

The queen cut him off abruptly. "Show him."

Reluctantly, Princess Louise removed the cloth, revealing a coiled whip and a length of chain.

Alamayou could feel them staring at him, trying to piece him together from what they knew, or thought they knew. *A man looks at everyone.*

He returned the queen's fixed gaze.

"This is what's said of you." The queen held up a newspaper. "In the *Telegraph*, and in the halls of Parliament. What have we done to bring this upon our monarchy? We took in a young man orphaned by war, not a monster."

She shook the paper furiously. "Had we known, we would have left you to your fate."

"Do we blame Alamayou for his father's actions?" the princess asked. "He wasn't the emperor."

"We are *aware*," the queen responded coldly.

The princess fell quiet.

"We don't hold you responsible for your father's actions, Alamayou. Only yours. Girl, does he understand us?"

Seely translated.

"Yes."

"Naismith has recommended that you be brought before Parliament to answer for war crimes," the queen continued. "He says there are reasonable grounds. It is clear he does not trust you, but we can engage a solicitor and argue you as an orphan of war. We have protected others, and successfully so. We did not cast them out like so many unwanted toys, no matter what you may have been told of us. But the war and your father's heinous acts complicate things. We are not sorry to have offered you shelter. We want to believe you are blameless for all that happened in Abyssinia. But you must clear yourself with us, and then with them. Or else you are lost. Are you prepared to do this?"

"Yes," Alamayou said. "But you must promise to keep Philip safe, no matter what happens to me."

The queen's face grew red as Seely spoke Alamayou's words. "Are you demanding from us? You are here by our charity, not by right. You've no basis to bargain with me like a fruit seller. Philip serves no purpose, and worse, do we understand he was in jail?"

The prince appeared stricken. A silence like death fell over the Private Audience Room.

Princess Louise reached for her mother's hand. The queen pulled it away. "How dare you?"

"Then I can't speak of what you want," Alamayou told her. "Send me back."

She sat as if made of granite. "Understand how easy it would be for us to turn our back on you. Clearly, this is what we are renowned for. Had we no heart, you both would be dead in the rubble of your country or the workhouses of ours. We are many things. Colonizer, cold, distant. A mother to regret. But we are not the murderer of your father, and we are not the murderer of your mother. Are you?"

Alamayou remained silent.

"Your insolence will not be tolerated." She summoned her secretary. "Have their things packed," she said. "They depart Windsor in the morning. Make the necessary arrangements and inform Parliament that no hearing will be necessary."

A pall of quiet descended after she left. The hall filled with her absence.

"What have you done?" Prince Leopold gasped as he stood from his chair.

"I fear you have put yourself too far away to reach, Alamayou," Princess Louise said.

Seely began her dutiful translation. Alamayou turned and left.

"He understands well enough," the princess said.

§

IN AN HOUR, SERVANTS under Simon's careful supervision descended on the apartment. A valet placed two simple cases atop the bed and stuffed Alamayou's meager belongings inside. When he finished, he set to Philip's, then left them alone.

"Are you insane?" Philip snapped as Alamayou sat sullenly in a chair at the window. "I don't matter. Why can't you get that through your damn head? Why would you do that? I'm nothing! A kaffir. What is my life, Alamayou? What's it ever been? Do you even know? I'm lower than a servant, and let me tell you of that life. I was born, I'll eat my way through a handful of days, and I'll die. And that's all. I'm not needed, you heard her say it. For you to risk your life for the likes of me, bloody Christ, I don't belong here in the first place."

Alamayou removed Philip's clothes from the case. "You don't leave. Only me. Write for me. Write to her."

"Don't do this," Philip told him. "Not for me. It's not worth it, Alamayou. This isn't my home. There is no home."

"Write."

Seely spoke Alamayou's words while Philip quilled them to paper, then they walked to the closed door of the Blue Room.

Alamayou rapped softly. "Please," he said to the wood, before slipping the letter under the door.

7 December 1868

Forgive my words. They come too fast and in fear. There are things I can say and things I can't.

I'm scared to go back and die, but I will if I have to. Philip must be safe. He saved me. He brought me all the way here to a new life. He's the only one who cares for me.

Say whatever you want of me. Monster. Murderer. But never say Philip serves no purpose. That he doesn't belong. He belongs where he can live, and I can know he lives.

Please see to him and I'll do whatever you ask of me. I was a stranger before him. He took me in.

Alamayou

They went to the great hall and sat beneath Alamayou's portrait of two princes. The light of the hearth cast shadows that found its ornate chestnut frame.

The hours left them. In time, Alamayou and Seely fell asleep and Philip watched over them. He didn't know what he'd expected to see, when he'd tried to imagine the moment he and Alamayou successfully bridged that damned ocean of language and were finally able to understand each other. Not this day, certainly. A runaway slave, talk of love, and defying the bloody queen of England.

Least of all, that Alamayou's first words before the queen were spoken to protect not himself, but me.

§

THE QUEEN CAME TO the hall deep in the night with Princess Louise in tow. She wore a simple dress of gray that flowed across the floor and small leather shoes that made a whisking sound with each step. On her chest was an unusual talisman of a brooch, Tartan ribbon, thistle fashioned from gold, and a pair of strung animal teeth.

The princess guided her mother to a simple chair beneath the portraits.

"Whatever happens," the queen said, "you will stand before us. You will tell us the truth. And we will see to it, no matter the outcome, that Philip Layard is safe and provided for. Is that sufficient for you and your sense of grandeur?"

"Yes. Thank you, Your Majesty."

"He's that important to you?"

"Yes."

"More important than your own safety."

"Yes."

The queen stared at him, though her eyes seemed to go straight through him, through the walls and on into the world, to a place no one else could see.

"Then it's time, Alamayou."

Alamayou turned to see Philip. He wanted to be sure of him now.

"I'm here." Philip held out his hands, one against the other.

"Not alone." Alamayou smiled.

"Not alone."

Alamayou closed his eyes. *Abat, anat, I've held you for too long. I can't carry you anymore.*

"Know this," he said as Seely began her translation. "God did not make me like them."

Chapter Twelve

7 December 1868

"MY FATHER LOVED YOU, Your Majesty. He called you his Christian sister."

The royals listened intently as Seely kept up with him. The queen's secretary wrote it all down.

"But my father wanted guns," Alamayou continued, "and cannons, and men who knew how to build them. He was always at war with the Moslem hordes in Egypt and the Red Sea lands. You said no to him. You sent men to tell him, no. He killed the man who spoke and made the rest prisoners. He let one Englishman sail away to tell you, so you'd know how strong he was. How he wasn't afraid of you. He hated you then.

"After that, there were a few years of quiet. No one came from England. I didn't trust the silence from the English. No one did. In those years my father was mad with rage, always. You ignored him.

"I was fourteen. I knew my father's anger very well. I knew what it could make him do."

"We embarrassed him?" Prince Leopold sat back in frustration. "He steals away two years from innocent diplomats sent on our behalf in friendship, and we take back his son. Mother, I'm sympathetic, but we can't go before Parliament with this."

"We will hear it all," the queen told her son. "Do not interrupt further. Alamayou, continue."

"When he knew your army landed in Annesley Bay," Alamayou went on, "he and his soldiers rode to his fortress at Meqdala. He told my mother and me that we weren't allowed to be there with him. Instead, he sent us to a small cottage on the next mountain, Amba Geshen.

"He banished us. My mother, because she hated him. You have to understand why. I didn't know the reason until we were on Amba Geshen. I'd always assumed it was because he was what he was. A cruel man. A soldier. But the women of men like my father's generals wanted those kinds of men, who took power and took them. Or they were given in marriage by their tribes for peace with my father, and they learned to love their husbands, or at least to suffer quietly.

"My mother did neither.

"One night on Amba Geshen, she told me that my father took her from her family, across mountains to his capital at Debre Tabor. At night he tied her to a bed and beat her until she stopped moving. That's how they made me. She was thirteen. I was her son and I didn't even know how young she was."

He glanced at Seely. Her eyes were closed as she spoke his words into the royals' language. He wondered how it felt for her to translate his mother's life, and whether she heard her own slave story in the theft of his mother's girlhood.

"He sent me away to Amba Geshen because I failed him as a son and a prince. I wasn't a soldier. I wasn't brave and could never kill a man. When he looked at me, he saw the end of his bloodline. At least, before the war. After the attack began, he came to know me, and then he saw something worse.

"It took us a week of walking to reach Meqdala and Amba Geshen from Debre Tabor. My mother, me, a guard, and a slave. I could see the fortress gate from far off. The fortress overlooked the Jidda Gorge and the plains beneath the Delanta Plateau. The fortress itself was cut from the mountain. A cavern at its bottom was stitched with iron and tied in a gate bearing the crest my father had forged—the David star and the Christian cross. My father created the crest himself. It came out of a dream he had of all the tribes of Abyssinia, sewn together by his own hands.

"It awed me that my father could build something like that. It made my father the man he was. To break and build from stone, you have to know stone, be stone. He told me, 'Stone holds no life but the dead, hard past.' That's what he was. Dead and hard, so his country could be built on top of him and not collapse.

"The guard brought instructions from my father. When we got to Amba Geshen and the cottage where we would live, we found a long pole lying alongside it. The guard erected it near the cottage door after attaching an old oil lantern to its top. When he lit it, the lamp light brushed the tops of the mahogany trees and danced across the cottage roof.

"'Why do we need this?' my mother asked him. 'It's not inside the hut and its light is too dim. It's too high to be useful.' But in a moment we saw a flame as small as a candle ignite in Meqdala, atop the next peak. As it flickered, I saw the shape of a window. Someone there lit it in response to the lamp burning above us. When he saw it, our guard lowered his lamp and put it out.

"The guard gave my mother a note, then brought a great chain into the cottage. He fit a manacle to her ankle and hammered it until it would fit. He ignored her when she ordered him to stop. He was doing what my father told him to do. He didn't have to listen to the queen anymore.

"My mother read the note, then handed it to me. It was in my father's writing.

"'Each day Alamayou will demand of you, "obey your husband, serve him, die for him." If you say you will do these things, if you say you love me, you can sleep like a woman. If not, Alamayou will beat you and put you in chains. This is a taste of it. Decide if it suits you. The guard shall light the torch to say that this is so. You are my wife now, and Alamayou is my son, or you're nothing.'

"The guard drove a stake into the floor of the cottage. When he tugged at it, it stayed in place. He fastened the chain to it. It would attach to the manacle that would go around my mother's leg each night. Next to it he lay a thick length of knotted horsehair. A whip.

"My mother went and sat at the cliff with her legs dangling over the edge. So close to the drop. I went to her and told her I wouldn't do it.

"From below, white clouds rose as if they were boiling over a fire. They were filled with gray, and with light. They swelled higher, and soon they covered the whole gorge between Amba Geshen and Meqdala, where my father and his army prepared for war with you.

"Lightning flashed in the clouds and the air smelled like burning metal. The skin on my arms tingled. A drop of rain hit me from below, then another.

"'The winds,' my mother said. 'They drive the storms like horses. My tribe is Lasa, and they told me stories as a girl. To see it now is a wonder. A dream. My people call it the "white dream."'

"She said, 'Whatever happens to us, think of me here where I will always be happy. The clouds take everything away. One day, you will call and I will not answer. I will be gone. Look for me in the clouds.'

"She went inside the cottage, sat on the floor, and put the chain on. She held up the whip for me to take. I told her no. She said she'd never obey him and she'd never love him. I went to the guard and told him I wouldn't, not ever. I wouldn't hurt her.

"There was a slave with us. His name was Rassam. He was gentle. Over our time on Amba Geshen, he taught me to draw and paint. I remember the first thing I made, the clouds. I told Rassam about them, the upward rain, the lightning in the gorge below me. I told him it felt like standing on top of a storm. He was in awe. He was so grateful that I'd told him. No one had ever been like that with me, until one was, here. It matters more than I can tell you.

"He showed me how to use a stick of pitch and a torn parchment. While I worked on my first drawing of the clouds, he made a drawing of me. My face in profile and my gaze out to the land. 'Facing the present and the future,' he said. Like a prince would. I looked so sure.

"I didn't want to hurt anyone. He knew that. He didn't care that I wasn't like other Abyssinian men.

"It wasn't love. Just...not hate. Just one person who didn't regret me. Even a slave."

He looked at Philip as the tears came, and he saw Philip's kindness, but something more, that made him want to burst with relief. Pride.

"You understand what it is that you admit to," Prince Leopold asked him.

"Yes."

"Mother—"

"We are listening," the queen said. "Only that."

"My father found out that the slave—that Rassam cared for me, and that I didn't kill him for it. He found out that I wouldn't whip my mother. I thought it was the guard who told my father everything. But I was wrong."

He smiled, a sad and crooked thing. "Even in chains, my mother hated the thought of me. More than the thought of my father. My father found out about Rassam from my mother. She'd sent the guard to him, to say that I was shaming both of them. On your Easter, just before the war started, my father brought us back to Meqdala. He sent my mother into the fortress and took me to a peak at the edge of the Beshilo Gorge, away from Meqdala, away from everyone. I remember looking behind me at the far point of Delanta sloping down into the valley. Wurq-Waha, like a scar across the land. I saw Meqdala's peaks hidden by these low, watery clouds. The light was high and the air was clean. Everything was so beautiful, so still and perfect.

"I thought he was going to kill me.

"My father stood on the wide ledge of Selassie peak, holding a telescope to his eye. This was his lookout point. It's where he waited for your army to come. 'There,' he said. He handed me the telescope and showed me the end to look through, and where to direct its eye. 'There you see the English, come to kill me.'

"What I saw stunned me. I'd never looked through a telescope before. It made a circle that drained the skies of color, like storm times. It brought the Beshilo Gorge to me. I saw your army everywhere.

"To come so far across my entire country and find us, you did things I didn't know could be done. You had to cut roads and rails into the ground. There were more men than I'd ever seen in one place. You leveled the whole world to kill us.

"I put the lens down. My father asked me what I saw. A sea of red. That's the only thing I could compare it to. He said he wasn't afraid, just tired. 'I'm weary of looking out across my country,' he said, 'waiting for God's hand to make itself known. I haven't seen it in anything. Why is that? I brought this country under God. But I stand here now, and I feel nothing. No joy. All these years, I've waited for nothing. I prayed for a true wife, a true son. Only now do I see God's hand, and look at what it is. A red vein of ten thousand murderers. No one will ever know me. Only a story with my name in it.'

"I saw pain in him. It was shocking. As if he couldn't hold up anymore and his heart was breaking—which was at least proof that it existed at all.

"Below us, soldiers and slaves massed on either side of Meqdala's gate. Even across the distance, my mother's brightly dyed cloth was vivid. My father watched her. 'Does she obey me?' he asked. 'Does she love me?'

"I told him no.

"He brought me back to Meqdala. His army surged inside our gate, stirred by his cries. The sun glinted from their knives and bayonets and rifles. They cried *salafa* in response to him.

Make ready for war. He walked among them to the parapets, where he could see the English forces. The red lines were everywhere, across the plateau in ranks, a growing camp on the far side of the field. My father called for prisoners to be brought out from their cells. The English and the Abyssinians who collaborated. The guards pushed them to the edge of the parapet, hundreds of feet above the gorge. My father took one of the Abyssinians by the neck and pushed him over the edge of the cliff. The rest of the captives wept quietly as they watched him fall. It looked like he was flying. He pinwheeled, colliding with the rock face, then slipped into pure cloud.

"'The rest,' my father said. They all went over eventually. Soon thirty men were gone.

"I watched. I didn't want my father to see me cry.

"My father came for me. He told me to whip my mother there in front of everyone. I was terrified, but I still said no. He looked at my mother and I swear, they both were ashamed of me then.

"My father brought Rassam out in chains, then ordered me to whip my mother."

"Alamayou," the queen interrupted him, "do you need a moment to compose yourself?"

Alamayou felt the tightness in his chest. He'd hoped speaking would loosen it a little, just enough to breathe, but it was only squeezing his heart harder.

"I'm almost done, Your Majesty." He managed a nod.

Almost to the fire, he thought.

He blew out some air as the room began a slow spin around him. *It can't harm you*, he told himself.

"My father put his hands around Rassam. Around his throat until his fingers closed. Rassam's eyes rolled as he went to his knees. I saw the veins in them fill. The whites washed over red, like your army. Rassam tried to pull my father's hands apart, but he was weak and my father was stronger than any man I ever saw. When Rassam's hands fell away, I saw it in his face. He knew he was dying.

'Don't,' he mouthed to me. Maybe he thought I would try to help him, because I cared about him. He didn't understand how afraid I was. I think the last thing he saw was me, not coming to save him. Not doing anything.

"Then he smiled. It was kind, despite everything. Despite his life, and now this.

"It took a long time. When I saw it leave, that old light that left his exploded eyes, I knew it was done.

"'Whip her or I'll kill you,' my father told me.

"So I did."

He took the whip from the royals' table as they stared. "It was bigger than this. Heavier."

Philip watched Alamayou speak his life—his true life—back into existence. He watched in awe, that so much courage could exist in one man. He didn't know what would happen to Alamayou now that he'd admitted to at least one of the accusations leveled against him—the whipping—and he hadn't even gotten to the fire. Surely the royals understood what they were hearing. Yes, he'd used the whip on his mother, but not by choice. Not by some cruel, sick flaw in his blood, like his father. Alamayou was guilty of hurting her the way a soldier was guilty of murder. He had no choice, no free will. He was compelled to act by the most primitive reason there was. Do what you're told, or die.

And there was the other admission, the one Philip couldn't believe he'd heard. Alamayou had delivered it with his head high, with no shame. With no fear. He'd stood before the most powerful woman in the world and let her see his heart.

You didn't have to, Philip thought. You didn't have to go that far. It was language you didn't need to use, and there are laws. They'll send you back and you'll die there, and for what? Why did you have to let them see what love looks like inside of you?

Because it wasn't for them, he heard Alamayou's voice say in his ear, in his thoughts. *It was for you. Remember, Philip? Not alone.*

I do remember. I'll never forget.

Alamayou set the whip back down on the table. His body wavered and he asked for water. The queen ordered a service of tea and plates of cold meats, and when it came they ate in silence. Philip chewed on a piece of pheasant that tasted like dust in his mouth. He watched Alamayou at the center of the room, picking absently at a cluster of grapes. Head down, at once oblivious and keenly aware that the chamber was arranged in a circle around him. There was no place for him to disappear to, nowhere he couldn't be seen.

"When I'd finished with my mother," he said, "my father sent her back to Amba Geshen. He made her walk so everyone could see the marks."

"Alamayou, you're exhausted." The queen set her plate down. "We can see how difficult this is to speak of. Tomorrow we can continue."

"No. Now. I need to say it all while I have the strength."

"We don't doubt that you have the strength," she told him.

At that moment, Philip would have lifted Windsor off the ground and carried it to Balmoral, had the queen asked him to.

"I went to him. He had a church, inside the gate of the fortress. It was the only stone structure there. He was inside, praying.

"I had his gun. I meant to kill him. That was the first time. There would be another. I didn't. I couldn't. He beat me until I passed out.

"When I woke I saw that my father had chained me to the stone of the fortress, at one of the parapets. He made me look from there to the plateau and the Falah. Your army was everywhere. The war would start soon. His aide, the *afe-negus*, took down his last wishes. That his body should lie atop the land for all his people to see, beneath carved, outstretched wings of angels. That he shouldn't be buried, because he'd return to earth in time, atop a throne of many-colored pillows.

"He called down to his soldiers from the parapet. 'This is the hand of God now upon us. If you love me as you love God, go to the English and cut their throats.'

"He ordered the gate to be opened and four hundred of his soldiers passed through. His first wave, to see what your soldiers would do. Someone inside Meqdala screamed. Someone watching their husband or son, maybe. I heard another voice, a song coming from inside the stone of Meqdala. Maybe the singer was comforting the screaming one.

"After a few minutes I couldn't see our soldiers. It was raining hard. My father forced the telescope to my eye. I looked through its circle, at Abyssinian men exploding. It was quiet because they were so far. They ran in every direction. They looked like they were screaming, then their chests burst. Their heads bloomed. Only then did I hear the sounds of bullets. By then the soldiers already lay on the ground.

"It was over so quickly. No one on the plain moved, nothing moved but the falling rain.

"I was at that parapet all night, in the rain. My father and his generals planned. I felt your army moving on the plateau. It was a rumbling beneath me, powerful enough to make the world turn.

"In the dark I found the spike and tugged at it, to see. I thought, if I'm strong, if I keep at it without caring about its noise and if I was brave enough to fight my father off, then it was possible. Out it would come and I'd run, the spike and chain dragging behind me. I'd run down the stone steps through the thousands of slaves, prisoners, and soldiers at the gate. I'd run out onto the field where no bullets would find me and the clouds would cover my escape. The white dream would take the light away. I'd never be seen. Soon I wouldn't be alone; others would be with me. They'd see me. They'd know me. We'd all run with wildness in our eyes, and we'd shed our chains and all that would be left of us was the blood that made us who we truly were.

We'd forget that there once was a place we thought was home. Home was ahead, and we'd run until we found it.

"Then my father came to me and said, 'I mourn the death of my son.' He unchained me, put me into the hands of soldiers, and gave me a shield and a gun. 'I'll open these gates again,' he said, 'and let the war swallow you.' Then he left me among a thousand Abyssinians waiting to fight.

"This is what war is. I saw men waiting, crying, saying prayers. They dug holes in the ground inside the gate and buried pieces of their lives. Rings, shreds of their wives' shammas. Some wrapped knotted blue cords around their wrists. This marked the wearer as a Christian. Whether they believed in the Christian words or not didn't matter. They put their hope of living through the next few minutes into frayed colored threads so the English would see blue against their black skin and not shoot them down.

"In the last moments before the gate opened wide, I saw men hold the hands of other men.

"I looked up at the man next to me, a stranger, to ask why. Why did we have to do this? He dropped his shield and seized my hand. His hand was terrible, wet, and hot like my father's had been after he'd strangled Rassam. 'Be free, Alamayou,' he said. Then the gate swung wide and we ran. It felt like flying, like the white dream.

"Above me, the high whistles of bullets. One whistle came low and that man I ran next to fell. I screamed but couldn't hear my own voice. It disappeared into the war.

"Men flew everywhere. They ran and fell, opened and bled.

"Ahead I saw red flashes from the peaks. Your cannons, all the men dying between you and me, the gap closing fast and not enough men in front of me to hide anymore.

"I bolted to my right and never looked back. I reached the treeline and plunged through swiping branches. Behind one of those trees, I came across a dying Abyssinian tribesman.

When he saw me, he smiled and held out his blue cord for me to take. He wanted me to have it.

"I stayed with him. He held my hand while dying. In that spot there was a quiet that I didn't understand, and I still don't.

"I watched his eyes empty, and I thought of Rassam, and whipping my mother. I still had my gun. I stood up and began to walk back to the fortress. I was going to kill my father, for all of it.

"Then your cannons fired at Meqdala. The roar lifted the whole plateau. I saw them streak across the sky. There were so many, and when they hit the fortress walls, everything blew into pieces. Everything collapsed. When it finally stopped, there was nothing left.

"I made it to what was left of Meqdala and looked for him. It took a long time but I found him. He was still alive. His leg had been crushed. He lay there, helpless, staring at me. I put the gun to his filthy head. I was so afraid.

"He smiled at me and asked me a question. 'What is it like to be loved by anyone?' He began to cry.

"I couldn't. I helped him up. Before your soldiers had crossed the plateau, I helped him away from Meqdala, to the cottage on Amba Geshen. We came around a curve in the path and I saw the flames just starting. The pole lay on the ground. The lamp was on top of the roof, where my mother tipped it to start the fire. She was already inside, sitting on the floor. When I got there with my father, she was just fastening the chain.

"I told her, 'We can give ourselves up to the English. We can beg for mercy. Where's the key, anat?' She said 'I loved you' to me. As if she only loved me long ago."

He could feel sobs breaking open in his chest but he swallowed them back. Not now. Not ever again.

"She looked at my father as the fire began to fall from the roof, all around her. 'We make poison together. Look what we've done. Look at all the death. Look at our son. There's no home for him anywhere. There's no home for any of us.'

"She held out her hand for my father. The only time in my life I saw her want him near her was in fire.

"My father was barely alive. But he went in. He fell to the floor next to her. He lay on top of fire to be with her. She took him in her arms and told him they belonged like this.

"They were both on fire.

"Then she held out her hand for me to come. 'Show us that God made you a man, Alamayou. Not a *gbra sadom*, a monster. God made you like him.' She began to scream.

"I reached for her and my hand started to burn. But it was far away, the pain. I wanted it. It was just like the men on the field. Just stepping forward, and again and again, until you disappeared. I saw how easy it could be. I saw how she was right. There was no home for me.

"I thought of it. It would be easy to simply continue, to walk in and burn like they wanted me to. Don't stop. Be free. It was only a choice. Men made a choice when they stepped on the battlefield. They chose not to turn or run. Maybe in those moments, some of them chose to be happy.

"And then I heard noises behind me and I saw Philip. And I stayed. I didn't go with my mother or father.

"I don't what will happen to me now. But I hope not to go. Not until I've had more time to find home.

"That's everything," he said.

§

PHILIP GLANCED AROUND THE room as silence overtook them. The queen's secretary put down his pen and closed his ledger. The prince stared out the window, his cane across his legs as the first time Philip had encountered him outside their apartment while Alamayou raged. The princess sat very still, her hands folded in her lap. Her eyes shimmered with wetness.

The queen seemed so much smaller than he knew she was. A ferocious, fearless monarch who sat atop an empire centuries in the making. Her lips parted to speak, but moments passed with no words. Her face was ashen.

"Leave us," she said at last.

Seely exhaustedly translated. Alamayou looked at the queen, trying to decipher what she was thinking. Her face was dry and hard, and her eyes went to a different part of the room when he tried to meet them.

Philip stood, ready to scream and consequently be damned. That was all she had to say? Leave? Why do this, then? Why make Alamayou cut himself open and spill his entire life out for them?

Alamayou took his arm, stopping him. "It's enough," he told Philip.

"Enough? We don't know anything about what happens to you."

"Mother," Princess Louise said. "We've much to discuss. Perhaps we can reach out to the solicitor and have him join us."

"All of you, leave us."

The queen turned in her throne to face the far wall.

Shocked, the prince and princess left their mother. Seely trailed after, and Philip next, still muttering in indignation. "I don't understand the point of this entire charade."

Alamayou hesitated a moment before leaving. The lady-in-waiting stared impatiently at him as she held the portrait room doors open for everyone to pass through.

The queen was facing the portraits. Her family, and next to it, the one he'd made, of himself and her dead husband.

"Come," Philip said, and he left the queen behind, passed through the doors, and heard them close behind him.

§

SEELY WAS TOO EXHAUSTED to speak for them anymore.

They returned to the apartment. At the door, Seely begged forgiveness for wanting a bath and some sleep. "Hard things," she said as she left. "You say hard things, Alamayou."

"I know."

"I hope they help you."

She left them.

Inside the apartment, Alamayou went to the basin and brought cool, clean water to his face. He felt empty, as weak as a newborn, as heavy as the stone Meqdala was built from. But he didn't want to lie down. He didn't want to sleep or stop. If he did, everything would stop with him. The queen, thinking of him. The princess, weeping for him. Philip, hearing him.

Philip was standing over the bag Simon had packed for him. This was what he'd intended to do. See to it that Alamayou could be understood and that he had the best possible chance of safety and hope for a life. Then he would leave. To what, he didn't know. His old life, maybe. Leaving the castle would be the easy part. Then he'd chance it on the streets like he did in Lambeth, where he'd grown up. He could steal like the old days, from the vendors and stalls, then resell the pilferings for pence. Or he could make use of what he'd learned from Dr. White. The legitimate and the not so. There were women, White had told him, who needed a steady hand and a secret-keeper in their doctors when they got themselves into trouble. "What sort of trouble?" he'd asked.

"The sort that leaves secret hearts inside them," White had said.

He'd learned how to find those secret hearts and still them. It was something he'd always hoped he'd never have to do. But if it meant his survival, he would do what was needed.

The bag was packed, the door to a new life was near. Not a soul in Windsor would care if he was gone come morning, off to Christ knew where with no hope of a life worth living.

He felt eyes on him and turned to see Alamayou watching him.

"Philip? Leave?"

In that moment Philip didn't see Alamayou in the apartment, but at the fire. The soldiers raced around the cottage, looking for a way in, while burning knobs of debris fell around the writhing bodies of two human beings. Bent figures, ablaze and screaming, but not trying to get out.

You turned to me then, Philip thought. *A man you'd never seen before and yet you wore the same expression you wear now. Fear, unimaginable sadness, and just a trace of hope, because of me.*

I saw you. Your hand in fire, yes. But it was too far to reach your parents and too far for them to reach you, because your other hand stretched toward mine.

Isn't that what hope looks like? he thought.

"Philip?"

Alamayou touched Philip's packed bag with his right hand. His fire-scarred fingers opened it and took out the first of Philip's possessions.

"Stay," Alamayou said.

"I'm staying."

He helped Alamayou unpack the bag first, then the other one they'd thrown together for Alamayou.

When they were done, Philip took Alamayou's hand and turned it over. He touched the smooth scarring, his finger rising and falling along the fleshy rivulets permanently etched into his palm.

"Does it hurt?" Philip touched his own chest, making a tight fist over his heart. "Hurt."

Alamayou smiled. "No. No more hurt."

THREE

Chapter Thirteen

3 January 1869

COLD WINDS SWEPT THROUGH Windsor's grounds. The freezing rain slanted sideways, bending the trees. In the gray light, a hot-air balloon hovered just above the steeps at Hyde Park. Despite the weather, an immense crowd gathered in the streets and on either side of the Long Walk, which had been opened by Her Majesty to celebrate the balloon's maiden flight.

From beneath umbrellas, they watched it rise on drafts of fired air. Its skin was the sepia of ancient maps. The balloon's passengers were reduced to black silhouettes by the falling rains. Small as mayflies, they waved to the city below.

The castle service came out to see, as did Philp, Alamayou, the prince, and the princess. They huddled together as the balloon drifted, casting its shadow over them as the wintry winds buffeted it about.

Some members of the castle staff broke ranks and walked to the gate, carrying mugs of tea and warm breads for the shivering soldiers waiting on the other side of the bars. In groups of two and three at a time, they'd come to Windsor's gate every day to stand in silent protest of Alamayou's continued presence. The *Telegraph* that morning had called for a trial to address Tewedros' war crimes, and it took the royals to task for remaining so conspicuously quiet on Alamayou's involvement. In closing, the editorial recommended that Alamayou be sent back to Abyssinia to meet whatever punishment his father should have received.

As the butlers, valets, kitchen staff, and maids returned to the castle, they passed Alamayou standing with the royals. Eyes down, they bowed to the prince and princess. Their side glances at each other, their smirks, and their turned backs made clear where their allegiances lay: with the men outside the gates, not the Negroes inside it.

"Come on, Alamayou." Philip wanted to get Alamayou back inside and out of plain sight before the crowd, emboldened by the castle service and the soldiers among them, started catcalling, or worse. The royals had enough to think about as it was. Restlessness in their subjects could only tilt their thoughts in one direction.

As they returned to the castle, Philip filled with admiration for Alamayou. He'd been brave in front of the queen. Brave wasn't even a large enough word to encompass what Alamayou had done. He'd been fearless, every bit the warrior his father wanted him to be, and not a drop of blood spilled. It was the sort of courage no one else would appreciate, and that was the part that posed the greatest risk. A man isn't called brave if he admits to killing another man or defiling a woman. He's called what he is, what he did, and he's punished. It was no less true when the offense had no name.

The prince and princess returned to Windsor too, but at a distance. They slowed their pace even though the prince seemed healthy enough. *No*, Philip thought, *this was purposeful. They didn't want to be seen by the people, and probably their own service, as getting too close to Alamayou. Bastards. Cowards. Stand right next to him. Learn a little something about bravery, and in the face of banishment and death, no less. The sort of death that couldn't be managed or put off by a medical bag and the best doctors on the continent.*

He knew what they needed to do that day. He had to at least try to be that brave, for Alamayou.

"Follow me," he whispered to Alamayou. Taking him by the arm, they veered away from the entrance to the ward and headed toward the livery.

"Where are we going?" Alamayou asked.

"We need to find our coachman."

§

IN THE AFTERNOON THE rain tapered off and a bit of silvered light bloomed open across the tops of the Long Walk's elms. The clouds thinned and the sky slowly shed its pale ash tone to become vivid, blue, and vast.

Alamayou, Philip, and Seely rode in Charles's trap through London's many neighborhoods. The city they saw from the coach held three million within a thirty-mile space. It teemed with filth and with life. Its people scratched out existences as best they could by collecting the bones of their dead and selling them to anatomy museums, or selling their animals to each other for food and fuel. They left their countryside homes each day for the fires of the distant city and the hope of work, only to die unknown on top of London's cobblestones while city towers and country estates rose around them.

It would have been impossible for Alamayou, on arriving at the docks of the Royal Victoria, to imagine such a place as Charles drove through. Its history and sheer breadth defied his attempts to grasp the immensity of the city. As Philip took them farther into London's soot-stained true heart, he felt that all the moments of his life since leaving the *Feroze* behind were like slats on a bridge, spanning his past and future, connecting one precariously to the other. He could look back and see how far he'd come, as if he'd left footprints on the hours that had passed. He could measure his life since the fire word by word.

Even his dreams spoke of how far he'd traveled from the man he was to the one he was becoming. His father and especially his mother still haunted him, but when he woke crying their names or their words, he was speaking English.

I've truly crossed over, he thought, *into this new world.*

At Windsor the air was clear and crisp after the rain, but as they reached the city's outskirts, the light over London became almost tactile. A bile-yellow pall shuddered in the space between roof and sky, fed by the city's many chimneys.

"You won't find anyone born to the likes of Exeter here," Philip said. "Or Windsor, for that matter, unless they're looking for trouble."

Charles brought them to the Lambeth neighborhood of Soho parish, where London's next age crept in from the edges on black, coal-fed smoke. To the east, the marsh; to the west, the old archery ground the locals dubbed the Butts, on which a workhouse stood. They arrived at the corner of Paradise Row beneath the tap sign, *Three Conies and Feathers*. Around them the Parletons made their way along Three Coney Lane to waiting meals of pie and mash. Across the green fields and roughened lanes full of broken glass and discarded horseshoes, nurseries and untended farms stood abandoned in the shadows of the factories that drew the men away over the years, never to return.

Though the rain had stopped, the city still trembled with thunder that rolled between tenements to shake the loose cobblestones beneath their feet. Lambeth shrank into the storm's lingering darkness even as candles flickered to life in the windows of flats and shops.

Down the lanes from the low house of the Feathers, with its sunken door two feet below the road, they came to a cluster of buildings five stories high and angled toward each other, making a star of the crisscrossing alleyways between.

"This is the flat where I grew up," Philip said, patting the brick work. "This was all the life my father was able to give me."

They entered one of the alleys. On either side, the tenements on Bailish rose, their rooftops overlooking the River Ouse.

"My father escaped to London as a runaway slave from the Caribbean," Philip said. "I remember him telling me how he hopped a ship and had to steal a white woman's purse to buy passage.

The conductor demanded a high price from the Negroes he smuggled below deck. People like us lived mostly seaside in Canning, Liverpool, or Cardiff. We were rarities in the city, but still faces like ours could be seen here in Lambeth, so he settled us here. A marriage to an East End girl, birth, death, and me. In that order."

Seely kept up a steady pace of translation. A quiver entered her voice at the mention of slaves, but she persevered.

They stood beneath a window on the Ouse side of the alleyway. "My mum died birthing my brother," Philip said. "December eighteen fifty. He didn't get a name. In her heart, maybe, but she never told anyone what it was. She took him with her. I was three, give or take. I don't much remember what she looked like. All I have of her is a memory of her smiling at me while I lay in her arms, as if I fixed everything just by living. I don't even know if it's a real memory or something I made up over the years. She feared the blue death, my dad said. I guess God in his infinite wisdom killed her some other way, eh?"

He paused as the sensations of his childhood flooded back. He'd first heard the word "plague" at thirteen, the year Parliament decreed all smell to be signs of disease, and London's future industries rose around his parish in response. New machines were created to beat back the plague. The air was collected by paddled wheels, pushed through pipes, purified with filters and water, and pumped back to the city's poor as a test, to see if the rich could be saved.

"We can beat the bloody Hessians," his father had been fond of saying, "so we won't be brought low by bloody gasses."

He'd look up at his father and think, *It'll all be right as rain before long. If my father says it, then it's true. He knows. He's found a way to live in a city that doesn't want him.*

Bloody idiot, Philip thought, there at his old tenement window.

Alamayou and Seely were staring at him.

"I remember there was a boy across this alley," he said. "He lived on the same tenement floor as me, just across the way here. We would meet at our windows. We made signals of candles and our hands.

A sunrise game of chase around the streetlamps or a race to the corner and back. I think of him at times. I'm not sure why. One morning, I waited at my window but he didn't come. After a few days, his window pane was fogged with dust, like it had been abandoned. It had. That was the first time.

"Each summer the Ouse overflowed and our flat flooded. All the sewers were good for was collecting the rains. I can't describe to you what it was that floated through our flat. A soup of the lives around us. I saw blood slicks that made the water dark, and I knew that someone close by had died. Like the boy across the alley here."

He smiled, a weak attempt. "I guess Lambeth was my first war, you could say."

"Philip?"

"Yes, Alamayou. Sorry. These memories."

"Your mother died. What happened to your father?"

"He mined coal at the Killingworth Colliery. The mine had him for seven years. His cough became like a lullaby to me. I heard it every night. All the men who worked the mines had it."

"Not you."

"No, not me. I never worked in the mines. He didn't want that for me."

A trolley went by the mouth of the alley, carrying revelers who hollered at them and held their flasks high. Their voices careened from the brick walls long after they passed.

"I told my father the boy across the alley wasn't there anymore," Philip said. "He asked me to take him to the window. I thought he wanted to wait with me until the boy came back, but really he just wanted to see a bit of the world before he died. He lasted another few days, maybe longer. He died there in a chair. That was autumn eighteen sixty-one. I was ten.

"The coroner came, and the sanitarium men. They fumigated the tenement while I sat at the window. They wetted our yellowed wallpaper with carbolic acid and let the paper curl, then stripped it all away to be burned. They brought these briquettes of brimstone and covered them in live coal. The stench made me gag but they didn't care. They took our curtains, our hung clothes, all our loose ends. They lay my father down on an oilcloth. The coroner said they'd return in a week to limewash our flat. Then it would be ready to let again. I suppose they assumed I'd leave and die elsewhere. Or else they didn't think at all of me. My skin, you know.

"But the coroner told me, 'Look away. Don't remember him this way.' He wrote a number on my father's arm with a stick of pitch, like you use to sketch, Alamayou. He wrote the same number into a journal. Then he whispered over my father's body, a prayer. God, I remember it. '*Yit'gadal v'yit'kadash sh'mei raba…*'"

"Old words," Alamayou said.

"Yes. Old words."

"My father knew old words."

"Did he?"

"Yes. Before."

"When you live in the middle of death, it's all you remember. I had ten years with my dad and that's how I remember him. How I see him. Tagged like a side of beef. I'd only met one man in all of London who'd spoken to me kindly, that coroner. So I wandered the city until I found him. When the lights of his flat dimmed I broke in and saw my father's body on a table. I sat there until dawn, at a window watching the city just like the window I grew up at. Watching the world go on without me. I knew I'd die soon. I could feel it, easy as breathing. When the coroner came in from his night's sleep, he wasn't cross with me. He showed me why the number. On a wall behind a curtain there was a map. Pins by the thousands, and a number on each. Each, a life. My father was in there. The coroner was mapping the plague. He was trying to do good. Shows you how much a street urchin like me knew about people, eh?"

He shook his head. "That's how it all began. My road to Abyssinia began when I became an orphan. By the time White found me in that jail cell, I was hard and mean. I didn't care about anything or anyone. If I wanted for something, I stole it. If I wanted for someone, I took them. I figured the only way out of my lot in life was my father's way. An oilcloth and a number. I didn't expect anything more."

"You didn't expect me."

"I'm sorry. You've come from so far and look at what sort of man you find yourself with. When I close my eyes it gathers round me."

Alamayou put his arms around Philip and let him lean against his shoulder.

"There's so much I've seen," Philip said. "London during the plague, when disease no one could see floated past our rooftops with no fear of God. Parishes where the poor like us were herded. Smoking chimneys that rained ash onto the Thames. That drunken bastard White gave me a kind of life. He was what he was, but so was I. He didn't give a damn about me nor I him, and when you have that in common, maybe that becomes a kind of caring after a time. I don't know. He taught me. He'd seen so much, done so much. He told me of a time when he was at sea, before the war. There was a seaman whose life he saved after the man fell overboard. His fellows plucked him from the icy water and brought him to the ship's infirmary. There was a Turkish water pipe, a trinket from a forgotten voyage. White filled its glass with collected rainwater and its bowl with tobacco. There was no warmth left in the seaman's body, and White listened but only heard the tides in his chest. So he lit the bowl and surrounded the seaman's bed with other sailors. They drew on the pipe tentacles and then blew smoke into the seaman's nose through tubes. Soon, the smoke pushed out the lungs' fluids. The seaman sat up and reached for a flask of whiskey.

"So many stories like that. He taught me how to be like him, and I wanted it. I didn't want to just die and be nothing."

He felt himself sink into Alamayou. His body shook with the violent unburdening of all that he carried.

"White passed himself off as a doctor, and maybe he really was one, I don't know. But he knew enough to get by and he took matters in hand. Each day there was a bit to eat and a drop to drink. In the poor times, that was something. Then I was at sea and at war, and I saw things the likes of us never see. It'll never be that sort of world for us, but I saw the body opened. The way breath looks when the ribs part ways with the muscle and the skin. And I wanted it. I wanted to know, even if putting my hands into the dead was no better way to live than sitting in my flat while those men washed my dad away."

A dark sky covered Lambeth. They weren't far from the pump at Broad Street. The heart of the blue death, the cholera outbreak of years before that emptied all the tenement windows of light.

"My dad died," he said. "So did my mum. I'm an orphan just like you. When you lose people, it's like taking a walk away from the world and me, I've always been the sort who doesn't come back from walks, you know? The only thing I ever dreamt of was who'd shovel my corpse one day. I went to jail. I went to war. Nothing else to me, until you. You're the first friend I've ever had, Alamayou."

Down it came. The curtain over his heart. And Philip thought, *I don't want to let it close me in a shroud anymore. I don't want to tell myself that loneliness is what I deserve.*

"Every day I think, 'Please, wake me in another body. Let me be anyone else.' Someone who doesn't look at the boy across the alley and wish for him, not to meet out and run wild in the streets, breaking windows and stealing potatoes from the carts, but for the feel of someone wanting me back. You give me something else to dream about," he said.

The sun set behind the tenements. They watched their shadows advance and it felt like no time was passing at all. They said nothing, only listened to Lambeth around them. At the mouth of the alley, two merchants paused, their carts facing each other as they groused about the poor day's sales. Somewhere beyond them, a squeaking cart rode atop the broken stone of the street, its owner calling out the price of medicinals.

The sound of footsteps crunching the graveled alley floor echoed from the walls. They turned to see who approached.

"Beggin' y'pardon," Charles said, hat in hand, "but we ought'a be gettin' back." He looked askance at the way Alamayou and Philip stood so close together.

When the coachman's eyes locked with his, Alamayou felt it. The desire to burn. To jump. To run, knowing full well there may not be any others running with him. But his arm stayed around Philip. As strong as his fear was at being seen, the fear in Philip was stronger. Alamayou felt it twitching through Philip's shoulders and into his own body like a current of lightning.

He needs me here, Alamayou thought. *Right here. It's what we do. We try.*

They followed Charles back to his trap. Under a sky of icy, distant lights, they rode back to Windsor.

§

A NOTE SAT ON the desk in their apartment. It was sealed with a stamped blot of melted red wax. The queen's seal.

Philip broke it open. "She wants to see you, Alamayou. In the portrait room."

"Not you?"

"No."

"Seely—"

"It says you. Just you. Be careful. Bring Seely so you understand what she says. She may ask you more questions."

He smiled thinly as he dressed. "What more to say?" he shrugged.

§

A TRAY OF CAKES sat on a side table near the burning hearth in the portrait room alongside two cups, a steeping pot, and some silver chalices of sugar lumps and fatty milk. Next to the queen was a pewter flask that was daintily small. When she opened it a heady smell emerged.

"*Tej*," Alamayou said.

"An Abyssinian beverage?" the queen asked. "This, we wager, is far superior. Claret with a hint of single malt whiskey. We feel the need for the sort of calm only good spirits provide. Especially in these strange, disquieting days."

Seely translated, but Alamayou remained quiet. He was content to let the queen dictate the terms of their discussion. He felt exhausted from anxiety over what she'd do with him, what words she would say, and whether they would mean the end of him.

The fact that she'd asked him to come to the portrait room, of all places in Windsor, opened a sliver of hope in him. His painting still hung on the wall. It had been here ever since the night they'd told each other the simplest, most terrible truth at the heart of their different, yet similar, lives. *Gone.*

How, he wondered as he watched her take a delicate sip from her flask, could she summon him here only to send him away? There had been words spoken between them in the portrait room that made the distance between them smaller. That had to count for something.

"We have so few opportunities to be alone," the queen said. "To simply be still and think of old faces and places we once saw. Pleasant things, trivial, one supposes. But what comes to us? Comfort and tranquil memories? No, only trouble and matters of great weight. We wish sometimes, to no good end."

She offered the flask to Alamayou. He shook his head. She set it down.

Seeing her reminded Alamayou of the first night, when the monarch of the western world slipped into her private portrait room an old, tired woman. For others, she was a leader, and she wore that title as effortlessly as she did her crown. But something about the room and the memories it held made the weight upon her shoulders almost visible.

"Seely," she said, "we remind you that what you hear is never to leave this room. Do you understand?"

Seely nodded.

"Very well. We wanted to tell you ourselves, you did very well. I understand now, the life you had. If crimes of war were committed, we do not believe you had a hand in them. Nor did you have any power or choice in what was done by or on behalf of your father. To us, it appears that you know things no one should know."

"Thank you, Your Majesty." Alamayou bowed gratefully.

"We lack the power to change the world, you know. Perhaps that is why your father chose his course. We know what is possible, what is not, and what is dangerous. Yet we cannot change the world that is out there, and if that world learned what you have already learned in your young life, well, the world would be a tragic, turbulent place indeed."

He couldn't escape the sense that something was missing from her words. She was holding something back. He could see it in the turn of her head away from him, away from the paintings on the wall. It was as if she didn't want any eyes on her, even flat, watercolor eyes.

She gestured to the fire. It waned.

Alamayou placed a log on and surrounded it with scraps of wrapped coal. He stoked it with the iron until its heat pushed back at him.

"You must hate them for what they did to you," she said quietly. "Your mother and father."

"No."

"Perhaps you should. They left you, after all. For a child, there is no worse betrayal."

"I don't hate them," Alamayou said.

"They left you."

"They died."

"No. They *left* you. They chose to, but they didn't have to. Not that way, not so soon. Do you see the difference? What they did, they did for themselves, not you. Your father chose to act rashly, to invite war and destruction. He didn't think of how best to protect you. And your mother chose not to run away when she saw that a monster ruled her life and the life of her son. She chose to stay with a man who chained her and forced her son to beat her, or die. Perhaps you think we're cruel to say these things to you, but this is what it means to raise children who have the strength to survive, Alamayou. Our mother brought us into the world and we were as broken as any babe. We couldn't walk or feed ourselves. We couldn't survive. And she did not change the world to suit our helplessness. She changed us. Me, to suit me to the world so I wouldn't be broken or helpless, but strong. She did this by walking away from me. That is different from leaving. There's all the difference in the world."

She paused for a sip from her flask.

"I don't think I ever knew kindness until I met Albert." She shrugged, a casual, strangely human thing to do, and it caught Alamayou so unawares that he could hardly breathe. She'd turned as she did it, toward the painting of her family, as if to apologize for her words.

"Are you afraid?" she asked him.

"Yes."

"Of going back? Of dying?"

"Of dying alone."

"Yes. That's worse, of that we can be certain. One tries to maintain the connections in their life, if one is lucky enough to have some. And then a cross word, a foolish choice, a terrible twist of fate, and we find ourselves alone."

"If I have to go back," Alamayou said, "if I have to be alone, at least I'll see the white dream again, one last time. At least I'll have that."

"We want to show you something. Come."

He and Seely followed her out of the castle and through the Middle Ward to an amphitheater atop the mound, and then up one hundred stone steps.

"Do we shock you," she asked breathlessly as they climbed, "that we can keep pace with ones so young? In our own home we are forever young. Don't forget it."

At the pinnacle, an immense quarter of cannon nested against the stone floor. More pieces were mounted around the rock curtain.

"This is called the Round Tower," she said.

Alamayou joined her at the parapet.

"From here we see, on clear days, Middlesex, Essex, Hertfordshire, Surrey, Kent, Sussex. Names of no meaning to you. These are the tribes. We see their houses, their churches. We hear their bells and we know they exist even if we can't see them when the fog covers everything. We come up here, above the fog and all that lies beneath, and we watch our people face the future. Maybe in Meqdala, your father did that, or believed he did. Look now, the fog comes."

Alamayou gazed out over a beautiful vista. Softly rounded hills threaded paths that from the height and distance looked to be more liquid than earth. They stretched as far as Alamayou could see, to the horizon line where the fog came in like a pale carpet.

"Is it like your white dream?"

"It is."

"Perhaps you'd like to paint it from up here," she said. "We shall see to it. Be sure to include that small chapel there. It's nothing important, but it's peaceful. I love to come here just to look at it in different lights."

"I'll paint it for you."

"Why did you tell me what you did, Alamayou?"

There it is, he thought. *The thing she'd been holding back.* Her question didn't ring with revulsion or contempt, and he was grateful for at least that much. Had she thrown her question at his feet like something dead and rotted, no one would have blamed her.

But there was a quality of anger in her voice. *Why did you have to make me know this about you? How can I look at you now?*

It was a silent world they surveyed from so high above Windsor. Nothing but the land rolling out to places he'd never been, and flocks of roused birds too far away to hear, and the trees bending in a soft, cold wind that grew stronger.

"You asked," he said simply.

"Don't play us for a fool. You understand very well what we want to know."

Alamayou waved Seely away. She retreated to the opposite end of the Round Tower. There, in the furthest curve away from them, she looked out at a country that he knew must seem strange and forbidding to her.

It gets easier, he wanted to tell her. A bit more each day. How much, that depends on how much time they allow you to have.

He didn't want Seely saying the words for him. They were his. They belonged to him because he'd earned them over his entire life.

"First thing anyone said to me here, 'Don't be you, Alamayou. Be what they want. Be them, other. Be you at night. Only then.' All my life is that. My abat, anat, finally they see me. What happens? They die. Better than seeing me. They choose death, not me.

"I came to London, to you. Now you all see. What will you do? Live? See more of me? I don't know. But there's one, he doesn't run from me. He stays. Abat, anat, think I'm a monster. He tells me, no, not a monster. A man. Don't go. Stay and live. Find home. He says he knows me. I give him reason to dream. *Me.*"

"Find home?" the queen said.

"Somewhere."

"You put yourself at great risk for Philip with that letter you delivered to my door. You understand that, don't you? It makes me want to ask, would Philip have done the same for you? Does he feel the same?"

"Yes," he said without hesitation.

"How do you know? How can you be so sure?"

She was studying him. She was wise, old, so tired, but in her eyes the ancient thing he'd seen leaving the dead was there, very much alive. It was life itself, awakened by the words he shared with her. She wasn't asking because she didn't know. She did know. She wanted to see that ancient thing alive in someone else. It was the way the old looked at a newborn, or a young couple so wrapped up in each other that they take no notice of the world around them. Wistfully, a little envious, grateful for having been there to see.

She wanted to see life give to another what it had once given her.

"I know," he said, "because he didn't let me burn. He didn't let me jump. He would fight even you to keep me here."

It grew bitterly cold. The queen's Woman of the Bedchamber brought a wrap. "We wish for tea and a book by the hearth fire," the queen said. "Our evening concludes. Do this for us now. Get some rest. There's much for both of us to consider."

"Yes."

She left him there, up so high. Not since Abyssinia had he been alone in a high place, where so much of the world he lived in could be seen.

In time he walked back to the ward with Seely trailing behind. He felt the full weight of his life now out in the open. All of them, the queen, Philip, he, were so skilled at veiling themselves, and yet each had peeled back a corner for each other.

He decided that he would go to the apartment and Philip with no thought of how any of it should be. Only that they'd talked of hard things without help, through silences, hands, and, finally, words. Whatever came next, he at least knew they were all sure of each other.

Chapter Fourteen

4 January 1869

ALAMAYOU WOKE THE NEXT morning to snow falling silently past the window, building a soft mound atop the hedgerow on the other side of the glass.

On the nightstand next to him, there was a silver tray and another note. *Someone had put it there deep in the night,* he marveled, *and I never heard them.*

He unfolded it and recognized Seely's handwriting at its bottom, translating to Amharic the queen's words above.

We thank you for yesterday. It gives us much to think about, and helped make some matters clear. Among them, this: you no longer need anyone to speak for you. It's time you stand on your own.

We know you will.

The apartment was empty. It was early by the look of the light outside, silvery and low. He was alone.

He dressed and went to the window as a petal of worry opened in his thoughts. At the Spur of the Walk, he saw a barouche-landau. Servants packed it with small suitcases while others gathered near the driver. Among them, the princess, standing with Philip.

He ran.

§

"DON'T FEAR," THE PRINCESS said as Alamayou reached the Walk, breathless. "A new life awaits you."

Seely stared uncertainly as valets put the last of her new things into the landau. She'd come to Windsor with so little, and now left with simple, clean clothes, perfumes from Paris, a journal, and a letter of recommendation from the queen pronouncing her well suited for positions as nanny or teacher.

"Why?" Alamayou asked.

"There are some loyal Parliament members who keep us advised of things," Princess Louise said. "Things we need to know. Ambassador Naismith was spreading rumors about the girl, that we bought her from a slaver for you."

He understood, though it pained him to see Seely go so soon. The queen wanted him to stand on his own for his sake, and for hers. There would be others he'd have to talk to, like Naismith and his colleagues, and if she decided to fight for him, he couldn't subject himself to the judgment of such men by relying on a former slave as a translator.

The worry he'd felt gave way to a hint of hope. Maybe Seely's departure meant that the queen had made up her mind in his favor.

"Will you be all right?" he asked Seely in English.

Seely smiled, one of the few he'd ever seen from her. "I live this way. Not knowing what the next day will bring. What about you?"

"What about me?"

"Will you keep saying hard things for the queen?"

"He will," Philip told her. "I know he will. He's far bolder than I."

Alamayou recognized the word. "Bolder."

"You, Alamayou. Brave. More than anyone I've ever known."

"He is," Seely said.

"When does she go?" Alamayou asked.

"Soon. There's a ship waiting."

"I ask, some time? Fast, I promise."

"I suppose that would be all right," the princess said. "But not long, now."

"Come with me." Alamayou took Seely's hand and led her back into their ward.

He entered their apartment ahead of her, feeling oddly lighter. *Come what may*, he thought, *we can claim a bit of Windsor for ourselves. Thanks to her, I have memories that live in London, the impossible city.*

"I owe you so much," he said in Amharic. "No one could understand me. I didn't know what was happening around me, what people were saying. How they felt about me. I learned through you. I can speak for myself now. I can understand how people see me. None of that would have happened without you. I want to do something for you, to take with you."

It didn't take long. It was crude, not something studied or cared for. It began with a circle and after creating that shape that would become Seely's face, Alamayou stared at it for a little while before continuing past it, adding color, adding contours of oils and a bit of chalk to make the green elms of the Walk behind her.

She was standing about five feet away, dressed not in the seaworn rags she'd come in on, but in a lace dress that a seamstress somewhere in the bowels of Windsor had crafted from nothing, from the spinnings of caterpillars. Whoever that seamstress was, she couldn't have dreamed her work would fall onto the bony shoulders of a former slave, being made into a thing of permanence and delicate beauty.

He shaded her cheeks to make them sharper and shaped her eyes into the almonds that he supposed Seely wished she had in life. *Now you'll never age*, he thought. *You'll always be here. Young, rescued from your once-life, and delivered however briefly to something you couldn't have imagined.*

May it continue for you, he thought as he finished. *I hope one day we'll see each other again, and we'll smile at our impossible fortune.*

Alamayou finished and gave it to her. She began to cry upon seeing it. "I've never seen myself as pretty before, but now I feel beautiful. Wherever my life takes me, this will be with me, hanging on a wall. Thank you for that. It's something others have, not me."

"I'll never forget you. You gave his voice to me. I think a life waits for me after all. Maybe a home somewhere. *That's* something others have, not me."

Her eyes darkened. "I gave you all their voices, not just his. I hope you find happiness, Alamayou, and I know you're a prince. You're above me. But it's wrong, what you feel. I won't say what your parents said. You're the bravest, strongest man I have ever met, to say those things out loud. I wish you hadn't. I hope you change. I hope you find a better way to live."

The low whinnies of the horses came, slow and dissonant. Their hooves beat restlessly at the ground. Seely wouldn't look at him. *Maybe,* he thought, *she was afraid of consequences for being so blunt, or ashamed. Or maybe she's simply being true to Windsor. Everyone here is warned against speaking too plainly, but what do all of us strangers come here for? To learn to speak, and then to use our new language to say what we couldn't say before.*

Such a strange place.

"Do you hate me for saying that?" She held the portrait tight.

She has what matters to her, he thought. *Not my friendship, or the warm blankets against winter, or a full belly and no chains. She has the moment she became beautiful, and look at her. She'd claw my eyes out and rot in a cell before she let me take it from her. You can't let go of such a moment when you finally have it. Having it changes you.*

"No," he said. "I think we're not so different."

He walked out, leaving her to stare at the painting.

§

HE LED SEELY BACK to the landau, helped her inside and stepped back as the driver closed the door.

"Where will she go?" he asked the princess.

"Naismith made it known he wanted to interview her," the princess told him. "She'll be on a three-penny steamer by nightfall, bound for the gardens at Cremorne. There's a man of good reputation and some wealth who's in need of a translator for his entertainers."

Seely held up Alamayou's painting of her to the landau window, a glow of pride on her face.

"Entertainers?" Philip asked.

"He owns a traveling band of some myriad entertainments, Cooke's Menagerie. Many of them hail from her part of the world."

Seely put her hand on the glass of the landau door as it began to roll. Alamayou pressed his against it, then let it fall away. The landau lumbered around the Spur of the Walk, onto the long stretch away from Windsor.

"He'll be good to her," the princess assured them, "or he will hear from us. But there's precious few places a girl like her can call home, I'm afraid."

The need overtook Alamayou to be somewhere high. Nearby was the Round Tower. He left for it as Philip watched the landau leave.

Scrabbling up the side of the mound to the top, he sat as chalk dust filled his lungs. It was not what he had hoped for. Somewhere to simply breathe.

He wondered if Seely would be made a gift yet again.

The landau rolled through the gate, then turned onto one of the paths he'd seen when the queen had brought him to the top of the Round Tower with Seely. It passed the small church. A figure moved through the graveyard as the landau pulled alongside the fence line and came to a slow halt. They approached Charles and stood there for a few minutes, talking.

A friend, Alamayou thought. *Someone else who, like Charles, worked their life away in the shadow of Windsor, pulling weeds from among the dead and keeping the modest chapel clean in case the queen stopped by.*

No one moved in the carriage compartment. A royal would have thrown the door open and demanded an end to the delay.

A royal, Alamayou thought, *would have a hand in where she was going.*

Whatever she was doing inside, Seely kept herself inconspicuous. Soon the figure waved farewell and the carriage rolled on, west to another life. Only after it was in motion did the whip cracks' sound reach him.

The farther they traveled, the smaller the landau got, until it disappeared into the earth.

§

IN THE AFTERNOON HE and Philip rode to the Royal Zoo in the princess's carriage. There was a crowd gathered at the zoo's gates, as word of a royal visit had gone round.

Cheers went up at the sight of the prince and princess. Many of the gathered Londoners were obviously poor. Their clothes were stained with the fluids of London's formidable industries and their raised hands held withering peonies and small flags of empire in hopes of some acknowledgement.

A keeper led them through the crowd to a special enclosure where a calf had recently been born to a mated pair of elephants. Inside the enclosure, the calf stood unsteadily next to its tuskless mother while she reached up to the high boughs of a tree and pulled its tender shoots down. The calf tried to nurse, but its mother's restless feeding frustrated every attempt.

Louise stood next to her brother, watching.

"Will the queen come?" Philip asked them.

"She's rarely seen in public these days," Prince Leopold said. "Certainly not for something as trivial as an outing with us."

"Has she decided? Have you heard anything?"

"I know you're anxious, as I'm sure Alamayou is," the princess said soothingly. "I've heard nothing and I doubt highly that we will until the queen herself is ready to be heard on it. Between now and then, we just have to wait."

"And while you wait," the prince said, "you might brush up on the manner in which you speak to royals. All we have in common is a roof, Mr. Layard."

"I ought to apologize."

"Indeed," the prince said.

"And I do," Philip said, "without reservation. You and your family are singular and you've shown us nothing but kindness. But I'm living each day in fear of it being his last. You don't understand."

"Having seen me bleed, I think you ought to know that I'm in an ideal situation to understand. Now, may I be allowed to free myself from this conversation? I'd like to watch a mother parent her child."

He returned to the elephant enclosure alone.

"My God," Philip said softly. "I've acted like a bloody idiot."

"Let him be," the princess said. "We all feel the strains of our lives. Ours are usually reserved for ourselves. Frankly, it does us good to see someone as knotted with worry over someone else. It's a reminder that such things exist."

After an hour, they departed the zoo and returned to the castle to freshen up before dinner. They came by a different route, one that took them through the winding lands that Alamayou had seen from the Round Tower with the queen and Seely.

"That tiny church there," the prince said as they rode by, "is where the queen slips off to sometimes, when she wants to pray without a fuss." He smiled mischievously, a child giving up a family secret. "She's so skilled at stealing away without telling anyone that it drives her service to drink. The staff at the church are used to her comings and goings. They stay out of her way in a manner that none at Windsor have ever managed to do."

Philip felt relieved. If the prince bore him any resentment for what he'd said at the zoo, it seemed to have dissipated.

"I saw it from the tower," Alamayou said. "Can I see inside?"

"It's no more than a cottage across the grounds from the Round Tower," Prince Leopold said dismissively. "It serves as a burial site and memoriam to no one of significance. It can't possibly be of any interest to you."

"It reminds me of something I saw in Abyssinia."

The prince told the driver to stop. "It's nearly dusk. Quickly, now."

Alamayou got out. He left the road for the chapel. Within steps the landau grew smaller, but still he could see the others inside, watching him from the warmth of the compartment.

He approached the ivy-covered rectory through a little garden of graves. At the weathered door, behind a copse of oak, he peered through a small square of glass.

Inside the small chapel's Gothic skeleton, all was grace. Quiet sunlight filled the inlaid tapestry paintings on the walls with a peaceful pale glow that encompassed the pews and the nave. High above, where images of saints and holies were fashioned of colored glass, he saw clouds floating across the watery blue sky.

I feel like the man I was at the porthole, he thought. *Straining to see the emerging city lights of London. How far away that is from me now.*

Bowing his head, he muttered to himself. It was no prayer, as he didn't believe in anything beyond what could be seen moving through life alongside all people. It was yet another failing in his father's eyes.

The old life gathered around him even as the new one waited back on the road, inside a fine landau.

He remembered his father's makeshift church, which had been built near the gate at Meqdala. His father had used slaves to cut the mountain's stone and shape it into walls. It was meant to stand forever. Once, its door had been open slightly in a way that nothing in his father's world was. It was as if he wanted his people to come in and be with him there. No one ever did, but Alamayou remembered the day he pushed that door open and went inside.

A cross filled the bulging stone of the facing wall. No packed mud or grit between the rocks; nothing visible held his father's church together. The otherness of the cross and the haphazard stone had filled him with fear that the whole thing would fall to pieces and bury him.

He'd gone there after his father made him whip his mother before everyone. He'd gone first to his father's tent and taken his father's gun.

He'd found his father kneeling on the floor. He'd never seen his father on his knees before, or after. The Christian Book lay on the ground next to him. His father read it aloud, and Alamayou understood that to his father, the words had to be more than thought. They needed to be set loose, to live in the world.

"Stop talking to your god," Alamayou had told him, "and tell me why you made me hurt her."

His father hadn't turned at his son's voice.

"I brought your pistol, abat. Let's see how well I've learned from you."

"If you're going to kill a man," his father said, "you should just kill him. You don't bluster about it and speak doomfata. Not until it's done. Now, come. Do it where my men can see what sort of prince I've raised. My army will be your army when I'm dead. Let them respect their *ras*."

Out on the field, one of the other generals brought his father a spear and a horse. "Gugs," his father told him. "A man's game. Remember the day I taught you? Bring a horse for my son!"

A soldier brought him a horse and he mounted, gun in hand. There was nothing beneath him but a goatskin and the torqued back of the animal, a brown and white of delicate beauty that had been covered in bright streaming ribbons, as colorful as his mother's shammas.

They moved to opposite ends of the field from each other as horses and soldiers made way for them. "She's my wife!" his father roared at him across the distance. "I'll do as I please with her! A man would know that. A man would be concerned with being the son his father wants, not a gbra sadom. A monster. That's what you are!"

"She would love you," he cried in response, "if you were like me."

The world reeled away from him as their horses charged at each other. He raised his gun, knowing that his doomfata words had leveled the ground between them in a way the English never could.

Around them, everyone stared as he raised his father's pistol. His hand shook violently. "*Fari!*" his father screamed at him. Coward. "Come! Ride at me until I'm dead."

He spurred his horse to go faster, his father's words in his head. Ride, don't stop until one of us is dead.

But he didn't believe those words. He hoped like a child that he'd ride and his father would just vanish, and the fortress and soldiers with him. The world would be a flat plateau and he would continue across it.

His pistol dropped. It wasn't rage that sent him headlong, but surrender. *Not every man is brave*, he'd thought, *and not every man goes home.*

His horse flew past his father's. He couldn't shoot. His father's spear caught him full in the chest, knocking him to the ground.

His father leapt off his own horse and pounced on him. His eyes were filled with blood and hate. He'd pounded his son with his fists. He'd said, "Die. Die." Each blow started further and further away until he'd felt nothing at all. He'd only heard the sound of his father screaming doomfata over him.

Alamayou shook his head violently, dispelling the memory of his father beating him. The colored glass of the tiny church had grown dark. The light was too low for him to see inside anymore. It was getting late, and he knew the royals wanted to leave.

So do I, Alamayou thought as he returned to the carriage. *It's time to be anywhere but where I am. In my past.*

§

THAT EVENING, ALAMAYOU AND Philip went to the State Dining Room where they were seated across from the prince, princess, and Corbould. The service filled the long table with roast game, fish, and tourines of beef broth while the royals engaged in a conversation of no importance. No one talked about rumors, scandals, or power struggles.

The princess expressed her love of travel, to Corbould's great fascination. "Certainly," she said, "our mother's fondness for Scotland is all too well-known."

"Mrs. Brown and that rot," the prince remarked as the service cleared dishes.

"We're disallowed friends," the princess said, glancing at Corbould, "as if a near decade doesn't sufficiently demonstrate loss or love."

The servants of the dining room brought in platters on a metal web, each its own terrace of finger cakes.

"I've become enamored with France," she continued as plates were set and cakes served with pearl-and-silver tongs. "I know it interests mother immensely, too."

"I've never been to Paris," Prince Leopold said wistfully. "How I would love to see it."

"There are villages by its sea," Corbould said. "Monaco, Nice. Villefranche. Quite lovely and restful. Maybe when the rest of what presses your majesties is past, you can all go."

"Maybe you could show us your favorite places there," the princess said.

"I'd be honored."

This, Philip thought, *is how people are at wakes. They eat and drink and talk in corners about something, or out in the open about nothing, and all the while the reason for the gathering is never spoken out loud.*

He could feel his anger rise together with his fear. The queen had spared him for Seely, and for that alone he ought to have been relieved. *I should be grateful,* he thought bitterly, *and go pen a note of slavish thanks to her.* But Seely hadn't been spared, no matter the princess's reassurances at the carriage. What sort of life was she headed for? She was an African bound for God knew where.

She couldn't be anything but a nursemaid or a nanny to a family. A decent one, he hoped, with a father not intent on making a bellywarmer of her. They would be reputable. They would be white. And that meant that Seely would be alone again, with no one there to see whether the queen's promise of a better life was kept.

He ate a bit of fish even as his stomach soured. He was safe, for at least one more day. Alamayou was safe, at least until the queen made her wishes known. There was no place for what he was feeling. But that was exactly the problem, wasn't it? No place.

"What's wrong?" Alamayou whispered, and Philip turned to him with a weak smile. *How far you've come with your words.*

"Nothing. Thinking about the zoo, and how nice it was."

Seeing that Alamayou wasn't convinced, Philip added, "I guess I'm waiting for the other shoe to drop on us."

He laughed when Alamayou looked up at the ceiling, frowning. Having that between them made him feel less foreign and alone.

Simon came to the doorway of the room, hands clasped. He waited for the royals to recognize him. Prince Leopold motioned for him to enter.

"Her Majesty asks that you join her," he told them.

"Where are we gathering?" Prince Leopold asked.

"She has requested that you come to the Blue Room."

"Extraordinary."

The prince placed his napkin atop his plate and got up, making heavy use of his cane for support. Leaning forward, he blew the table candles out.

Alamayou and Philip followed him to the door. Alamayou paused, waiting for the princess to follow them.

She rose with Corbould into the shadows of the State Dining Room. She silently mouthed words to Corbould and Corbould responded in kind. They smiled at each other, their eyes locked.

Alamayou looked away. What passed between them belonged to them only and needed to stay where he'd found it. Out of the light of Windsor.

§

THE QUEEN SAT IN a modest chair in the Blue Room, near the hearth. Spent wood still threw off heat and soft orange light. Six more chairs had been arranged in a semicircle for Alamayou, Philip, the prince and princess, her secretary, and Lord Grant.

They all sat before her, uncertain and silent.

"Lock the door behind you," she instructed Simon. "Be sure the corridor is kept clear until we advise you otherwise. No one is to come near. Nothing we speak of ever leaves this room unless we bless it. Not even the outcome. Our notes of this will be sealed."

Simon did as he was told. The door locked and the sounds of his shoe heels faded away.

"We have made our decision," the queen said. "While we are certain you have opinions and advice for us, we wish to tell you, our decision is a final one."

Jesus, Philip thought, *look at her. Look at her eyes, for the love of God. It's as if she wants to bloody hide from us. She's doing it. She's sending him back.*

He forced himself to remain calm. He was in the most intimate, the most secret place of this queen's rooms, and if he didn't will himself to sit and wait to hear her say it out loud, he'd leap up and take Alamayou, break down her locked door, and run. *Just like you once thought of running, Alamayou, until it all burns away and then we'll be home.*

Alamayou saw it, too. In the queen's pale, still face, he saw the possibility of his death in Abyssinia, and he wasn't sorry for any of it. Not for telling her of his life before Windsor or of his true heart. He had been given days after the fire, after the rail. It hadn't all ended. That meant something.

He prepared himself for the queen's words.

"We have made arrangements," she began, "for Alamayou to go before Parliament tomorrow and tell them everything."

Her decree passed over all of them. Philip wept quietly, shaking with relief. The prince stared at his mother, dumbfounded. The princess smiled so slightly that it could have been mistaken for thought, or for nothing at all. But Alamayou saw it flicker across her face as she glanced at the far window that looked out onto the grounds.

"Everything?" Lord Grant asked hesitantly. "Your Majesty, please forgive me my impudence. But what we heard, death and…and the other. There will be names put to it. War crimes. Deviance, the nameless offense. Against all of that, you'd place the prestige of your crown. Are you certain?"

"I'm glad," Princess Louise said.

"Glad?" Prince Leopold exclaimed. "I don't want anything to happen to Alamayou. Understand that. Nor do I want to see anything happen to the monarchy or to my family."

"And so?" The queen directed her question to the prince. "What would you suggest to us?"

"I'll paint you a darker portrait than our solicitor, mother." The prince took a kerchief to his damp brow. "Your rule is called into question in the *Telegraph*. Soldiers come to our gate. Now the country will hear of this. You'll be heard on this. On him. I know his is a sympathetic story if we concentrate on what was taken from him and not on, as Grant puts it, the other. And I know it's that loss that tugs at you. So, too, you have lost. We all have. But you aren't seen in public by your people in a generation and they tire of your mourning—"

"You speak to us as if you know anything about us," she said coldly.

The prince's face reddened. "He was my father, too."

"You sad, selfish boy." The queen rose from her chair. "You say they tire of my mourning? He was my husband. There shall be no other. Ever. Do you understand that? A life of no further love. That is my life. That is what England expects of me. I do not have the luxury of life, or art, or all the things you pine for. I never have.

I am watched and measured and parceled out to those who would see me according to their expectations. I do not exist but for what they make of me. And I endure it so that you don't. You'll go to Oxford and they'll not know of your illness. Your sister will marry well. Your children and their children will have envious lives. And it will all be upon my back. Do you see this?"

"Yes," the prince said meekly.

"All I have, all that is left to me, is the weight of my word given in the name of what I believe. I have listened to him, and, having done so, I believe him. So, too, will Parliament. So, too, will you. Because I say so. Now, I wish to be alone. I've said quite enough."

They got up and left the queen to her thoughts. As soon as the door to the Blue Room closed behind them, the prince and Lord Grant broke off from the others and walked to the ward, speaking in hushed, urgent tones.

"He's afraid for his mother and himself." The princess walked away from Alamayou and Philip to a window in the corridor. "He well knows that those who oppose us might use every means necessary to undermine us, including revealing his secret. If word of his condition became common knowledge, he'd not be allowed into Oxford. He couldn't marry for fear that he'd pass down the flaw in his blood. He'd be shunned. He's royalty, true enough, but it's easy to forget that he's young."

"As are you," Philip said. "And yet, you agree with the queen."

"Any dutiful daughter would do the same."

She was distracted by something outside. Her words were as far off as her gaze, so Philip left her to her reverie. It was enough that the queen had given Alamayou a chance to fight on, terrifying though it was to imagine going before Parliament and saying what Alamayou had to say.

Alamayou lingered a moment longer beside the princess. He glanced out the window to see what she watched so intently.

There on the snow-covered grounds, Corbould sat before his easel and painted the Round Tower.

"Artist like you," he told the princess. "He paints it for you."

"I know."

She turned to him, and he was sorry that he'd stayed. The first hint of crumbling was in her eyes, along with the struggle to hold the tears off until she could be alone.

"He's a commoner," the princess told him. "He has no title. No subjects. Which means he has choices. Don't be misled by my mother, Alamayou. What she goes through, we all go through. We are what the world makes of us, not what we make of ourselves." She returned to the window. Her breath steamed the glass. "He's nothing like me," she said.

§

INSIDE THE APARTMENT, ALAMAYOU went to a covered easel. Removing the oil cloth, he stood aside so that it could be seen.

"When did you do this?" Philip asked him.

"One night when you slept."

"It's extraordinary."

In faintly hued oils, Alamayou had painted his father's fortress at Meqdala as it had been before the war. The field was as lush as Windsor's grounds. No bodies lay atop it.

Alamayou had portrayed himself in that painting, in a dreamlike dusk, standing before the fortress's gate. Next to him was another figure, black like him.

Their painted selves stood together in an Abyssinia untouched by war. Their hands were clasped.

"It's yours," Alamayou said.

"I can't accept this."

"Why?"

"You made one for Seely. It meant goodbye."

"This," Alamayou told him, "is like the one for the queen. Not goodbye. Something to see every day."

"Something for the both of us to see. Only on that condition will I take this and hang it somewhere. Not here, mind you." He brushed Alamayou's arm and smiled. "Thank you. For this, and everything else."

"For what?"

"For every night. What you did for me. Making a demand on the bloody queen that I stay here, as if you were the emperor of Africa."

"Ras," Alamayou said.

"I don't know anyone else who would have done that."

"But now?"

"Yes. I know a brave, good man who would do just that. As would I. I hope you know that, Alamayou."

"You would do the same for me?"

"Yes, that's what I said."

"I want to be sure."

"Be sure, Alamayou."

"I am, Philip. You speak English well."

§

CROSSING THE GROUNDS UNDER a vast net of cold, brilliant stars, Alamayou passed the spot where, in the daylight, he'd seen Corbould painting. It was late now and everyone was asleep, but he'd been restless and had come out in hopes that a walk would calm him. The frigid air didn't ease his mind; if anything, his thoughts raced faster. It was as dizzying as the sensation he'd had at the Beshilo, at the *Feroze's* rail. This time, it was the new language pulling at him, teasing him with the thought of falling. All the words.

Choices. Tell them everything. Deviant. I'm nothing like him.

He thought of the expression on the princess's face at the window earlier, as she had watched Corbould paint. He'd seen such an expression before. The memory came to him in Amharic, a relic of the dead past. It had been in his father's eyes. His mother had been the one to cause it. *What must it be like*, his father had asked him, *to be loved?*

He'd seen it in his mother's eyes, as well. It was while she watched the white dream come. And now this princess, her eyes full of the same astonishment.

Love comes for all the weak and wanting hearts. Royal, commoner, orphan. It didn't matter.

It was late when he reached his apartment door. Philip had been asleep when he'd left for his walk, so he meant to creep in as quietly as he could. Their ward was far more isolated than the others, by design so that no visitors strolling through Windsor's halls in search of royal life might instead run into two Negroes setting up house in an apartment of their own. As a result, only their own sounds filled the ward at night. The music of the service—a bucket's squeaking wheels, the slap of spilled water upon hard flooring—were silent by the time the sun went down.

He opened his door and paused, overcome by the need to remain awake, to take this new life in as if he'd never see it again.

Across the room from where he stood, he could see the sighing trees through the apartment window. Their shapes slowly shifted with the winds. The moon shone clear against the pale stone of the castle. Beautiful, and cold. To the right of the window was just a hint of the boundary wall and the ribbons of streams cut into the earth by recent torrents of rain.

Someone strode unsteadily across the frost-crisped grass. He could see them from the doorway, through the window pane. The figure turned once to look back at a closing door in the East Wing. Its interior light extinguished. It had only been a faint glow of gold, as if cast by a single candle. A secret sort of light.

He went to the window, careful not to wake Philip.

The small wavering circle of a lit splint brought the figure out of the dark. It was the queen, he was sure of it. The night and the moon's impressionistic light played a trick, making her shape appear as long as a sexton.

The queen hastily crossed the frigid grounds. He caught a last glimpse of her when she snuffed her splint, her face lunar in the rising cloud of smoke and the eye of a red coal from the tip of her match. Then she was gone at the spur of the main path, and the castle grounds fell into a wintry stillness.

He heard the creak of the entry door to the ward and saw her slip inside. He went to the open apartment door and listened, certain of where the queen was going. After a while, he heard footsteps and the sweep of her long coat against the bare marble floor of the hall. A door opened far down the corridor. When he heard it close again, its soft latch popping the ward's cocoon of quiet, he went down the hall to the portrait room.

A light ignited under the closed portrait room door. Firelight.

He softly rapped on the wood, then entered.

The queen was in her chair, her silhouette trembling before the new fire.

"No sleep for you either," she said, seemingly unsurprised at his presence. "Tomorrow you'll stand before Parliament. You should rest while you can."

"No sleep. Too many thoughts."

"Yes, we know that state of mind well. Come. Sit awhile."

He pulled up a chair to the orange glow of the hearth. Servants had prepared the room for her presence. A pot and a cup sat next to her, untouched. The steam seeped from the teapot lid and curled on the air.

"What have we done to you?" she said, almost to herself. "We wonder. To make you lay your life out before them. It's a difficult decision that we reached, Alamayou."

"You give me a chance. You listen to me, believe me. A stranger. You took me in."

"And yet those are only words."

"All of life is only words. Then you give words to another, the words belong to you and someone else. Your life is known."

"The words we gave to our son earlier were not kind. We regret the words, but not their meaning."

She turned her chair to face Alamayou. To see him.

"We are aware," she said, then shook her head. "I am aware that my children think I'm cruel. I see more than they think I do. I see them walking on their own power into a world far larger than Windsor or England. That world makes way for them because of what *I* have made of them. It acknowledges their strength. It does not choose precipitously against them. Me, my coldness, that's what's responsible for this. I know well what it is that I've set into motion. It began before me and will go on after I'm gone. I place them above everything else, even their love of me. Listen to me on this, Alamayou, because I know this more than I know anything. Survival depends not on love spoken in plain sight. It depends on love spoken silently, deep in the night, when no one is there to witness your heart come apart. Only at night do you become the secret that you truly are. And yet, this bitter truth is one I'm asking you to violate tomorrow, in front of the most powerful body of men in the world. And I don't know if it's the right thing to do or not. The price of my failure is you."

Sounds of movement came from outside. The cumbersome turn of wheels across ice and gravel, the wheezing of horses and the straining squeals of an overburdened cart. *Deliveries*, Alamayou thought. Food, firewood, supplies, anything was possible in the endless stream of commerce that entered Windsor every day at all hours, like animals coming to a watering hole.

The queen gazed up at the family portrait. "I lost my husband in a winter month. Why is that a harder thing, I wonder? He'd been ill for a long time. I loved him, and when he got sick it was as if the country finally realized I could feel anything at all. It took the worst sort of hell to convince them that he mattered. That I mattered."

She reached for her teacup. He took it and filled it for her.

"I remember girls picking armfuls of white lilies just to tie them together in garlands and bring them to the castle gates while the bonfires burned all night in fear of the plague. I was separated from him, you see. I couldn't see him or be near him in his final days. The court physicians said I could catch it, so I was kept away from him. He was alone in the room where you visited me. The Blue Room. All I knew of him was the closed door and his voice from inside. His last breath was a sound I didn't hear. He died by himself."

She set down her cup. "Do you see now, why I decided that you should do this?"

She watched the flames. They found a new green shoot in the kindling and spattered.

"Prove to them that I matter," Alamayou said. "The way you prove to them. The way I prove to you."

"Yes," she said, "and I am so very sorry. Your life is in play now, and for what? I don't know."

"Love."

"I sit here, Alamayou, and I don't know if one such as you can understand love. Maybe you do know, or maybe you know nothing of it. You find someone, and you'll give anything for their love returned to you. You'll live when they touch your hand. In their eyes, you'll see a bright hot star and you'll know, it's yours. And if they leave before you, you'll die. You'll wish you could, but the heart is a stubborn machine that doesn't let you give up so easily. You'll wish you could know that bright hot star once more. Just once. And yet, you'll wish you never knew it."

The firelight slowly died, but Alamayou couldn't get up to rekindle it. She was facing him now, her gaze ferocious. She meant every word to burrow under his skin, take root, and grow. Her face slipped slowly into shadow in time to the waning hearth, and it was if that light pulled away from her.

She looked so dark. She looked like Philip, so much so that he sat back from her, startled. It was the gloom, the embers, and it was her plaintive gaze, her open and unadorned need to know that what she'd lost, someone else had found.

"Is that him?" she asked. "Is that what you see?"

"Yes. You say 'star.' I say 'home.' Both the same. Something no one believes we have, or should have. We don't say it in words. We just live, and that makes it true."

She fell quiet. His eyes adjusted to the gloom and found the painting he'd done, its shape and small figures, the white dream rising behind them.

"I'm afraid," the queen whispered. "I don't want to fail you, Alamayou. I don't want to be the reason you get hurt. If Parliament doesn't accept what you say, they'll send you back. We'll fight, but if we can't, we'll lose you. It will be as if I did it. My hand."

"No." His hand touched hers and she clasped it gratefully. "This. This is all your hand does for me."

He saw her crying, and he wanted to take all the pain out of her. But he wanted it to go on as well, to grow louder and more violent, to rise up and take him like the fire and sea meant to do.

She sees me, Alamayou thought, *and she cries for the day I'm gone.*

"And so." She rose, unsteady on her feet. He took her arm and helped her to the door. "It's settled," she said. "Neither of us will fail the other. You will speak to Parliament tomorrow evening, and they'll see. You'll make them see, Alamayou. I know you. Make them see you as I do."

He opened the door and stepped back for her. She walked past, down the darkened hall to its end. "Get some sleep," she called before turning the corner. "Your queen commands you."

§

AFTER SHE WAS GONE, Alamayou went out to the spur of the Long Walk. It was almost morning, and the first signs of the sunrise tinted the sky in burnt red and sienna, resting like a stilled ripple of sea along the horizon line where the cartmen's traps kicked up dust clouds as they filed in.

He turned and walked back to the ward. Counting windows up and across, he found their apartment and the Blue Room. The queen's silhouette kept watch over Windsor.

It struck him that he needed no light, no moon, to find the way back to where he lived. *I know this place,* he thought, *and it knows me.*

The queen was right. He ought to sleep while he could, even if it was only a few hours. The day would bring with it a test unlike any he'd ever faced. Nothing in Abyssinia could have prepared him for the sort of war he had to wage, and win. He'd never been further from the man his father wanted him to be. A soldier, a killer of other men.

And because of that, he'd never been closer to becoming the sort of man he wanted to be.

I'm lij, he thought. *At least for one more day. A prince of Abyssinia, fighting for a life where I'll no longer be lij. Just a man, allowed to live like anyone else.*

He couldn't bring himself to go back to the apartment. He wanted to wait for the sun to crest the horizon and see for himself its red rounded dome pushing up into the sky as it turned bright and hot. When it did, he would be under it. Then Philip would wake, come to the window and see him here. *Yes,* he thought, *the world has to listen to what I want from it, just this once. Philip will see. The prince and princess, the queen, too.* He wanted them to see him standing unafraid at the precipice of the day they'd all helped him reach.

A man looks at everyone or no one, his father said.

Or he looks past them all, abat, to the life waiting beyond them, and he walks right through them and claims it for his own.

Chapter Fifteen

5 January 1869

IN THE AFTERNOON, SIMON helped Alamayou dress for his appearance before Parliament. He outfitted Alamayou in shale trousers, a long frock coat, polished boots, and a silk scarf. "For every war," Simon told him, "there is a uniform. You'll at least look the part of a gentleman. Is there anything else you need?"

"No. Thank you."

"There's no cause to thank the service."

"Thank you."

"There have been others, you know. Sara Bonetta Forbes. The Indian. They come and go. Her Majesty's heart is big. That's what I thought when you and the other one washed up on our doorstep. Big heart, more dark orphans of one storm or another." His lips tightened, as if the words had gone sour in his mouth. "I haven't seen her like this before, though. Not with any of them. Clearly there's something about you, lost on me though it may be."

"She's afraid for me," Alamayou said.

"Yes, she is."

He used a horsehair brush to clean stray threads from Alamayou's coat. "They may well be rough on you, you know."

"Yes."

"More than a young man deserves, I'd say, though it's not my place. Just go speak to them as she's asked of you, and don't make a mess of it. I may have my differences with you both, but you're nothing compared to the bloody politicians. I'll not tolerate you breaking that good woman's heart, you hear?"

"I won't. I'll try, Simon."

"Off with you, then. Don't go and get yourself killed."

Outside, two carriages waited on the horseshoe drive. One took Alamayou and Philip while the other carried the Imperial State Crown, the Cap of Maintenance, and the Sword of State. They were traditional symbols which the queen would use to open the Parliamentary session.

A third extravagant coach carried the royal family.

The sun set as their caravan passed through the quiet city on the way to Westminster. The last golden light shone across the Thames onto the Middlesex Bank. Soon the towers rose above London's skyline. The Royal Standard flew between their torchières.

They pulled up to a crowd waiting at Westminster's gates. A group of men gathered behind the bars near the Sovereign's Entrance. Ambassador Naismith stood among them.

The royal coachman handed out the queen, followed by Princess Louise and Prince Leopold, who leaned heavily upon his cane. Another bout of weakness was upon him.

"Welcome, Your Majesty," the Lord Speaker said, bowing deeply with the other members of Parliament. "You grace us."

"We would not have missed this opportunity to bear witness," the queen said.

The MPs led the queen and her entourage through a lush garden to the entrance beneath the King's Tower. A burst of magnificent chimes drew Alamayou's eyes to a grand clock soaring to the clouds, its architecture in stately, perfect rhythm with the music it made. Its pinnacles were decorated with statues of saints. The clock face itself was shaped like a rose, with petals fringed in gold and windows lined above and around it to the slate roof and a spire made up of a crown, flowers, a cross, and an iron pyramid. When it chimed, the clock tower sent its bells across London and her canopying sky.

Naismith walked alongside Alamayou and Philip. Alamayou knew he was being observed closely.

"Nothing like it anywhere," Naismith commented. "I've always thought of it as no different than England herself." He picked up his pace and walked ahead to the entrance. "Fire almost destroyed her nearly four decades ago. It's a horror, what fire can do. Don't you agree, Alamayou?"

"A building," Alamayou said. "You can build again. People are different. Once they're gone—"

As she paused to admire the lovingly manicured Speakers' garden and attendant path, the queen glanced in his direction and nodded encouragingly. She held a gloved hand up ever so slightly. *Say no more.*

"I don't expect you to understand how important permanence is to our culture," Naismith said, "but to us, it's a tragic loss when something as old and important as this building is damaged, for any reason let alone because it rots from within."

He placed his hand on the surface of the tower wall. "Anstone. It was quarried in South Yorkshire and Mansfield, Woodhouse and Nottinghamshire. Those names are the stuff of legend. It was brought across the Chesterfield Canal and the North Sea, the Trent and the Thames. Our history is in this great clock tower."

"My father felt the same way about Meqdala," Alamayou said. "It fell."

The queen passed Naismith on her way into the Sovereign's Entrance. "We don't dwell on weaknesses, Ambassador. We see wisdom in the stone. Wisdom brings with it the wear of the effort to acquire it, and then to bear its weight. We cannot help but observe how light and unblemished you are."

The princess followed her mother. She smiled at Naismith. "Are you not pleased that your queen chose Session to emerge?"

"Endlessly, Highness."

He stepped into the line of Parliamentary Lords and nobles heading to the western slope of the Upper House.

Inside the entrance, Alamayou and Philip found themselves at the foot of twenty granite steps, flanked on either side with uniformed men of the Cavalry Household Regiment, the Blues and Royals. They unsheathed their swords to form a tunnel of razors.

Attendants ushered the queen into the Robing Room at the south end of the palace axis, where she sat in an ornate Chair of State. Behind her hung a purple tapestry stitched with the Royal Arms.

Two servants robed her in ermine and silk. They placed the Imperial State Crown on her head. It was encrusted with precious jewels and its base was a pattern of *fleur de lis* and half-arches surmounted by a cross. The cap itself was bordered with snowy white fur.

"We shall be there with you," she said as her attendants closed the doors.

Others brought Alamayou and Philip to the Norman Porch, where they were told to wait in the foursquare landing beneath a ceiling intricately inlaid with cross vaults, lierne ribs, plinths, and columns clustered together like a stand of ribbed oaks.

"Philip." Alamayou pressed his ear to a closed set of doors. He heard the thrum of voices. "So many."

He began to pace the stone in frantic rings as sweat broke out across his face.

"Do what you've already done," Philip reassured him. "That's all you need to do. Pay their white faces no mind and give them no more power than they already have. You've got the queen on your side."

"To speak to them is leaving," Alamayou said. "I feel it, Philip."

He slid to the floor, near the entryway. Behind him, the rising tide of men in the chamber made the door quiver.

"Listen to me, Alamayou." Philip sat on the cold stone next to him. "Make them understand, you're not what they believe. You're what she believes. You're what I believe. We can't be what we truly are. Maybe in our quiets. But at no other time. I know you. You're just like me. We were children who prayed they'd wake up and be a different sort of boy, and now we're men who know that prayers don't get heard and they don't get answered, and so we've made peace with being alone until now. Are you like me? That you can't be at peace because of me?"

"Yes."

"Then this is the price. You understand what I'm saying."

He searched Philip's face because the courage was draining out of him and taking his new language. A terrible cold filled the void left behind. It was a frigid, spreading sensation that infected every part of him.

It's what drowning in the sea would have been like, he thought. *I'll lay out my life like a map for the men in the other room, and they won't believe me. They won't see me.*

Or they will, a voice told him, *but not like the queen. Not like the princess, not like Philip. They'll see you the way I did, lij. Gbra sadom. And they'll hate the monster they see.*

Philip put his hand next to Alamayou's. "Remember the rail?"

Alamayou's eyes widened.

"No," Philip said. "Not at night. The next morning. Your hand next to mine. You didn't understand yet, but I was telling you, see, we're alike as shadows. You're not alone. Not while I'm here next to you."

"I remember. Not alone. I called it from the window of the apartment when you were leaving."

"After the rockets and that miserable fortress model, right? I'd been thrown out by then. I was walking, but I stopped because I thought I heard you calling to me. But now we're here and look, there's our hands, again. Telling our story."

"I see them. Every night I see that story. Know that, Philip."

"This is all we have, Alamayou."

"I know. Maybe somewhere, though. It could be different."

Their hands brushed each other and remained.

"Then live," Philip said, knowing full well where they were and who they were around. He knew his words could make the road to Alamayou's damnation smooth and fast if someone were to hear, so he kept his voice low. But he needed to speak. He couldn't be silent anymore.

"Live," he said, "and come back to me. You and me, we'll find home. I swear we will. We'll close the door and there'll be no one else. Just us. Just what we want to say and do, and no one can hear us but each other. And the world will fall away and we won't care. Our world will still be. We'll still be standing together, but you have to live to make it there, Alamayou."

The double doors opened. "Parliament awaits," a red-coated soldier announced.

§

THEY FOLLOWED THE GUARD through the Royal Gallery, past the feet of Caen stone statues under a ceiling paneled in Tudor rose and lions. Their path soon crossed with that of the queen's, and they fell into rank behind the princess and her Honor Guard escort to the end, in the Lords Chamber.

The chamber was cavernous. Its red benches brimmed on all three sides of the room with members. To the right were the Spirituals, the bishops and archbishops of England's Church. To the left, the Temporals, England's masters of the purse and the law.

A gold Canopy and Throne stood at the south end, next to the chairs of state. The queen took her place on it while the prince and princess sat next to her. The Lord Chancellor sat on the Woolsack, an armless red cushion. The House mace hung menacingly behind him.

There was an empty lectern awaiting Alamayou. He crossed the floor and stood behind it as the sea of white faces stared at him.

The queen feared for him. He could see it in the rigid stone of her expression, and in the way her eyes went wide at the sight of him at the head of the Parliamentary session.

The princess and prince, too, they feared. Leopold clutched his cane tightly enough to splinter it. Louise's radiant beauty was hidden behind a raised kerchief. The light glimmered in her wet eyes.

He waved at them to let them know he was ready.

Naismith sat among the Temporals. A stack of papers was tucked neatly under the arm of his coat. He studied Alamayou intently.

Alamayou returned his steady gaze, his father's long-ago words in his head. *A man looks at everyone, or he looks at no one.*

The Lord Chancellor raised his hand for quiet. "God save the queen!"

The Chamber resounded with the blessing.

The queen raised notes of her own. "We come to you not only to open Parliament, but pray to open Parliament's heart. We thank you for convening so that you may hear from a young man. A stranger, brought to England to find the peace so absent from his turbulent life. We ask that you listen and see in him what we see. Someone who deserves a home with us."

She set down her paper and nodded at Alamayou.

"Alamayou," Naismith shouted. "Are you ready to answer the charges awaiting you in Abyssinia?"

"Yes. I am."

"And you're comfortable speaking our language. You understand fully?"

"I do."

"Then the floor is yours."

A deep breath. "Yes," Alamayou said to them all.

And then they began, the words of his true life.

Chapter Sixteen

THE CHAMBER WAS SILENT when he finished. Several uncomfortable moments of stillness ticked by. Parliamentary members stared at each other as the queen's eyes roamed the room, searching for signs of their intent.

Naismith finally broke the quiet. "We will discuss all that we've heard today, and then we will render our judgment. There are, to be sure, serious allegations before this Chamber. They must be addressed in the appropriate manner and in due course. It, therefore, remains an open record."

The queen stood, dragging the rest of the Chamber up with her. She removed her crown and left it on the throne. "You have your answers. He remains under our care and we will keep him safe while you see your way clear to the right and only outcome. Free him of these unjust accusations. We expect nothing less, gentlemen."

"Is there anything else you wish to add to your account, Alamayou?" Naismith asked.

"No."

"I have something, for your auspicious record."

The Parliamentary members turned to see Prince Leopold leaning unsteadily on his cane as he stood. "When he came to us, he was a stranger. We took him in. We listened to him. Some of us, closer than others. But now there can be no doubt. All of you have heard him. I have heard him."

He smiled at Alamayou. "He's not a stranger any longer."

§

PARLIAMENT'S DECISION CAME SHORTLY after midnight.

It arrived in the hands of a courier who delivered it to the castle in a simple, sealed envelope. Simon accepted it and brought it to the prince and princess first.

"I ask for your guidance," Simon explained apologetically. "If it's bad news, I don't know how Her Majesty will react. I'm just a butler, in the end."

"It's for us to do," Princess Louise said.

She sent word through the lady-in-waiting asking for an audience with her mother. By the time she and the prince closed the door to the Blue Room behind them, word had spread through the castle. Parliament's decision on Alamayou's fate had come down.

§

"'FOR THE CRIMES OF war, and for the crime of deviance, it is the decision of this body that the prince Alamayou be remitted immediately to Annesley Bay, Abyssinia, by ship which shall be requisitioned for the purpose of transmittal in a day's time at the Royal Victorian docks. In Abyssinia, Alamayou shall be held in custody until the conclusion of a trial under Abyssinian law.'"

The queen put down the letter. She took off her glasses and set them on the table next to her, then picked up her teacup. Her hand shook, spilling some tea onto her black dress.

"Damn it all!" She hurled the cup against the wall, shattering it.

Princess Louise knelt to pick up the shards of porcelain.

"To hell with that," the queen said, regaining her poise. "Summon Grant. We need to discuss our options now that Parliament has utterly betrayed us."

"Mother," Prince Leopold said tentatively, "forgive me. I'm as heartsick as you about what's happened, but this was to be expected. I don't know how we can fight for him. He is what he is."

"He'll die." The princess picked up the last of the broken cup and placed it on the tray. "Let's be plain. There won't be a trial in Abyssinia. Or if there is, it will be a farce. What law? Who is even in charge there? Our governor? He's a figurehead. Alamayou is heir to the bloodline of a despot who was hated by every man, woman, and child in that godforsaken country. For that alone they'll hang him. We can't pretend we send him to anything but his death."

"Be quiet," the queen said. "Both of you."

The knell. The bells were hushed, that the queen and her children heard ringing. Not the majestic peels of St. George, but rather the slight ones of the tiny church outside Windsor.

They listened to the frail bells. In the moment of their ringing, the lands around Windsor felt empty. The tops of the clouds outside the portrait room window held all the light within them, and the earth below gathered beneath the graying bellies of them and grew dimmer.

"In our life," the queen said, "we have opened our heart a precious few times, and it always comes round to punishment. Always. There comes the moment when our heart is turned away. Our own people think us cruel. But we opened our home and our heart to him. And now, we'll fight until we can't any longer. We must try, or else everything that's said of us is proved true. Whatever is thought of us, we would do the same were it one of our children. We would walk to hell and home again."

"He's not one of your children," Prince Leopold said.

"No, he's not. But he's no longer an orphan or a stranger, as you yourself said."

She went to the door. "We owe it to him that he hear this from us."

§

THE QUEEN POSTED SIMON to the corridor outside their apartment, under instruction not to open it or allow anyone near.

"This is how you will refer to him," she told Simon. "Should anyone come to their apartment and inquire, all is calm. He's ill and is not to be disturbed. If we receive any further communications from Parliament or Ambassador Naismith, we will hear of it immediately and no one else."

After the door was shut, the queen gave Parliament's letter to Philip and Alamayou. The room fell silent while Philip read it.

"Do you understand?" the queen asked him.

Outside the apartment window, the morning came in a slow growing violet sheen to the east. Sliver by sliver, the snow-covered garden and the lawns revealed themselves. The light crept into the room, sliding across the floor and to the painting Alamayou had made for Philip.

"I understand very well," Philip said.

"Alamayou, do you understand what they wish to do?"

"Yes."

"Then understand this, as well. We are not here to bemoan, but to think. No one else hears of what we discuss. Now, what do we know?"

"We know the staff is already suspicious that Parliament ruled against us," the prince said exhaustedly.

"You've seen them ferrying tea and food to the soldiers at the gate," Princess Louise added. "We know where their sympathies lie. It's not too much to presume that one of them might be speaking to a compatriot in Parliament's service, or to an MP."

"Which is to suggest what?" the prince asked.

"That if we choose the option of helping Alamayou escape, Parliament and Naismith will know about it and we'll be crushed under the weight of scandal."

"Were we speaking of escape?"

"It's one choice that bears close scrutiny." The princess poured tea for herself, her mother, and her brother. "Do you not agree?"

"No," Leopold said. "No, I don't. I can't."

"We could house Alamayou somewhere near, or send him as far away as we possibly can," the princess continued. "Maybe not here in London. He'd be found. Peharps that's true of anywhere on the continent, in time. But if he lost himself in a city we may never see him again. Cities have their ways with strangers. Though is it better that way, I wonder? His fate is certain if he's found. Maybe it would be better that he disappear, for his sake and our own, in such a way that we never know of him."

"Country before all," the prince said. "How can you even speak of this?"

"There is fighting them," the queen said, quieting her children, "and there's sending Alamayou away. Any other option brings this monarchy down. Make no mistake. And don't think we haven't considered assisting his escape already, and may still. But if we come to that, it will be because nothing else has worked, and we then weigh whether his life is worth the end of our reign."

"Just bloody stop, all of you!"

Philip crushed Parliament's letter in his fist. He couldn't stand any more, listening to them speaking of Alamayou as if he were a chess piece to be moved at their whim. The apartment spun sickeningly and he felt his bile rise. Sadness, regret, even guilt, all of it he saw in the faces of the royals. The queen especially. It only made his anger burn brighter, and when the words came flooding out of him, he didn't try to stop them.

"Why?" he screamed at the queen. "Why did you make him say what he said? For what? Nothing! Send me away. I don't care. This is his death and I won't let you take him!"

"We share your sentiments on this—" the prince began, but Philip cut him off.

"Sentiments? Options? You're murderers if you let them take Alamayou. On *that*, make no mistake. I saved your life. I could have let you die. I didn't. He didn't. This is a debt you all have to pay back. He didn't ask to be brought here. He didn't ask for any of this."

"And where do you think he'd be if we hadn't?" the prince said.

"This is difficult enough without our being at each other's throats," the princess said. "Our solicitor will be here in the morning, first thing. It's our queen's intent to explore every option. You've heard her on this. Every damn one. She'll fight and she's formidable."

"More words." Philip dismissed her with an angry wave of his hand. "In a turn of the earth he'll be under arrest and on a ship bound for Abyssinia, and you'll be where? In a castle, eating and sleeping with others tending to you."

The prince jabbed at the air with his cane. "Now see here—"

"*Enough.*"

The queen rubbed her temples, trying to ward off the merciless pain growing behind her eyes. While they all argued, a deep resonating shame swelled in her chest, and it would surely burst if Alamayou were to turn from the apartment window and just look at her.

But he hadn't turned.

"Alamayou?" she asked quietly. "Please, you mustn't give up. We're standing with you."

Alamayou walked past her, past all of them, to the apartment door. He opened it and left without a word.

"Wait!" Philip cried. "Let me come with you—"

The queen held up a hand, stopping him. "Give him time. We've much to discuss. Let him breathe free of us, a royal family helplessly flailing about."

"That's you," Philp said. "Not me. I may not be as bloody highborn and smart as the lot of you, but I don't talk. I act. That's what he needs now."

He left to go after Alamayou.

§

ALAMAYOU STOOD AT A parapet atop the Round Tower, looking out at the rolling countryside. The soft chiming he'd heard came from the church he'd stopped at. It was so small, so modest, and yet it was capable of holding so much. Even memories of his old life that shouldn't find a place anywhere in this new world.

Standing on top of the Round Tower felt no different than standing at the parapet of Meqdala and looking out across the gorge at the cottage on Amba Geshen, the way he'd done the night before the attack began. Chained to its wall as the war moved into place around him, in the form of Abyssinian soldiers at the gate and English soldiers across the Falah, he'd tried to pretend that he was a stranger and not part of any of it. The cottage was just a small place where someone lived. It didn't mean anything and was hardly worth taking notice of, let alone remembering.

His eyes filled, making the church shimmer in his vision as if it were on fire.

I'm not ready.

There have been times when I thought I was ready. I don't know what comes after. I've never believed what you believe, abat. I don't believe in heaven, God, or angels living in the clouds. I only believed in the clouds I saw, not yours.

I did believe you once, when you said I was a monster. For so long, I thought you had to be right about me. You were emperor of the visible world. You couldn't die. What didn't you know?

Since then, I've seen things that someone like me was never meant to see. An unimaginable city. Royals of another country. Castles and a life beyond what I knew. Even you never saw what I've seen.

I've come to know someone who I matter to. Now I'm not ready to die. But I'm going to. I can feel it.

Maybe I should. Maybe you were right about me after all.

He stepped closer to the parapet. It was wide enough to stand in but low enough to climb easily. *Up here,* he thought, *I'm high enough to end everything. No one has to fight for me anymore. They don't need to risk everything for someone like me.*

The world below pulled at him. It wanted to have him. He climbed up.

You were wrong about so much, abat. But maybe you and anat were right about this. Maybe there's no home for me anywhere.

He held himself steady as the frigid wind lashed at him. It roared in his ears and erased the gentle ring of the church bells. It took away the dream of the life he thought he could have. Long, full of years, alongside another.

Philip.

We can have it, but you have to live, Alamayou.

He hesitated. The noise in his head felt like the war. Two opposing forces fighting for a foothold that would break the other. On one side, his old life telling him he never should have left on a hopeless search like the one he was on, for a place to belong.

On the other, too soft to be heard, Philip telling him to be a hard son of a bitch and live. *Live like you already have been. Don't you see? What do you think you've been doing since Meqdala fell? Surviving. That's how life starts. You're born, you breathe, and it's a struggle. You eat, and it's a struggle. And on the way, you learn to care, and love, and suddenly you're living. Suddenly you want to.*

He leaned forward, then back, teasing the world below with the possibility of claiming him. *I've survived,* he thought. *I didn't want to be there among them, crossing Abyssinia for months, leaving the shores of my land for the first time in my life to float on top of the sea, all the way here. I didn't know where I wanted to be. Just somewhere deep and lost.*

I was so scared, abat. Anat. The way you always saw me. A scared, weak monster. Men crawled like insects through the masts and ropes of that ship. Blades of cloud drifted by on their journey to other places. Philip told me things I couldn't understand. "Home." Philip's hands couldn't find a way to make me understand that word, not until they swept the deck of the Feroze, *then the ceiling of sky, and then pointed at my heart. 'Gone, Alamayou.' He waved it all away. My whole life from then on. Everything.*

He was wrong, anat. I didn't lose everything. I didn't realize it then, but up here, right now, I see it. If I stayed with you, if there'd been no war, I would have jumped from Meqdala, or the cliffs at Jedda. You would have killed me one way or the other, abat. And anat would have watched. Don't think I don't know.

Death stopped for me when I finally left the both of you.

§

WHEN PHILIP FOUND HIM, Alamayou was standing near the parapet. Philip's heart raced, thinking Alamayou was there again. At that place where jumping seemed the only way left to him.

"I'm right here," he said. "Behind you."

"I know you are, Philip."

He joined Alamayou and together they took in the dawning countryside.

"I was afraid when I saw you just now," Philip told him. "I thought you were going to jump."

"I still could."

"Then you'd be dragging my sorry self right down with you."

"You wouldn't."

Philip took hold of his hand. "Try me."

"I have. Twice."

"That's right. You have." He let go. "And I'm going to trust that you make the same decision now."

As the sun rose higher, it opened up more of the land. Dusty roads frozen over, leading to small clusters of villages with chimney smoke curling into the cold sky. Small writhing dots on the white hills that were herds of cows, searching for green shoots beneath the snow. Tiny figures in carts, making their way.

"I've always had fear," Alamayou said, "since I came here, that it's a dream and I never really left. I think it started at the rail that night."

The black liquid shadows of birds passed over the Round Tower, breaking into his remembrance. They flew beneath the rising light, and when they dipped in a mass down to the ground and the church, they resembled falling bodies.

"I was so sick."

"I remember," Philip said, wrapping his arms around himself to ward off the deep chill. "You had a horrible fever and I thought you'd die."

"You never left me, even to eat. I couldn't understand what anyone wanted of me. I looked to you, as if you could say any of it in words I could understand. You moved your hands and gave me my second English word, after 'home,' 'drink,' when they brought me medicines. Remember?"

"I do. You were as stubborn then as you are now. Practically had to pour it down your throat."

"I asked for new words and you would find one that you could make with your hands. We learned. Stars were fingers painting dots on the ceiling. Sleep, eat."

"That's how we figured out how to speak to each other. Listen to you now."

"At the rail that night, I thought I saw my father and mother."

They'd been at sea for weeks. On the night before they reached London, the seas were calmer. The *Feroze* and the other ships had crossed into a different place, one where the air moved in a new way. Fog covered everything. It clung to the tops of the waves.

"I was still sick with the fever and I couldn't stay in the cabin anymore. I went up into the last bit of light, thinking that maybe I might see the place they were taking me. I thought it would look like Meqdala because I'd never seen anywhere else. It would look like abat's fortress. The world would look like everything he'd ever built because he could reach that far. Then I remembered, he couldn't reach past his own death.

"Everywhere was the sea, but I couldn't tell. The waves swept past and the fog took it all away. There was no end to anything, no matter where I looked. I couldn't even see the other ships.

"I thought I heard someone calling my name. I know now, it was the last of the fever, making my mind sick the way it made my body sick. But I thought I heard anat. Then I thought I saw her."

He closed his eyes and she was there again. A shuffling figure struggling to walk across the deck to him, burned to a twist of a human being.

"Alamayou," Philip said. "You never told me. I would have said it was all the fever. I would have helped you understand."

"I saw her walk past me to the rail. I followed her because she asked me to. She used her hands to tell me, like you did. I thought it meant she loved me.

"But when I got to the rail, I saw abat in the water. He was waiting for her and for me. The clouds parted; they made room for us. He floated on top of the waves like a piece of Meqdala after the rockets. 'Come with us,' they said. It was so easy to believe, Philip. It's what they'd say to me if they could. It's what they said in the fire."

He put his hand on the parapet stone, steadying himself against the feeling of falling. It was still rippling through him.

"I could see how easy it would be.

"But then I heard something on deck, and I knew that the new sound was true. It was real, not the fever. I turned and saw you. You held out your hand for me, the way you did before. The hand that told me things. I saw your black hands, Philip, reaching for me before I went after my parents.

"When I turned back to the rail, they were both gone. There was just a bit of light, and if they'd been real, they would have seen that I stayed behind, on deck. They'd see me choosing the world to come, not them and their white dream.

"I want more time," Alamayou said. "I don't want to die."

"And you won't. I swear to you. Come inside before you get sick again. God knows what you'll see then."

He climbed down from the parapet and they went back to the apartment, where the royals waited for them.

"You look cold," the queen said.

"I was," Alamayou told her.

FOUR

Chapter Seventeen

THE ENGLISH LANDSCAPE GARDEN at Clermont was a maze of crisscrossing lanes, trees, and carefully tended swaths of greenery. Floral sculptures in the shapes of animals, spiraling trellises, and patterns that curled like the chambers of seashells lined picturesque walking paths. A stranger to the grounds could easily lose his way and wander for hours, and Rabbi Ariel was every bit the stranger.

Princess Louise slipped her arm through his and led him around the gentle slope of the lake, every so often breaking the serene quiet of their stroll with a gesture at one of the neighboring estates.

Ahead of them, a cluster of children raced through the trees and around a small pond, sending the geese into panicked, skittering flight across the top of the still surface.

"Orphans," Princess Louise said. "We bring them here from time to time. A bit of beauty and peace in a turbulent life is necessary, don't you think?"

"I do, and what better place can there be? It's beautiful here."

"It is, isn't it?"

They paused to rest on a bench. "Do you see that estate?" she asked. "It's home to Helena, my brother Leopold's widow. Our mother purchased it for her. She's a good woman. She loved Leo when no other woman would have him. His blood flaw, you know, and how it swam upstream through the royal line. It's common knowledge now, but not then. Everyone else found the thought of his disease repellant. Not her. They had two good years together."

She smiled as a valet struggled to catch one of the younger girls, a towheaded beauty, in a game of tag. It only took the valet a moment to pull up short, huffing while the girl rolled on the grass contentedly.

From their spot beneath the lakeside rotunda, Rabbi Ariel admired the scene before him. Across the lake was an amphitheater where old plays were put on by Oxford's finest thespian classes beneath boughs of ringed tree groves. The lake fed canals and dams and was as quaint as any enchanted forest in one of the children's bedtime books. Sighing beds of reeds, cattails, and cottony wisps undulated in the gently lapping water. The lake washed to the foot of the grounds and moistened the roots of ancient elms.

All was silent. Rabbi Ariel heard only the wind threading the leaves and the occasional giggle. The children had continued on and were far away across the grounds.

"What will happen now?" he asked.

"Parliament will have its say. And my guess is they'll demand that their original sentence be carried out, that Alamayou should be sent back to Abyssinia."

"You do believe it's him, then. The man who speaks to you from a prison cell, who told you everything from the shape of Windsor to the meaning of an orange. You believe he's really Alamayou."

The valet almost had the girl but, clever child, she feinted right and left the helpless man grasping at air. She turned and laughed as the valet took a seat on a bench and pretended to pass out.

"Yes," Princess Louise said. "I believe it's really him. If ever I doubted him, all doubt left me when he again recalled his life in Abyssinia. I remember him as a much younger man, speaking of his father murdering that boy, and his mother beckoning him to the fire. I remember his eyes then. I saw the same eyes between the bars at the Old Bailey."

"So there's hope?"

"Only this. What my mother didn't do the first time. A pardon."

"Does she know of him yet?"

"I sent word to her."

"What does she say?"

"Nothing. She's said nothing. I've asked her through her service but she hasn't yet responded to me."

"You haven't seen her yourself."

"Don't act surprised, Rabbi. Growing up, this is what we knew of our mother. Once every month or so, we would have an appointment with her so she could inspect us as we made the circle, or practiced a dance, or read from Tennyson. We would see her at functions. News of our education and our health came through nurses and nannies, teachers and her service. She wasn't cruel. It's just how these things were done. She was raised the same way, and it's all she knew. I can still remember the woman she used to be, but she disappeared long ago, when I was still a young child. I remember one night, I had a dream that caused me to cry out. She came to me and said, 'You're too old for nonsense.' That was the last time I remember her coming to me herself, and that was also the last time I let myself truly need her. I haven't felt for her since. Not until recently, when she became so ill. Now she needs me to care for her. I've become the mother, it seems.

"Death is very near to her now," the princess said, looking at him as if he could explain how her life had gone through so odd a reversal. "I know I'll see her soon enough, but in truth it may be too late by the time I do."

This is all wrong, Rabbi Ariel thought. *While Alamayou sits in prison, looking at his death yet again, I'm sitting by a lake and watching the swans land, fold their wings, and settle back into their gliding passage across the surface, and a child still at the beginning of her life runs beneath the cold, bright blue sky. I'm talking calmly with the princess about a doomed man.*

He's not just a doomed man. He's my friend for thirty years.

"You can't let her die without seeing him," he told the princess. "Once she meets him, she'll believe him and she'll save him."

Princess Louise laughed bitterly. "My mother believed the very same thing of Parliament."

"Then why didn't she pardon him?"

The little girl ran past them, waving at the princess as she chased a wayward swan from the shore to the Belvedere Tower.

"Her solicitor explained it as a matter of legal permissibility, or some such, but that's not truly why. Her court, her counselors, and her closest advisers all told her that the repercussions would have been too great. Even Leopold told her that he feared what would happen. And she listened."

"Then I beg of you, Your Highness, tell me why you called me here."

The girl's head of countless curls disappeared in a thicket of lushly cultivated sunflowers.

"I think my brother would delight in his own children," Princess Louise said. "I think he'd pause at each mention of their names to marvel. Such a wondrous thing, to see aspects of ourselves in those we love, don't you think?"

"My late wife and I, we both loved the same music. The same paintings."

"It's not that."

The child's peeling laughter made them both turn to see the valet carrying her aloft.

"Over the years, my mother told me of the night she and Alamayou spoke of love. 'The bright hot star,' as she called it." She shook her head. "I always thought it an odd, romantic notion and completely out of character for her. Not at all like the woman I grew up with. Perhaps I felt a bit of envy, if I'm being completely truthful, that Alamayou saw glimpses of her secret self that I never saw. And I'll never truly understand why he did. But some other part of me wanted to believe in love the way they described it to each other that night. That it finds us all at some point if we can just be patient, live our lives, and try not to drive ourselves mad with the wait. It doesn't find us all, Rabbi. I can say that now. My husband is a decent man. He's not cruel to me nor to others. I shall not ask for more, and I've learned the tender art of not looking for more. I thought I saw it once, with another. But it doesn't matter now."

"Corbould."

"May I tell you something, about him? It's such a silly and stupid conceit now that I look back on it from this far away in time. But then, I felt certain that I could always see into Edward. Right into him. Into his lungs and veins, into his heart and his thoughts. I would always know if he thought of me. If his love ebbed one day and surged the next. I'd know by the color of his paints or the tilt of his head. But I knew nothing at all. He was kind and patient to a young girl with whose mother he wanted to curry favor, and perhaps he did care a bit for me, but when he left court, I never heard from him again. That was an odd and uprooting thing to accept, that I could feel so strongly and yet be so wrong. In that moment I learned. My heart is quite apart from the rest of me. I don't expect it's so different for anyone else, including my mother and Alamayou. And so, for all this time I've presumed love to be fiction. A lie parents tell their children at bedtime.

"Corbould's gone now. He's just another person who has passed out of life. *That* is where I've seen it, Rabbi. I've seen true, real love only in death. Isn't that sad? I saw it in my mother when my father died. I saw it in her when Leopold died. Yes, I saw it when Parliament acted with Alamayou. These were losses she couldn't stop."

She stood. "That's why I'm not going to rest until she hears Alamayou herself. Let the fact of him give her the peace I never could."

He watched the princess summon the valet over. He brought the little girl so Princess Louise could brush the curls from the child's face while he still carried her.

"Wait to hear from me," Princess Louise called back to Rabbi Ariel.

He waved to the princess in acknowledgement of her request. Alamayou's best chance, he knew, was a lonely princess who'd spent her life trying to fill the holes in two hearts. Hers, and her mother's, even as her mother sought to fill her own heart.

Such a wondrous thing, she'd said. To see aspects of ourselves in those we love.

Yes, he thought while watching the princess and the little girl, two fatherless daughters cuddling each other against the cold. *It is a wondrous thing to see.*

Chapter Eighteen

8 January 1869

IN THE MORNING, THE queen called Alamayou and Philip to the Grand Reception Room, a space more than one hundred feet long and forty feet high. There, she waited with the prince, princess, and Lord Grant beneath a set of massive Gobelins French tapestries.

Taking a seat on the other side of a marble table almost half the length of the room, Philip felt at once dwarfed and humbled by the power on display. He supposed that was the queen's purpose, to convey her strength to them all.

"We wish to know our options," the queen said.

Lord Grant was neatly dressed in a fitted gray suit. His hair was parted and oiled. A treatise lay open on the side table before him, together with a thick sheaf of papers. He consulted them frequently and spoke calmly, with great authority.

"The moment Parliament handed down its findings," he said, "a ship was commissioned for the voyage to Abyssinia. It's docked at the Royal as we speak. I must tell you, their decree states that he will be brought to that ship before dawn tomorrow."

"We need no reminding of that fact," the queen said. "We have time to weep in private. Now is the time for planning."

Alamayou felt a strange stirring to have it all over with, to face it now while he had even a little strength in his body. As he stood at the window of the room listening to Lord Grant begin to recite laws, rules, and ways to fight within their bounds and outside of them, he felt his heart turn at the idea of going back. He sent himself to that ship—it looked just like the *Feroze*—to its decks and tiny cabins, a belly full of some other country's broken pieces, and a rail. He sent himself across the sea to Abyssinia's shores at Annesley. He gave himself over to the men of all the tribes who would be there to see him.

He would give them everything if he had to go back. All the stories of his father and mother. He would give them the war and the fire, the Rassam drawing, and the whip in his hands. He would hold nothing back. Because he'd lived with every door closed, and now he saw what his life looked like when one opened to let the light in.

He would describe everything except Philip. Philip was something other than just life. That would remain inside, only seen at night.

He listened to the queen and her solicitor debate a future he no longer felt sure he'd see.

"We can seek asylum," Lord Grant continued. "We can make a formal complaint about the oppressive and malicious treatment he received in Abyssinia before and during the war, and how there exists no reasonable basis to believe that such treatment forms precedent for what should befall him if he returns. If we are to believe the accounts of the populace and their sentiments toward the late emperor, his fate is dark indeed. We might well explore whether sufficient grounds exist to assert formally that he's a ward of England and the Crown. But that won't, in all likelihood, change what took place yesterday in Parliament. Or why it happened, which is perhaps the more important issue."

He fell silent.

"Do continue," the queen prompted him.

"Well, I… How does one put this delicately?"

"One doesn't," the queen interjected. "We believe we have heard all there is to hear. We do doubt highly the ability of a barrister, even such as yourself, to shock us at this point. Cause time to slow, perhaps."

"Yes, of course. Forgive me, Your Majesty. As I was saying, I am concerned. There is the matter of the deaths of his parents in the fire, and his role in it, as alleged. Before, Alamayou's was a credible account of that fire and how his parents came to their ends. It refuted what others sought to make of it, and served as a basis to believe that he played no part in it."

"But now?" Princess Louise asked. "Has something about the fact of what happened changed? Because I'm aware of no such thing."

"As to the facts surrounding the tragedy on Amba Geshen," Lord Grant said, "I'm in complete agreement with you, Your Highness. What's changed, and I stress that it's my role to advocate our side of things, feelings notwithstanding, and then to advocate against that position to ensure that it can stand up to scrutiny. As I was saying, what's changed is not the account, but the one who delivers it."

"Perhaps with time and effort," Prince Leopold remarked, "you could achieve a greater degree of opaqueness."

"Yes, Your Highness. Plainly stated, Alamayou is what's changed about all of the issues. How he's perceived. With all that's come out about him, I just don't know anymore." He cleared his throat and put his papers down. "Your Majesty, you graciously asked for my opinion and I'm humbled by your trust, of course. In my discretion, I mean."

"Yes. Most of all, that."

"Yes. Of course. As I observe your personal secretary isn't here with us, we can be assured that nothing we speak of will survive beyond this day. Let me speak plainly, then. The allowances for you and your children must be considered. Parliament approves them, at times causing the expenditure of much political capital and no small amount of quite public displays of resentment. We know this. Depending on the makeup of those factions in either chamber who are prone to downplaying the importance of monarchy, or the sentiments of a public at varying degrees of comfort or poverty, monies flowing into the monarchy's chests are either understood or railed against. There's the matter of your legacy, which is no small thing. Your place as the people see and understand it. They'll hear of this, of course, and sooner than we think. It exists at present as rumor, the stuff of editorials. That won't last long. Already we've seen the good men of our military gathered at your gate in protest of the young man's presence here in Windsor. That will undoubtedly worsen a hundredfold when word of this escapes. And then? You place yourself, your children, and the monarchy at risk for such a young man as him. Is it wise? This is the question I can't answer."

"We hear clearly your own wisdom on this question," she said.

"You do, Your Majesty. I'm sorry if I offend. I am first your servant and think only in your interest. But I am a Christian."

"We too are Christian, sir."

"Of course, Your Majesty. I mean no offense."

"Everything you tell us, we don't doubt the wisdom. But we're aware of the reasons why we will surely fail and bring ruin to our good name. From you, we wish to know how to fight and win."

Lord Grant swallowed some water, grimacing as it went down.

"A fight you can have, Your Majesty. I just don't see a path to victory."

"Just say *something*," Princess Louise blurted. "Nothing in the law is clear and sure, you've said so yourself on more than one occasion. Why now? Is this the law, or your sense of morality at play?"

"Her Highness gives me much to consider," Lord Grant said.

"We don't have the luxury of the time it will take for you to consider it," Princess Louise said curtly.

"Very well. It's not clear, one way or the other, whether a royal pardon could work, were you to even consider so drastic and public a step. A pardon essentially cancels the stated will of Parliament. The ill will that would engender alone must, I would argue, call for very sober contemplation indeed.

Abyssinia isn't a colony, for one thing. For another, Alamayou has not yet been convicted of anything."

"The hell he hasn't," Philip said.

"Philip's right about that," Princess Louise argued. "Can there be any doubt of the outcome of a trial in Abyssinia? They'd execute him on the spot."

"Are you suggesting we colonize Abyssinia to secure a fair trial?" Prince Leopold asked.

"Don't be so foolish, brother. What I am suggesting, though, is that we hide Alamayou away where Parliament won't find him. *Ever.*"

"Are we back to this, then?"

"*Yes*, we're back to it. Because we're up *against* it."

The princess placed a tightly rolled document on the table. It was tied with ribbon and bore marks of having been folded, then opened and smoothed, over and over.

"Dear God," Lord Grant said as the princess untied it and spread it across the table.

"If we're going to talk about everything," she said, "then let us be smart about it."

It was a map of London. Its every landmark, its waterways and streets, the ways around its heart. The ways to get in and get out of it.

The first drops of rain spattered against the window. The princess rose as the wind picked up, rattling the glass. She opened it ever so slightly and listened to it howl through the trees. The room filled with the smell of storms, clean and cold, coming to wash the trodden snow away and then freeze the ground beneath a sheen of new ice.

The air curled the map up, ruffling it before dying down.

I saw a map like that once, Philip thought. *Full of pins. All the dead clustered like constellations.*

"I want us to take this moment," the princess said, "and truly think about what it is we're considering. Listen to us.

We've closed the doors and locked them. We've sent the secretary away and will not write any of this down. We speak to each other with one eye on deceiving Parliament and one on the door to make sure no one's listening. We're conspirators. I'm a princess and I'm suggesting smuggling a man out of Windsor. And yet, that's the least of the sins being whispered about in here. We're speaking about knowingly sending a human being to his death. Must I say what that makes us? All of us? In light of that, and in view of the fact that our words die here the moment those doors open again, I suggest we gather a list together of places where he can find refuge, and then a list of those people we can count on to keep him safe and in secret."

"Such a list," the queen said, "can be prepared."

"Good," Philip exclaimed. "I know the streets better than anyone you'll find and better than a map can ever show you. Leave it to me."

"They'll hunt him down," Prince Leopold said. "What do we think will take place when Alamayou is to report to a ship bound for Abyssinia, with guards there to document the execution of Parliament's resolution, and he never shows up? They'll send soldiers in arms through the streets of London looking for him. I want to save him as badly as any of you, but it will be a damned invasion of our own people. Or are we going to smuggle him across our borders and set off an international scandal?"

"They wouldn't dare," Princess Louise said as her face paled.

The prince slammed his cane against the table. "He's a war criminal in their eyes! What would you expect them to do?"

"He's not—"

"I know what he is and what he isn't," the prince cut her off. "We had our chance to convince them of what we know, and we failed. Do you hear? We failed."

"Then we fix what we failed at some other way. Philip, can you promise to get him away safely?"

"I can or die trying."

"Take a good long look at that map," the prince said. "Imagine every street and alleyway filled with soldiers. Our loyal men, all searching for the two of you."

"Or we can stay here," Philip said, "where they already have found him."

"Your Highness," Lord Grant said, his face dropping as it went crimson, "I beg of you, never repeat what you've said beyond these four walls. I'm your solicitor and bound by duty and privilege to hold your words confidential, but you're speaking of sedition, defiance of Parliament's will, and possibly treason. Half of that is the will of the MPs. The other half will be that of the people. Such actions, if they're discovered, will bring your monarchy and your family to the brink of collapse."

Their voices rose as their arguments collided against one another, and in the middle of it all, Alamayou and the queen found each other's eyes. They stared at each other as if no one else was in the room, firing off volleys of *sedition* and *execution* and, from Philip, *betrayal*. The others there with them fell beneath the slick, smooth surface of an inky black sea, sank to the bottom and died, and it was just them.

Alamayou heard them as he heard the wind outside, howling and formless. He went over to look at the map. From Westminster and Parliament's houses, where it had begun the day before, he traced the path carved through the city by the Thames. Its current passed under all the bridges, Westminster on to the Waterloo, Blackfriars, Southwark, London.

What he saw was worse than the specter city he'd first glimpsed from the *Feroze*. That day, the city had been like seeing the mountains at Wurq-Waha beneath a ceiling of cloud. Peaks of an impossible size, but his eye could hold it. This, this was like opening up the body and trying to find a speck of dust among all the blood, the veins, the muscles layered upon muscles upon bones, and chart that speck's course from the head down. He saw knotted nests of lines that were each streets teeming with people, carriages, animals, homes, windows, life unspooling out against one wall and on the other side the same, and on and on, never ending until the sea.

Every last cell of the mapped city hated him. The London he saw laid out across the table, dissected by roads and rails, would look for him. Those knots of streets and waterways and paths would tighten around him like a vise. The city would swallow him as the sea had yearned to do the night before London's silhouette came visible from the deck of the *Feroze*.

Somewhere just past the border of the map, somewhere on the air of the room, was the sea that had brought him here. It couldn't be seen, but he knew what it could do. What it would do. That much was clear, no matter how loud everyone screamed at each other over his fate.

The sea would take him and he wouldn't return. The men who sailed him away, they'd come back. Philip would go somewhere safe. The queen had given her word. He tried not to give in to the voice that told him, *But she gave the same word to you, gbra sadom.*

If he so chose, and if the royals would have him, Philip could return again from wherever he went.

But I won't. I'm the bright hot star, shooting across the sky over London and the sea, and in Abyssinia I'll fall. Then, even the sky will forget me. The queen, the sickly prince, the princess who even now screamed at her brother and the solicitor, they'll grow old and die and what they have of me will die with them.

Across the room, Philip looked up to see him. He shook his head because he knew. He could see the words forming in Alamayou. They understood each other so well.

Philip, your world will turn away from this and from me. I want it to. It does no good to put one hand in here, where things can only die, and one in the world that can still find a place for you if you look. If you try. That's what we do. We try.

The breeze from the open window cooled his hot face. He looked down at the scattering of dead leaves that the wind had picked up from somewhere outside and brought in to lay at their feet. When the air stirred them again they hissed across the floor, momentarily flying before falling again, too heavy to stay up for long.

He spoke the words. It was inevitable that someone said them out loud.

"I have to go," he said, silencing the room.

"You don't." Philip's voice cracked.

"We'll send an emissary with you," the prince insisted, his voice rising with the effort to keep up his bravado. He placed his hands on the marble of the table as if to draw its strength and its immovability into himself, to bring to bear on the hopelessness of the man standing before them. His cane rested against his chair, unused. "Lord Grant, provide some assurances of what our pardon might accomplish."

"It gives at least some cause for hope, Your Highness."

"Oh my God." Princess Louise bowed her head.

"Our emissary will have our pardon with him," Lord Grant said. "The very moment your trial even starts in Abyssinia, the pardon will be presented and this nightmare will be over."

"Then you'll return to us," Prince Leopold said hopefully. "That's exactly how this will come to a conclusion. You'll return home and it will be as if all of this never happened."

"Home."

"Yes, Alamayou. Isn't that right, Mother?"

"They'll kill him," Philip said simply.

"Come to us," the queen said.

Alamayou did.

"From the moment they tear you from us," she said, "I'll fight them. I swear this to you."

"Your Majesty," Lord Grant said, "you ought not promise what cannot be done—"

"To the very last moment."

"I know you will," Alamayou said, thinking, *God, I'm tired.*

Alamayou wavered where he stood, but they were all so intent upon him and he didn't want to let them know how much it hurt just to remain where they could see him, while the end of all he'd hoped for swirled just over their heads. There was a new terror blooming in every moment he stayed here with them. The hopes he had of days and years yet to come, they'd all felt so plentiful before. Now they felt hard, dry, and rare, like blooms dying inside the cracks of Abyssinian stone.

Philip put his hands together, trying to evoke an old language even as his face fell.

Don't try, Alamayou wanted to tell him. *Don't look at me and see me old and gray next to you, painting a tree or a cloud while you tease me about something we've said to each other a thousand times over. Don't hope for time once it's been taken. Your hands together can't keep either of us from being alone.*

"Fighting will destroy your family," he told the queen. "For me, don't. You've been good to me. What they say now is right. All of it happens if I don't go. It happens to all of you. I'm just one."

"How can you *say* that?!" Philip screamed at him.

The queen's gaze at him was as intense as it had been that first night, when she came so close to his painting, when she held out a hand to be helped to her knees, to press herself up to it as if wanting to step inside it and be with her husband again. All through that night while they sat, exchanging the occasional word or gesture, she'd stared at his painting. He hadn't been sure if she'd even seen it, truly, or whether something in her moved away from the painting, the room, Windsor itself, back to a different day. She may have been staring at the past, but she came back that night.

This gaze at him was different, he thought. A long, last look.

The others fell silent. They bowed their heads, careful not to stare at their queen as she wept for Alamayou.

"Please," the queen said quietly, "don't speak to me as if I'm doing a noble thing. I cannot be the reason you go back."

"You aren't," Princess Louise assured her. "It's them—"

"Everything that befell your mother befell you, too," the queen said. "Everything that you did, you were compelled to do." She glared at the Lord Grant. "Including love," she said. "If anything shall be written about our discussions today, you'll be sure to include that."

"I will, your Majesty."

"Your Majesty," Alamayou smiled. "Don't. You gave me so much."

"You act as if we're simply sending you home. This was my idea. I made you do this. I told you, 'say it all,' and I will have to live with that. And I cannot."

Alamayou raised his scarred hand to wipe the tear from her cheek. Every day pain ran through the hand, though he'd stopped thinking of it. The pain at the stretching of his fingers, reaching for painlessness, had long ago submerged, out of his thoughts.

These were his friends, he thought. They wept for him. Only Philip turned away, his entire body shuddering.

"When your Albert died," Alamayou said, "you were there. Not inside the room, but there. Near."

She fumbled with her teacup. The princess brought a napkin to dab at the silver tray it rested upon.

"Clumsy," the queen said quietly. "It's what remembering does. We lock these things away, you see, but it can be so unexpected, what comes of looking back."

"But you knew when it was done," Alamayou said.

"Yes."

"You didn't wonder."

"No. We knew."

"That's the hardest. That you love but don't see. That you won't know what happens. That's the part I'm afraid of, Philip."

"I can't," Philip whispered hoarsely. "I can't."

He ran from the room.

Outside the window, a child danced a solitary jig from stone to stone in the garden. She wore white. Twirling atop each footfall, arms spread open, she held her balance and defied the stones to make her fall.

The queen, her children, and Alamayou, all of them watched the girl dance the day alive.

§

"THERE'S NO HOPE FOR you if you go back," Philip said in the apartment late that afternoon. "You understand that, don't you?"

Despite the dusk hour, the day was still impossibly bright. The light took on a threadbare, dusted appearance.

Alamayou sat at the apartment window, painting. In faint colors he'd recreated the portrait room. A hazy fire burned in its hearth, and the outlines of two framed images hung on its wall. In the corner, all but off the canvas, was the arm of a chair, and the hint of a woman's black sleeve resting on it.

Outside the portrait room window, he brushed in long shadows over the lawn to the garden and the paving stones. The dancing girl was gone.

"I'll tell my story," Alamayou told Philip as he finished. "Maybe they'll hear. They don't know me. Most Abyssinians never saw me. Those who did, I'm different now. I could be not known. There's a chance."

"You're wrong. They'll send you diplomatically. Do you understand? A ship with orders to deliver you. They'll likely jail you for the whole damned voyage, to ferry you back to Abyssinia and hand you over. Your own people will take you. There'll be a trial, if you're lucky. And then what? Gallows? A gun to your head? And a piece of paper from the same queen who bloody invaded them is supposed to do something?"

"Or maybe I can jump from the ship when we see land. Swim away where they don't know me. I'll be careful at the rail—"

"*Stop* it! Stop making a bloody joke out of this!"

They gazed out at the world outside their window. It seemed as the dead do in paintings, Alamayou thought. Wise and eternal.

"This is no different than standing at the fire," Philip told him. "You're killing yourself, Alamayou."

He moved Alamayou's canvas aside and knelt before him.

"We can run," Philip said. "Let's go. Now."

"No. The man, Grant and the prince, they said we would be hunted. *They* would be hunted. The queen, all of them. You. Especially you. If I don't go, what happens to you? Who do they hurt instead? If not me, the one like me, who helped me. No, Philip. No."

"Listen to me. We can be exactly like what you wished for in Meqdala. We'll run and we'll lose everything of ourselves. Our names and our lives. I know how to survive on the streets. I've done it. We can leave right now. You only have until dawn before they come for you."

"We'll never have peace. We'll never have home."

"What do I do then?" Philip screamed at him. "Tell me! What would you have me do?"

Outside, the sounds of Windsor at evening rose. The chimes of the stable, the buckles and water buckets, the footfalls across the darkening walks that led to its every corner.

"Close your eyes," Alamayou said, "and listen."

Philip closed his eyes. In that moment, it became clear. The world in motion was cold and vast and indestructible. It opened in dizzying ways, to release plague, to swallow the dead offered up in war. But, too, it opened to take in strangers and care for them.

The world opened there in the apartment, if nowhere else, to make room for them to breathe. It shimmered so brightly that the only way to see it bathing them as their words fell was to close their eyes and let their language be silence.

"Be a doctor," Alamayou said. "Help people like you helped the prince. Live. If I come back, live with me. If I don't, live for me. That's what you can do. If you say you will, I'll be ready to leave when morning comes."

Walking away from Alamayou, Philip went to the bed. Beneath it was the medical bag the princess had given him as a token of appreciation. He opened it, touching each item inside reverentially as his mind raced and all the years of his life buckled under the weight of the months at Windsor. Under the simple grace of knowing Alamayou.

His tears fell in to be absorbed by the balled tufts of cotton. They were so like clouds, he thought as the cotton swelled.

"You can do this, Philip. So strong. Strong enough to hold me through it all. You have to be. I'm scared to go. To die."

"I think I understand now," Philip said, "what needs to be done, and who needs to do it."

He reached inside the bag and rummaged through its many pill vials, ointments, sutures, and clean linen until he found what he was looking for.

Chapter Nineteen

3 January 1901

WE COULD RUN.

Lying on his cot, Alamayou watched the sun set through the bars of his cell's window as Philip's words lingered in the air. In thirty years there hadn't been a day when he didn't reach back into the dead past for a moment of it, some action taken or words spoken, and turn it over in his hands until hours had suddenly disappeared and the world had gone on to the next day without him. That last day in the apartment at Windsor more than any other moment of his life. More than the fire, the rail, the war.

And of that day, those words. *We could run.*

Listening to the twilight noises of Newgate prison, he gave in yet again to the need to hold those words. *Yes, we could have run. We could have lost ourselves in London or crossed over into a new country and begun to build a life. We could have found a flat in a city somewhere. Each day we'd listen for news that the queen and her family had toppled because of us. Every night, when we watched the sun go down and the city around us come into its dark life, our hearts would start pounding and our mouths would go dry and silent for fear that that night would be our last before we were found.*

Or we could have found a cottage somewhere in a green valley, on the outskirts of a village far away from everything and everyone. At night, we'd tell each other that we felt safe. We would never imagine the way that cottage would look if it burned to the ground with us inside.

Anywhere we could have run to, we would be two black men, together, and for that we'd be hunted. Every day, every night.

But if we'd run, we might have had one more of those days and nights. Or two. Maybe that would have been worth everything.

"Get up," a voice ordered him from outside the cell. "There's a carriage waiting for you."

The guard unlocked his cell door, then stepped aside to let Rabbi Ariel pass.

Alamayou took the items the rabbi offered him with a puzzled expression. A straight razor, a towel, and fresh clothes.

"Hurry," Rabbi Ariel said. "I don't know how much time we have."

Washing and dressing as fast as he could, Alamayou gathered his few possessions and followed Rabbi Ariel and two more guards through the maze of cell-lined corridors to Newgate's entrance.

Princess Louise waited there in her landau. Spotting him, she opened the carriage door.

"Is she all right?" Alamayou asked.

"She lives," Princess Louise said. "Alamayou, she wants to see you."

§

ALAMAYOU GOT OUT OF the landau and followed the princess. The rabbi kept at a safe distance, his mouth gaping at the spectacle of Windsor.

As they passed through the shadow of the Round Tower, Alamayou glanced up at its parapets. He turned toward the ward where their apartment had been, and found the window they'd stood together at so many times to gaze out at the world they'd become a part of.

Such a strange thing, he thought. None of them were unique moments. People stood at their window and watched the world every day. And yet, who had moments like ours, anywhere?

A few steps ahead, the princess paused. They were close to the Upper Ward. "It's for you to find the way from here," she told him. "She wants you to come to her in the room where you first saw her."

"Another test," Rabbi Ariel grumbled.

"I trust your service won't mind the sight of someone like me wandering the halls," Alamayou said.

"And will you be wandering?" the princess asked him.

"Only for the moments it takes to walk to the portrait room, Your Highness."

"They've been told that we'll be hosting a guest," Princess Louise said. "I'll be right behind you, as will your rabbi. Rabbi Ariel, of course, you're welcome to come in."

"I should hope so," the rabbi said, trying to hide his excitement. "Too cold out here for an old man."

Alamayou led the way into the castle. He marveled at how it all came flooding back to him. There were new interiors, fresh paint, and decorations of a different era. As he took in each room, the surfaces sloughed away like dead skin, revealing to him the sights he once saw on a daily basis. They passed a ballroom and he winced at the bulk of the table, at the many chairs lining either side like the legs of a millipede, because at the far end he saw himself so much younger, sitting and not understanding as Naismith and the royals exchanged the first words that had led him to everything that came after.

Those chairs were once filled by our younger selves.

He glanced at the princess, at the fine lines on her face and shades of gray in her hair, at the beauty still visible beneath the soft folds of skin around her mouth. *And two of those chairs were filled by those who are gone...*

They passed the State Room. He could still see the linen streamers, the mess he'd made of the photographer's Abyssinian backdrop, the camera, and the carte de visite it gave birth to.

"May I just take a moment?" he said after they'd come to a new hall.

"I thought you might want to," Princess Louise said. "It's open. Not too long now."

He touched the wood of the apartment door. Voices came from other corridors and on landings. Doors opened in other parts of the castle to let people come and go with no idea. A long, mechanical sigh rose from somewhere outside, the whirr of a machine that didn't exist when the apartment had been theirs. Another machine song joined it, a new motor car erupting into gas-wheezing life far down the Walk.

He wished there were no people and no noises that didn't belong to the old world. No new tapestries and paintings and renovated, rebuilt, refitted skin on the walls to make the castle something it wasn't. A citizen of the times. *Damn it, that's not what it is, or should ever be.* If you want to build from stone, you have to know stone. Be stone. If you want to be timeless, forever a monument, then be the history you stand on. Don't move. The world does enough of that for all of us. You, you stay here. Don't change, don't age, don't die and be remade.

The new world shouldn't be allowed in this place, he thought. *Least of all this room. All of it should be sealed off, like me.*

Nudging the door until it swung silently open, Alamayou stepped inside as the past accumulated in him.

"However you remember it," Rabbi Ariel said, "let it be that. No one can take it from you, no matter what you see."

The apartment was exactly the same.

He went in fully as the breath caught in his throat. The bed, the covers, all the same. The curtains on the windows were the same pale shade; he remembered that in the castle he'd seen back in his time, this apartment was the only room not to be covered with the queen's mourning shades.

The covers still hung low. They'd make a good hiding place for things, as they had for the medical bag Philip had secreted there.

He went to the window, and though the view had changed— new trees, new flowers, the landscape rolling slightly differently to accommodate changes to the contours of the castle itself—it was still the world he saw every night while he painted.

"Why?" he asked.

"It's the only room like this," Princess Louise said, "besides the Blue Room. She did it for you, Alamayou. Her other dead prince. We'd better go if we want to speak to her. Her strength fails her so quickly now."

They moved away from the open doorway into the sunlit hall. He lingered a moment longer, closing his eyes and listening to the voices in the room as the rest of the castle fell away. *Our world,* he thought.

I've had a good life, Philip. I want you to know that. It's hard every day not to know you. I've learned to live with a sort of joy, of having a hole in me bigger than can ever be filled. Who can say they had something, even for a second, that carried so much of them away when it left? Few of us. In my lifetime, only one other. Her.

One night, we closed our eyes right in this spot, and we let our language be silence. Do you remember? Who could have known that she would have heard us and understood that what we made in here had to remain here, untouched?

Standing at our window each day was common. It was not poetry or painting, just the stuff of life. And yet we made something, Philip, that a queen wants to keep preserved for all time.

§

AT THE DOOR TO the portrait room, Alamayou knocked softly.

"Come," a soft, trembling voice said.

Opening the door, he stepped inside and felt as if he'd stepped into the moment he and Philip first saw her. The room was almost as dark as it had been that night, with a dim fire in the hearth that cast a throbbing glow across the walls and windows.

"Your Majesty." He bowed deeply. "Thank you for seeing me. I'm so grateful."

She sat near the warmth of the hearth, and when she raised her hand to acknowledge him, it caught a bit of the fire and made her skin appear lit from within.

He came closer, stunned at what he saw on the wall above the mantle. Her family portrait and his painting of the two princes, where she'd hung them long ago.

"They're never far from me," she said. The quaking in her voice made a smear of her words, but he understood her. She was bent, frail, breathing with difficulty. A shawl lay loosely over her shoulders. Even the simple weight of that cloth seemed to push her farther down.

"May I ask about your health, Your Majesty? I wish you a speedy recovery."

"There won't be any recovery. We accept the fact of it."

The light in her eyes was as fierce as he remembered. He saw the glow of the fire in them, and the room, and even a suggestion of himself, dark and looming. He thought he saw the grace she spoke of in them, too. The awareness of how close her death was to her.

Was I as accepting as she is? he wondered. *Was I as composed on that day she and I found each other amid all the fighting over sending me back?*

"I don't know where to start," he said, his body shaking unstoppably.

"Sit with me."

He took the chair next to her. At the far end of the room, Princess Louise and Rabbi Ariel sat on a bench near the wall.

I remember Philip sitting there that night. Watching us here by the same fire.

"We have heard the account from our daughter," the queen said. "You wish to give us peace in these, our last days."

"Yes, Your Majesty. I do want that for you, very much."

"Enough to place yourself in the danger you now find yourself in? For me?"

"Yes."

"All so I can die knowing that I didn't fail you. I didn't send you to be killed by telling you to go before Parliament and lay out your life before them. All of it."

"Philip was the only one who ever believed in me enough to say, 'tell it all.' I'd do it all over again, I swear to you. If only because it meant you didn't see me as something to be ashamed of."

"And so you come to me now, to tell me the same thing. That my hubris and arrogance, placing you in that position, hasn't made of me something to be ashamed of."

"It never did. It never will."

A flicker came across her face. The stirring of an old memory and, with it, the pain it had left with her. Just as quickly, it was gone.

"I've heard almost all that I need to," she told him. "But one thing remains. If you are who you say you are, you're the only one who can answer. Where is Philip Layard?"

Alamayou reached into his coat pocket and took out the only possession he'd ever cared about, the only thing to come with him from London to Paris and back again.

The yellowed letter fell open along its creases.

I've almost said it all, Philip. Not perfectly, but I've said our lives in full. I've grown all these words over the years and now all I have to do is cut myself open one last time, find my secret heart, and show it to the queen of England.

It's time to set the last words loose and see them live in the world. Your words.

"He's here," Alamayou said, holding Philip's letter.

Chapter Twenty

9 January 1869

"I THINK I UNDERSTAND," Philip said as he reached inside the medical satchel. "I truly do. You can't go back."

Alamayou turned to him, to comfort him.

He saw only a flash of white in Philip's hand. It came at him too fast and pressed against his face, filling his lungs with a sickly sweet odor. He struggled but Philip had him, and he was so strong. He always was.

The paintings and the lands outside the apartment window all descended. The sounds of Windsor doubled, chimed like bells, then grew thick and fat like the chloral-soaked linen clogging his nose and mouth.

"I'm sorry," he heard Philip say from far off, as his vision slipped into the clouds.

§

I can barely hold the pen as I write this, so I must be quick. And yet I have to say it all. This letter has to make everything clear. It's the last time I'll ever be able to talk to you.

You never felt the linen in my hand, Alamayou. I held it to your nose and mouth. The chloral seeped into your skin and into my own. The fumes overcame you. I felt myself grow light and dizzy, but I knew to hold my breath. You didn't.

My right hand's gone dead from it, as I need it to be. In a moment I'll stick it into the fire I've built up in the hearth. When I go to the ship tonight, they'll see a bad right hand, and they'll take me for who I must be. You.

Your eyes flutter. You're fighting to see me, but it's no use. You're leaving me. Your arms flap weakly at your sides. The grip of the chloral has you and nothing can make it let go. Nothing but time.

When you wake, you'll have this letter and all it holds. The last language we can share.

Alamayou, listen. There are things I want to say to you.

There's this—you'll wake later tonight. When you do you must leave. No one will give a thought to me. I'm nothing. At least, I was before you.

Tell no one where you're going. Just get as far away as you can from London. Don't let anyone see you.

And this:

Remember me.

Until Abyssinia, I lived as if no one was listening and no one could ever possibly care, and so my life was meaningless. A hapless road through a world far larger than someone like me deserved.

I know now, I've lived for you, Alamayou. I've lived for this moment. It's the map by which I found you over time. And I have found you. At last.

It's right, then, that here with you, this road ends.

You weren't what I dreamt of, on those occasions when I dreamt of someone who would finally see me and not run, but remain, know, and care for me. You're more than I dreamt of. Now, you're all I'll dream of, across the sea.

As you would say, it's enough. This.

I don't understand it, but I can't live knowing that you do not. What I can do is die knowing that you did not.

By these words, I leave you, Alamayou. In bed, in our apartment at Windsor, in the predawn hours of this the ninth day of January 1869. What awaits me I can't say. But at your side I learned.

Love is language. It comes to us before we can speak it. It demands our fluency. Learning it undoes us, or brings us home.

May these words bring you home. I know I found home, with you.

Philip Layard.

§

3 January 1901

PHILIP'S LAST WORDS WERE out there now, for the first time since the night he'd left the letter for Alamayou to find when he returned to consciousness. The words were a part of the world.

The queen's face was inscrutable. She stared past him to the door, as if expecting to see someone there.

Tears fell down his cheeks. *Finish it*, he thought.

"When I woke, it was nearly morning but still dark. Philip had been gone for hours by then. I read his letter and ran away. I didn't know where to go. I didn't know anything but this: get to the water. Stop him and together, run. Whatever might come, let it all come. We can run.

"Charles, your old coachman, found me on the Walk. I told him what Philip had done.

"He hesitated only a moment, then told me to take what I couldn't live without. Some clothes, Philip's letter. Everything else, even the painting of Philip and I—I left behind. We fled under the last hour of nightfall.

"We sped through the city as the light grew. Charles gave me money. He told me I shouldn't ever come back. 'Ye make a life somewhere else. Alamayou can't be seen again. If he is, the family'll not survive the scandal. No one'll care for Philip's whereabouts and ye know well that's true.'

"I knew. The world would never hear of him.

"We reached the Channel. Charles couldn't stay, but I hesitated in the carriage. In there, my life at Windsor could still be found. In the corner was the spot where I saw Philip's London, his Lambeth, the flat and the tenement where a long-ago boy once came to the window and waved at him. Outside was the Channel and a future I couldn't name.

"I asked him why Philip had done it. I suppose I needed to hear it out loud, somewhere else, not just inside me. 'Why?' Charles said. I'll never forget the way he asked me that, as if I was an idiot for not knowing. This old white man, who ought to hate me on sight for saying what I said. 'I seen it in war,' he told me. 'I learned what men do when they come t'know one another, go through 'ell and only th' other t'speak it to. Only th' other t' trust it with. Then comes a man with a blade or a gun, an' the one stands in front of th' other, and they die and we th' living ask why.'

"He shook his head at me. He pitied me, maybe, or more likely he welcomed me into a small brotherhood. I wonder what he thought he knew. He said, 'Th' answer's th' most natural reason there can be for such as Philip sacrificed. An' that reason has found ye, among all. He loves ye. And no matter what anyone might think, I'll not know a love like what ye know.'

"He left me there.

"I got out, into the deafening chaos that was London at the Channel crossing. I queued and was told to go to a farther point where other lessers gathered to wait for the ferry without upsetting decent passengers. I waited there with the sounds of many nations ringing in the air. All of us, so far from home.

"After thirty minutes I paid my pence and boarded the ferry. Taking a seat away from the others, I turned to the water. Shrouds of rain hung over a distant point on the water that we'd eventually sail under. There at the rail, I thought of Philip and where he might be. How far, how close. Somewhere beneath the clouds, there was a ship crossing the sea with him aboard. Bad right hand, black of skin. Everyone would see him aboard that ship and they'd take him for me. They'd have their instructions. Bring him to Annesley, and then come round again. Come home without him.

"What a sight I must have made. A Negro with nothing but the clothes on his back, a shoddy bag, and a letter gripped as if it would save him, weeping as the daylight broke open over the water.

"We crossed. I didn't even know where it was I was headed to until the ferry arrived at the other side. As I got off, I was met by a gendarme who asked me something I didn't understand.

"'*Une citoyenne?*' but my vacant gaze must have told him.

"'Are you a citizen of France?'

"'No.'

"'England?'

"'Yes.'

"'Your name.'

"I held his letter in my hand. I looked at the water, then the sky. The same sky would be above him, the water below. For a little while longer, we still shared the world.

"'My name is Philip Layard,' I said.

"I came to Paris and kept to myself. My heart learned. In daylight it remained quiet, so as not to draw attention. But I saw Philip in every window, in every dusk. At night, I read his words in the letter. I thought of every conversation we ever had, through Seely and just us, together. With our hands and with our words. I memorized his life and made it mine.

"On a winter day in eighteen seventy-one, I happened upon a Parisian newspaper at a café on Rue Barre where I occasionally stole half-eaten pastries and cold coffee if I didn't have enough money to see me through. I took the paper because of the name I spotted in the rightmost margin, near the bottom. 'Alamayou.'

"I wandered the city and eventually reached the Marais, holding the *Journal* out to every passing stranger and begging them to tell me what it said. Finally, I met an old man who spoke enough English that we could understand each other a little. He told me his name was Ariel. 'Lion,' he said.

"I liked him right off, and each day since.

"He fed me, spoke briefly of a service he needed to lead in the temple below, and then read the article to me. It talked about my history through the day before Parliament. It said that I boarded a ship in the dead of night, like a common coward. My identity was confirmed by the color of my skin and the state of my hand.

"It said that the ship arrived in Abyssinia in approximately three months' time. Upon their arrival, the crew was met at Annesley by thousands of Abyssinians belonging to every tribe. A tribal leader, a *dejazmach*, read the accusations against the son of Tewedros on behalf of the people. He asked questions, but the prince only said one thing, over and over. *Manoriya bet.* Manoriya bet.

"They beat him to death there at the harbor and threw his lifeless body into the sea.

"I imagine they asked Philip the obvious question. Why did you come back? He knew a little Amharic, from me. He could have said, 'I didn't do anything,' or 'I'm not a monster.' What he did say, they took as a reference to Abyssinia. They didn't care and they couldn't have known what he meant. 'Why did you come back?'

"Manoriya bet. Home.

"Over time, I learned enough French to strike up conversation. Where it didn't seem out of place, I brought that name up into the open. 'Alamayou.' In a few years I received only questioning expressions. Alamayou had disappeared.

"Now you see," Alamayou said. "I live because of the one who loved me."

§

HE POURED SOME TEA for the queen. While he'd spoken, her eyes had flitted to his hand in search of the scars.

After he set her cup down, he held out his right hand for her to see. She turned it over and looked at the fire damage there.

"Love." Her voice trailed off. "It's folly to think we can bring old loves back, isn't it?"

"It's folly to think old loves grow old just because we do, Your Majesty. I close my eyes and he's forever young. And so he'll be when I close my eyes for the last time. Whether now or later."

They smiled at each other, at how the years had changed them and yet left their perennial foolish hearts untouched.

I'm the idiot, Alamayou thought, *carrying paintings in my eyes and expecting the world to bend itself into those colors.*

He looked into her cloudy eyes and saw that she understood him, utterly; she carried paintings of her own. Her bright hot star, and his.

All that time, he'd considered his life a mystery waiting for someone to untie it and let it unravel completely, but here was an old woman, more powerful than anyone and anything but time, and she was every bit the mystery he was.

"We wish to be in our room now," she said. "Exhaustion overtakes us. It's a terrible thing to be this old."

"Let me summon your lady," Princess Louise suggested.

"He will take us."

She held out her teacup for the princess to take, then waited expectantly for Alamayou. He linked his arm in hers and led her out of the portrait room, exchanging looks with Rabbi Ariel as he passed.

Through the windows of the corridor he saw Windsor's gates open to let in a procession of dignitaries arriving by landaus numbering in the dozens. "My deathwatch," the queen said, shaking her head. "Tomorrow we depart for Osborne House. It's where I want to die. The grounds there, my room, the Durbar Wing. That's what I want to see at my end. I've had a lifetime of mourning in the Blue Room. It's enough. A speech tomorrow and then I depart."

At the Blue Room door she slipped her arm out of his. "To this moment," she said, "I've been mulling what it is I should say to everyone tomorrow. How does one say goodbye to the world one created?"

"How to say a life."

"Yes. That's the dilemma, exactly."

They smiled wearily at each other. "There's been a pain in my heart all these years for you," she said. "I don't feel it now."

"Then I'm so glad I came, whatever else may take place from here."

"Wait here a moment."

"Your Majesty, I've nowhere else to go."

"On that point, you're quite wrong. You've everywhere to go."

She stepped inside the Blue Room under her own power. It was excruciating to watch her walk, far more so than watching Prince Leopold at his lowest ebb. She was so fragile. Her legs quivered to the point that he feared she'd fall with each step.

Somehow she made it to her nightstand, where she picked up an envelope and brought it back to him.

He opened it. His eyes filled with tears.

"I must rest," she told him. "Be here tomorrow, for my speech. I wish to see you, if I have the strength to look up. One never knows the great heights one might ascend."

"I will. Your Majesty, the date on this—"

"It's been waiting quite a long time. I assure you, it will do the job. I've checked. I'm old, but not enfeebled. We still rule, after all."

"May you always," he said, the words catching in his throat.

"Embrace the oath you spoke in our courtyard. 'I live.' We welcome you back, Alamayou."

She closed the door.

§

RABBI ARIEL AND THE princess stood when he returned to the portrait room. He handed the envelope to the rabbi.

After everything, he thought, *it's only right that the old man be the first to read it. He is, after all, my friend.*

The rabbi unfolded it and began to read. The smile slowly spread across his face. "Oh, *mayn zun.*"

Rabbi Ariel gave it to Princess Louise. She nodded vigorously as her eyes filled. "January ninth, eighteen sixty-nine. My God, she wrote this the day you left."

Their arms encircled him as he spoke the queen's pronouncement aloud.

"I'm pardoned."

Chapter Twenty-One

4 January 1901

THE FOLLOWING MORNING, ALAMAYOU woke to the sound of drums.

He bolted from his bed and ran to the window, his mind feverish with the thought that he would see his father's soldiers setting their fires across the plains and pounding their negerit, the war drums.

Frith Street was filled with carts and carriages. The wheels thundered across the cobblestones as Little Britain came alive. It was still early and the light was only just pushing in from between the buildings, into the open.

On the table next to his bed, he found his letters. Philip's and the queen's pardon. The rabbi had tied them together with a bit of silken string from his tzitzit.

Two lives, bound one to the other by a piece of blessed twine.

The aroma of cooking breakfast reached him. In the kitchen, Rabbi Ariel spooned some eggs onto plates set out next to a rasher of toast. Alamayou sat down while the rabbi poured them tea. Over the years, the rabbi had begun at last to favor the stronger British blends. After a cup or two, Alamayou found him as chatty as a grand dame.

The rabbi was pensive as he sat down next to Alamayou. "I think a part of me always knew there was something more to you. Your story was in your eyes, since the day you came up to me in the Marais."

His age-spotted hand shook as he reached for a piece of toast. "I miss Philip. He was my friend. But I can say, yes. I know him. Or I knew him. I'll always call him friend. As I do you, now."

"I miss him, too," Alamayou said.

At that moment, it seemed to Alamayou that they were about to say all things they'd never said in thirty-odd years of living in each other's company. The silent dinners, the days spent working alongside each other at the synagogue, the innumerable hours of their lives that passed by unremarked upon, now came to them in the room on Frith. Maybe, after all that time, those things needed mentioning. Each of those hours lay under a lie, after all, the way a baby rests under a blanket and dreams of no particular thing, moving in sleep to a melody the watchful parents will never learn about.

We'll stare at each other, Alamayou thought. *Or he'll strike me, the way he ought to do. I'm another son gone to see the world, never to return.*

"I'm sorry," he said as Rabbi Ariel's arms folded around him. "I'm so sorry."

"This is no confession," the rabbi said. "This is a testament of life. Of love." He smiled and wiped his eyes. "You're almost done, my friend. My new old friend. Come, we should be making our way to Windsor. A prince shouldn't keep a queen waiting. But here, this belongs to you."

The rabbi placed the carte de visite on top of the letters, above Philip's last words. *Love is language.*

§

THE QUEEN'S ROUTE AWAY from Windsor was well planned. By the time Alamayou and the rabbi arrived at the castle, anxious crowds had come from everywhere to say their goodbyes. Her procession, once it left, would travel by closed landau from Windsor to Paddington and across the parks to Buckingham. There were stopping points along the route where dignitaries, kings, princes, and governing heads of state from all her colonies waited to pay their respects. She'd pass Westminster Abbey with an Indian brigade of cavalry for escort. Scaffolds of her subjects some ten miles in length snaked back through the city from the castle gates.

Alamayou and the rabbi were admitted and found their seats in a box behind Princess Louise. Across from them, old men in the Parliamentary section glared and whispered to each other.

Alamayou wondered if, underneath their wrinkles and gray shocks of hair, he would find the same men who'd joined Naismith in calling for his banishment.

They were both bundled against the chill. Rabbi Ariel wore an ascot, the only bit of color Alamayou had ever seen on him. "One keepsake of London that you can't call a tchotchke," the rabbi said.

It made the old man look almost jaunty. He seemed entirely pleased with it, Alamayou thought, judging from the way he spied himself in the glass of carriages and shops on the way, smiling at what he saw.

He caught the rabbi smiling at him, too, on more than one occasion. Once, it was a sad smile. Once, puzzled. Soon, he hoped, he would look up and see forgiveness.

The queen's balcony doors opened. The curtains of the room lifted with the frigid air. The crowds outside fell silent as word spread.

In a moment she emerged, took hold of the balcony rail to steady herself, and spread a sheet of paper atop a small lectern. She glanced across the grounds and at the throngs sitting in the boxes.

She saw Alamayou and nodded.

Clearing her throat, she began.

"Who can say what love is, in the end.

"We expect so much. We expect to know how and when love will find us, and who we'll be when the day comes. We expect the seasons to unfold and all the years to follow as promised, and all the births and deaths will come in an orderly and proper fashion, and life will stay in the room we've built for it with our plans. We don't expect our hearts to go wandering off and get lost, or broken, or mended again.

"We're reasonable creatures, but we don't understand how all that we are burns away with time. The homes of our childhood fall or are rebuilt for someone else. Our century's mechanisms for holding memories, the paintings and photo plates, the grainy voices unspooling across the black wax rings of Edison's dreams, one day fade. The ones who knew us and loved us in spite of it all are lost to the years. With each extinguishing light, so we extinguish, little by little.

"A life lived reduces us to the last keepsake, the last memory. Is that where we've been keeping our loves, even ourselves, all along?

"I can say that I am your queen. A mother. Once, a wife. My physicians reduce me to the smallest visible parts, the blood, the cell. Science takes us further with each passing year, and soon we'll be little more than rumors and specks of physics. We'll see what can't be seen by the simple eye, and we'll consider that God particle and ask: *Is it me?* Have I left enough for you to know me? For my children, grandchildren, and those I've been fortunate enough to call friend, to remember me by?

"I truly didn't know how to answer this until recently. But now I can, and so I leave you with this, the thing I've learned so late in my life. What I leave of myself, what all of you will carry of me, is what you carry of your own family and friends. It is how we call all of our most precious memories, hopes, and dreams up from the secret places we keep them when we wish—when we *need*—to hold them one more time, or one last time. What we leave of ourselves is love, spoken by any means necessary. In the end, love is language."

Alamayou closed his eyes and let the cold wind try to find a way in. It would try and it would fail, because nothing could hurt him now. She'd seen him. His secret heart had been called out by name, to the thousands.

Did you hear her, Philip? She just told us we're home now.

She smiled, and Alamayou thought the sight of her smile, filling as it did with memories the way the balloon on Hyde Park once filled with fired air, was the most beautiful thing he'd ever seen.

"To all of you," she said, "we are blessed for knowing you. We carry you with us wherever we may go from here. God bless you all, and save you all."

Hands emerged from behind the curtains. They reached for her to help her back inside.

Around them, the crowd began to cheer. It spread through the boxes into the courtyard and beyond the gate, sweeping down the processional route like a wave. The day was clear and bright, and the gathered didn't leave. The sun glistened from the windows. It didn't feel like mourning. It didn't seem possible to any of them that their queen would be gone soon. Something new had been born on her balcony, not seen since, of all things, the plague years, when children came with flowers for their monarch despite the terror of disease. They'd dared when their families didn't, because the woman they scarcely understood, who lived behind the gate, lost someone and they wanted her to know she wasn't alone.

Now the queen had given that gift back to her people.

Alamayou listened to Louise and her siblings and their children talk about the upcoming trip to Osborne House, about nannies and nurses and matters of the state that would have to wait for their return. He knew they meant the return from the queen's funeral and all that would involve. He knew that he would be there, with the rabbi. He would weep with them because, like them, he would lose someone he loved.

But this day, she'd given him back what he'd given her. Peace.

Princess Louise gestured for him to come to her. They walked toward the castle.

"She wants you to go to Osborne House with the rest of her family," the princess said.

"I'd be honored. May the rabbi come, too?"

"He may. He's a good man."

"Don't tell him that. I'll never hear the end of it."

"I'm not deaf, you know," Rabbi Ariel said as he followed them inside. "Maybe she'd permit an old rebbe to say a prayer for her."

They gathered in the portrait room while the guests outside made their way home. Their clothes and possessions were brought over from Frith Street and packed. Over the course of the afternoon, they ate and talked while, across the city, the audience swelled in anticipation of the queen's final ride.

Dusk gathered at the windows. Alamayou built a fire.

The portrait room door opened and she came inside.

"We wish to take the paintings with us," Princess Louise said. "It's time. Alamayou, a carriage waits for you and your friend. We are so glad for your company. Come."

§

THEY CLIMBED INTO THEIR carriages, and as the sun set they left the Round Tower and the Walk behind. Alamayou leaned out to feel the cold air on his face. He saw the queen through the window of her own landau, staring back at Windsor as it fell into the distance. Seeing him, she held up a hand. He held up his own, and for a moment he thought he saw Philip's, raised alongside his. *Not alone.*

He thought of those two hands alongside each other, resting on the *Feroze* rail. Their first language had been silence and distance. The language of their fathers, which didn't prepare them for what they found in the world once their fathers were dead.

Then their hands spoke their first shared language. They couldn't say enough, or say it right, because they knew nothing about each other and had no way to give each other that first piece that would open the door.

Until they found the words.

I can answer my father now, Philip, for both of us: God did not make us like him.

In our time, in that bright hot star, we found all the words for what we were. Love was language. The language we spoke in daylight and the language we spoke at night. Our language brought us from a cottage on fire, across the sea, and further than we could ever have imagined.

"Are you all right?" Rabbi Ariel asked.

"Yes."

"When it's over, will you stay in England or come back with me?"

"I don't know. I really don't."

"It's good to know that you could make a life for yourself in either place, eh? Something to think about."

"It is."

Alamayou sat back as the world moved around him. The rabbi was happy as a child as they passed waving onlookers. Occasionally he waved back, to their utter confusion.

Alamayou thought about the rabbi's question throughout their journey to the Isle of Wight and Osborne House. He walked the beach below the gardens and watched the sea carry in from distant places, and in the evening of their arrival, he sat alone in the Durbar Room and stared at the portraits hanging alongside the chimneypiece and peacock over the mantel. When it grew dark, he built a fire while the rabbi studied his Talmud nearby.

The old man's incantations filled the air, but all Alamayou heard was the rebbe's question turning over and over in his mind. *What comes after this?*

The only answer there could be for someone like him was, *I don't know.* There had been a time when the same question haunted him. Wandering the streets of Paris while a ship took Philip to a death meant for him, the next day and the next could have been anything, and that felt like being damned.

But now, he thought before the Durbar hearth, *this blank canvas feels like possibility. No, rebbe, I don't know what all the rest of my life will be. But there are a few things I can at least hope for.*

I hope for you. Your friendship, now and every day after. I hope for peace to settle around the queen and her family. I hope you get to say that prayer while she can still hear you. She'll find comfort in your voice, and in your words. I know I always have.

Grant her light.

A servant came to the room, followed by the queen in a wheeled chair pushed by her daughter. As Louise brought her mother to the fire, a line of grandchildren filed in to kiss her while she sat, still and frail, staring at the paintings.

To their eyes she was ancient, small and sick and even frightening. *The young fear anything old,* he thought. *It's too close to death and too far from them.*

But he could see the queen's bright, clear eyes, full of knowledge and memory. As her descendants said their goodbyes—the littlest ones were too young to understand, yet they cried anyway at the sight of so many grownups in tears—the queen smiled at them. She waved weakly.

Alamayou brought her closer to the hearth when the last one left. He draped a blanket over her legs and turned her so she could have a better glimpse of the paintings. Princess Louise and Rabbi Ariel sat together against the far wall, watching.

Kneeling before her, Alamayou asked her if she'd like to hear a story. "Perhaps I can tell you about my life after London."

She smiled, nodded, patted his scarred hand.

He told her about his unlikely years in Paris, of painting and tending to the sick, and of a years-long friendship with a curmudgeonly old Jew who had a prayer for her. The queen listened, gazing away. The sight of the carte de visite of him brought the last words he ever heard from her.

"The years," she said in a voice that shivered and rasped. "Where do they go?"

Wherever it is that the ancient light goes, he thought, *I believe we'll find all our years there.*

It would be dark soon. By then he knew they would have spoken the names of the departed ones. Leopold, Albert, Philip. They will be quiet after, because there are no words for some things. Then tomorrow will come and they will see what comes with it, and what departs.

And should anyone pass this room and peer inside, drawn by the hearth light under the closed door, they'll see us by the fire, sharing a night language we've come to know well. Speaking of home.

Acknowledgments

WHILE RESEARCHING JULIA MARGARET Cameron's photographic work for my first novel, *The Luminist*, I came across the melancholy image of a young black man she took in July 1868. I knew nothing about him then, but his haunted expression remained with me. He wore the colonial's notion of African garb and was made to cradle a small white doll. He sat regally, yet everything about him spoke of isolation and a palpable longing. I set his photograph aside in order to finish that novel, but I knew I'd return to him eventually. I couldn't look away from him.

What I subsequently learned of Alamayou's life formed the backdrop of *The Night Language*. He was the only son of the Abyssinian emperor, Tewedros. Orphaned by England's invasion of his country, Alamayou was taken back and made a ward of Queen Victoria. He didn't speak the language. He'd never set foot in another land, let alone one that had decimated his home and his life. He was only a child. He died at seventeen, of pleurisy.

I found various meanings attributed to his name. One was "I have seen the world."

It turned out that the image I'd discovered had been created shortly after his arrival in England. Everything he'd come through—war, seizure, a perilous sea voyage, the very first moments of a new life built around his otherness—filled his eyes. So too did a fierce desire for a future that, in his short time, he was never allowed to have. He died in a strange land and never knew real friendship, or adulthood, or love.

I've taken great liberties with the known facts of Alamayou's life and the lives of those historical figures who populated his world. It's customary to offer apologies for that sort of thing, but I wrote *The Night Language* to give Alamayou another story, and his story another ending. I hope I succeeded.

I'm grateful to Rare Bird, Tyson Cornell, Julia Callahan, Hailie Johnson, Alice Elmer, and all the kind folks who read about the growing love between two young black men in Queen Victoria's court and said yes, this novel might come to mean something to someone. Thank you for the home and the chance.

To my extraordinary agents Melissa Chinchillo and Christy Fletcher: two novels into this eclectic literary career of mine, and every day you believe in what I write and why I write it. You patiently waited while I found this story draft by draft. You've fought for a place for me, and I'm so lucky to know you as agents and friends.

I deeply appreciate early draft readers Shilpa Agarwal, Kate Sage, and Caitlin Myer. Your generosity and insights were invaluable and gracious.

I'm so proud to belong to the Los Angeles literary community, which has been a wellspring of friendship, support, inspiration, and awe. I love our tribe.

To my mentor and friend Susan Taylor Chehak, who continues to be an inspiration to me as a writer: I'm forever grateful.

Of the many sources of information I came across while researching this novel, I must single out and profusely thank the Getty Archives and the Victoria & Albert Museum in London. Philip Marsden's meticulously researched biography of Tewedros evoked the emperor's Abyssinia in loving detail, while Tsehai Publishers' reprint of the diary of a Victorian journalist who accompanied the British on their invasion of Abyssinia in 1868 painted its downfall from the invaders' perspective. Both enriched my research tremendously.

To my daughters Ariel and Kavanna, it's not just your names that show up in this novel. The joy, tenacity, fearlessness, and empathy you bring to your world and mine is on every page. I love you and am so proud to know you.

My father Jerrold didn't live to see me published. I hope he's proud. I can say now, I am like him in all the best ways.

Finally, this book is dedicated to my wife, Dr. Nina Savelle-Rocklin. Writers are frequently told to write what they know. I know about love because of you. Always and forever.